MIND OVER MURDER
JANNA ROSE MYSTERIES
BOOK 1

JAKE LYNCH
ANNABEL MCGOLDRICK

Copyright © 2025 Jake Lynch & Annabel McGoldrick

Layout design and Copyright © 2025 by Next Chapter

Published 2025 by Next Chapter

Cover design by Lordan June Pinote

Original cover photograph by Fisher Studios, Oxford

This book is a work of fiction. Names, characters, places, and incidents are the product of the author's imagination or are used fictitiously. Any resemblance to actual events, locales, or persons, living or dead, is purely coincidental.

All rights reserved. No part of this book may be reproduced or transmitted in any form or by any means, electronic or mechanical, including photocopying, recording, or by any information storage and retrieval system, without the author's permission.

To Finn, with our hopes for the future.

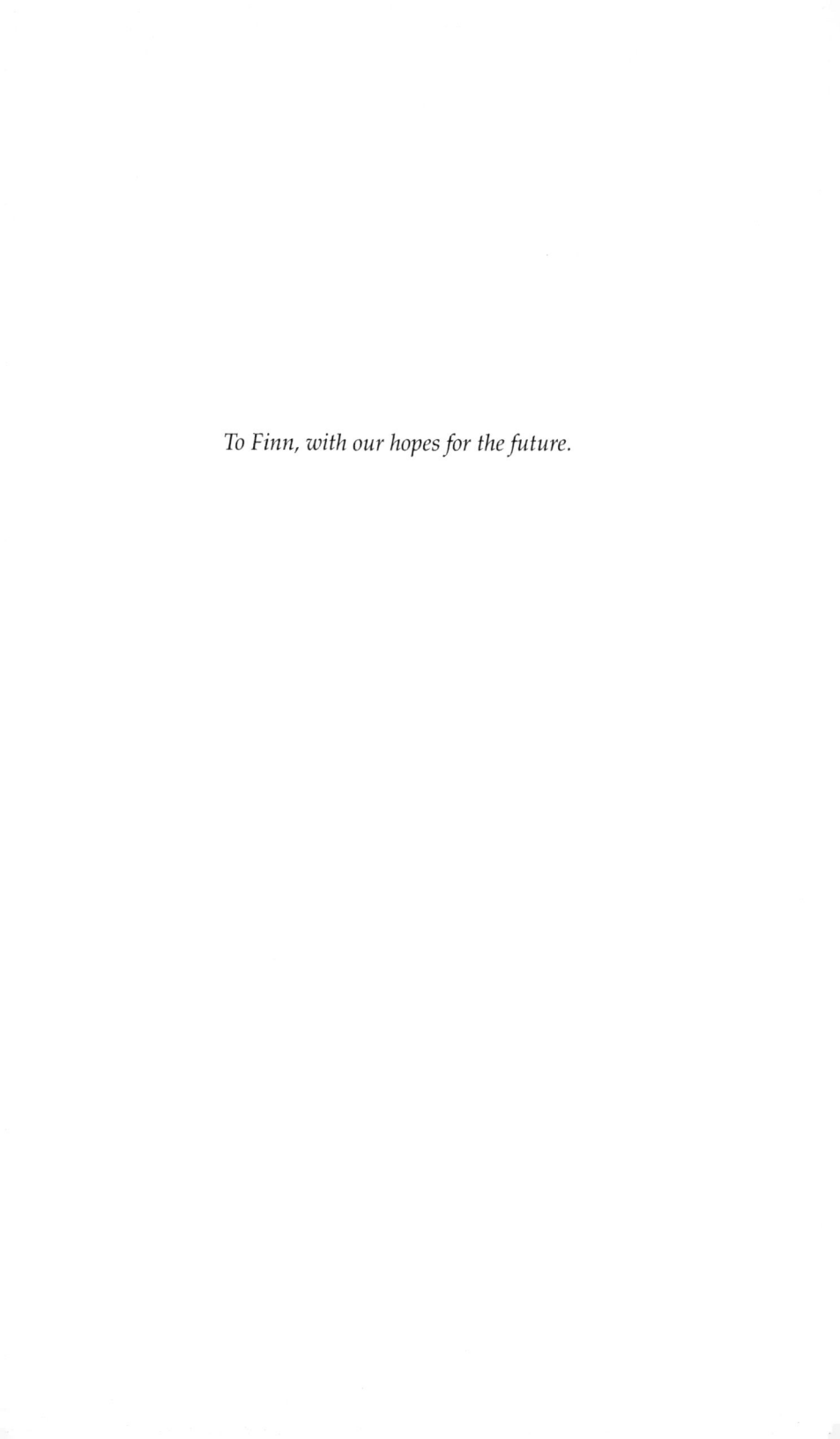

AUTHORS' NOTE

In some instances, the demands of fiction have overridden precise verisimilitude in the portrayal of EMDR techniques and procedures. In such cases, responsibility definitely lies with Jake, not Annabel!

ACKNOWLEDGMENTS

Thanks to the global EMDR therapy community for the vital work of helping clients to process unaddressed trauma, to prevent and minimise harm to themselves and others. Thanks to Megan Kerr of the Writers' Greenhouse in Oxford, for a stimulating novel-writing course and expert reading of the draft.

# CHAPTER ONE

As I parked my bike outside West Oxford Community Centre that day, crows perching in the bare beech tree overlooking Botley Park rose in unison, as if responding to some hidden disturbance.

I watched the dark shadows melting into a rare glimmer of March sunshine, then turned to lock up. At that moment, a taxi, a silver Toyota, drove into the car park. A faintly audible skid as the brakes were slammed on.

Joining several already there, I now noticed, from the same firm, Regal Cars. Attending some kind of trade convention? Or collecting a big group from across town?

The driver, slight and middle-aged, in grey flannels and a dark-blue zipped cardigan, jammed a flat cap on his head while striding towards the single-storeyed red-brick building. I slung my helmet by its chinstrap on Bertha's handlebars and followed him inside.

Drawing out the small poster from my bag, advertising as a friendly female neighbourhood therapist, I stopped at the cork wallboard in the foyer and searched for a space, or an expired notice I could legitimately remove.

But voices from just ahead in the Centre's main hall were

growing louder. I pinned up my flyer, pre-cut strips with my email address protruding below for would-be clients to tear off, and stuck my nose through the open door.

"This whole bloody city is grinding to a halt – and you want to stop us getting even one more road?!", the newcomer was shouting.

"What is this really about, man, huh?" another said. "We're all good Muslims, we drivers, you know? We just want to make a living, and you're stopping us, you Greenies." The word was shot through with contempt. "It's Islamophobia!"

"This is racist!", a third chipped in, quivering with rage.

Beyond them, I could see signs being created with paints and cardboard, protesting against the Osney Mead plan. Bits of a nearby industrial estate had long been sliding into disuse. I'd read about the scheme to redevelop it in my old paper, the *Oxford Mail*.

Taking pride of place in the colourful array was a banner with a choking anthropomorphised Planet Earth and the words, "Stop the Bridge of Doom."

Sarah, the Centre manager, stood between the antagonists, trying to lower the tension with the classic palms-down gesture. Beyond her, a handful of "Greenies" watched impassively. They'd made a booking, she was explaining, so were entitled to use the space. "We all share the same planet, mate," I heard one of them call out. "Muslims and everyone else."

Flat-cap man darted further in and wrested a placard from the hands of its startled maker, flung it to the floor, hawked audibly and spat on it, then just as quickly darted back. A volley of "heys!" from her comrades, and the official raised her voice.

"Right, that's enough. I'm going to ask you to leave, or I'll have to call Security." Turning reluctantly, the drivers began to file back out. One treated me to a scowl as I stood aside to let them pass.

I was due for a meeting later with Kevin, a City and County Councillor who's also my landlord and upstairs neighbour. As a side-hustle, I help with his correspondence and comms. He'd know why the proposals were generating such strong feelings.

Before moving on, a pair of dark eyes at the back of the hall briefly met my gaze. Their owner lifted a hand to the side of his head in the shape of a telephone and mouthed: "Let's talk." But that could wait. It was time for sustenance.

I stifled a moan of pleasure as the first spoonful of warming liquid tingled my tastebuds. "Special from Banja Luka," Miri called it. One of the choice recipes she'd brought along when leaving Bosnia as a refugee in the 1990s, and now offered at the Thundering Bay Café. Best thing about the whole Centre, for my money.

"Getting too thin again, Janna Rose." Her verdict after surveying me through narrowed eyes. Just after her trademark greeting of a peck on both cheeks. "You sit – I bring soup. You eat all, bread too. I come back to check."

Sarah had taken the next table, seeking solace in a decaff latte. She fanned her face with a hand and puffed out her cheeks as we exchanged sympathetic looks.

Plumbing the cloudy depths with a spoon, I'd spotted okra and carrots, and was wondering about another root veg – parsnip? – when the glass door to the paved dining terrace rattled with a clatter.

Taxi driver again. Luckily it was locked. No great demand for outdoor refreshment just yet. He glared and jabbed his finger at the manager like he was the Terminator or something, turned on his heel and stalked off. "Bloody hell," she said. "Hope *they* don't come back."

Suffused with comforting warmth, I parked myself on a black vinyl chair in the small consulting room at the end of the corridor that led past the toilets and greeted the client, Cara, with my usual opening question.

"So – what sort of week have you had?"

The young mum had signed up through a charity, The Listening Project, where I donate an hour per week. "Don't ask." I gave a sympathetic murmur. "It's Kyle – again."

Out of money to renew her mobile data plan, she could no longer make outgoing calls, even to book a doctor's appointment. So the previous day she'd arranged an early finish at work, collected her son from school and taken him to the GP's surgery in person.

"We have to get a diagnosis for him," she explained. "Teachers are always on at me, saying he's playing up in class. He's only six, but there's times I can't handle him."

The low moment came, apparently, when the young tyke broke a toy in the waiting room.

"I was mortified. I just wanted the ground to swallow me up," she said, face pruned in anguish at the recollection. They'd had to come away without Kyle seeing the doctor.

"Right, so you felt embarrassed, and that made you get up and leave. What if we start there?" She mumbled assent. "OK, now close your eyes and go inside. Now run through that scene at the doctor's like a movie, and press pause at the worst moment. Tell me what you see, what's the picture?"

"Another kid wanted to get the toy, the one he'd broken, and Kyle started pushing him away and shouting at him. Used the F-word, he did."

"And what are you noticing in your body?"

"There's a real heaviness in my chest."

"Right. And what thought goes with that?"

"I just keep hearing myself say, 'you're a bad mother.'"

On a low formica table in front of her, I'd placed two tear-shaped blobs of grey plastic, connected by cables to a box sprouting dials and switches.

"OK, pick up the paddles, close your eyes again. Bring back that picture, feel that heaviness and hear those words, 'I'm bad.'

I'm going to switch this on, so then just notice what you notice." I set the controls to pulsate.

We sat and listened companionably as the pulses stimulated first her left hand, then her right, then cautiously explored further. Where did that bad feeling come from? The incident at the surgery or, as I strongly suspected, further back? At length, a shadow seemed to lift. Her plump face assumed its habitual setting of placid contentment.

As Cara got up to leave, I had a brainwave. "Could Adrian take Kyle to the doctor's?" Now her frown returned. "He works at that builder's yard, Hewsons', doesn't he? I passed there the other day, it said they're closing at lunchtime on Fridays. Might take some pressure off you."

"Ah, but that's his fishing time." Right. So that's what forklift drivers did to unwind. Or un-prong, maybe. She noticed my momentary look of – what? – frustration tinged with scepticism. Couldn't quite hide it.

"He's good with the housekeeping. Reckons there should be a bit more of that soon. But he's got to have his own space an' all. He's off to the river then, with his mate."

Somehow, something didn't feel right. But I've learned to suppress any instinct to meddle between married couples. After all, it's not as if my own record in that department is anything to shout about.

CHAPTER
TWO

Coffee was chuffing through the stove-top moka maker when a flap, rustle and thump from the front door announced the arrival of the post. Brief interval, before my next appointment, for a quick squizz.

Parked myself on the venerable leather armchair I've hoiked about from one abode to the next – for, ooh, a mere couple of decades – and set about earning my rent reduction for the month by sorting wheat from chaff.

Well! Interesting. The Osney Mead "gala launch event" was next week. Lindsey Miles, head honcho of the developer, Brayford Construction, was requesting the pleasure of Kevin's attendance.

Presumably that's what the placards and banners were for, that protesters were creating at the WOCC. The Councillor would be torn. Supporting jobs in the patch would risk putting environmentalists offside.

Still a few minutes to go… I straightened a picture on the sitting room wall, careful not to scuff the dusky pink emulsion. Framed modern still life, since you ask. Stylised orange snapdragons with black-veined deep green leaves.

Propped on maplewood bookshelves opposite: willow-patterned china plates. Hoarded by my old mum, from Gran, so never had the heart to get rid. Treated them to a perfunctory wipe.

Suitably caffeinated, interval duly filled, I stood, at the clunk of a car door and chirrup of remote locking from outside. The client had arrived.

Emma Kesteven took a seat in the office that overlooks the small front garden of our converted Victorian end-of-terrace house.

Intros and prelims over, I got us started with my opening question for newbies: "What's the one thing in your life you want to change today?"

Emma replied with a convoluted account of discontents in her work as an office manager. "My boss treats me like a servant. I mean, how many coffees do I need to bring, to get a simple thank-you?" As it transpired, nothing in Emma's life was "simple" – but I didn't find that out till much later.

She'd been at fault in a data security breach, when confidential company records were compromised. As she recalled the incident, I noticed her fiddling with her fine gold necklace.

"I'm shaking when I step out the door to go to work. I can't sleep, I can't concentrate." She swallowed hard, tucking her dark blonde hair behind her ears.

I took a punt. "Sounds like it's triggering some old stuff for you?"

Emma settled back into the soft cream leather of the swivel chair and sighed. "I've thought about that. Feels like I've been stuck in this place for a long time, ever since I can remember really."

So now, in her mid-thirties, this was getting serious. "Right, I'm going to get us to play detective, to work out when these patterns started and how they've got stuck. So to do that, I need to find out more about your history."

Emma recalled growing up in a home where material comforts were provided by her wealthy father, and her struggle for attention in competition with the demands of his successful building firm. Not to mention an older brother who could do no wrong.

Back in the present day, she'd threatened to leave her job, even getting as far as sending her boss a resignation letter. The deep sense of freedom was immediately overladen with guilt, and fear of losing her salary.

"How did he respond when he read it?"

"He said: 'This isn't a resignation letter, because you still love me.' Honestly, it's like dealing with a little boy sometimes, he's always trying to manipulate me."

Crossing her legs, she sat back and sighed again, letting one of her smart low-heeled office shoes dangle off her stockinged toes as she brushed away tears from the fine, fair skin of her cheeks.

I resolved to move Emma on as quickly as possible, in future sessions, to installing positive cognitions: countering the trauma by attaching it to good memories and things that worked well in her life. That would give her something to fall back on in those difficult moments.

How many therapists does it take to change a lightbulb? Wrong question. Does the lightbulb really want to change? Doom and gloom from the past act like a dimmer switch.

"Right, good start." I looked over my notes as she stood up to put her coat back on. "What did you say your company's name was, by the way?"

"I didn't," she replied, with a nervous little laugh. "Brayford Construction. Office is in town."

Brayford?! Right. I was feeling a strong hunch coming on. "And your boss?"

"Lindsey. Lindsey Miles." I made a show of writing it down, as if hearing it for the first time. Interesting again. I had to guess this Lindsey character would be under a lot of pressure, what with the launch coming up. Maybe that was why he was being so tough on her.

CHAPTER THREE

I should tidy up in the kitchen – and launder. Mug rings on the oiled oak worktop were conspiring with a coffee stain on the duvet cover to guilt-trip me into housework. Nah, sod it. I needed some reflection and processing after a day's thrupping. Time to run.

Pulled on a green-and-pink patterned pair of Sweaty Betty's finest – from, gosh, could it be four years ago? It could. The elastane had long since lost its snap. Set off along Oatlands Park, our very own green space on this side of the main road. The path now just about exposed as the seasonal flooding receded.

So, husbands, eh? And bosses. Perennial figures in therapy sessions. A certain type of chap seems to crop up in both categories, reminds me of dilapidated yoga pants. Might look the part, but offers absolutely no support, boom-boom.

Dido's dulcets rang in my earbuds. Stuff about rent, commitment and getting one's just deserts. Which brought me to those eyes, watching from the back in the WOCC's great hall earlier. Daniel.

Over the years, we'd been on; off; on again, then finally (?) back off. Spanning both marriages, on my part, and squeezes I wouldn't care to count, on his. Didn't seem to break his heart, that last time, as the song went – but had I really minded? (Note to self: put on the more upbeat playlist in future.)

A Newsquest graduate traineeship rotated me through regional papers, three months a pop, soon landing back in Oxford, where I'd grown up. On the *Mail*. Whose office I was just passing on the right. Not a flicker inside. Much-reduced staffing these days.

Jogging along Osney Mead now, the still-functioning bit. Yards hiring out cars and small industrial plant; the fish market opposite the cash-and-carry, with its garish orange sign announcing openness to the public.

Daniel and I had been set to work in partnership, running the Investigations Desk. Turned out the best fun was investigating each other.

Next came the dun-coloured brick and faded blue wooden panels of the Queen's Centre – venue for the development launch, I remembered from the invitation.

He'd be there, no doubt. Holding up one of those placards outside, probably. Might go into one of his occasional *Guardian* columns, commissioned when the comment editor wanted a radical perspective.

Now finding a second wind, I steadily bore down on the hulking outlines of redundant buildings, concrete blocks plonked in their driveways to prevent travellers from parking up and claiming occupancy. Past obscure university departments and an old printworks and, just short of the road's dead end, a footpath down to the river.

Outrageous, how many redolent place names Oxford contains. Recriminations over loves lost took me all the way to – wait for it – Folly Bridge. And back, via the lock and past the community-owned hydro, grinding away in the torrent.

They had open days at weekends when you could get a close look at the massive propeller inside its wood-and-glass housing. Always gave me the shivers, even when the flow was normal. From the path, I could hear the giant turbine threshing away, steel blades shearing through the floodwater. Whump-whump-whump-whump.

Next, you had to slalom your way around chest-high bars intended to prevent lycra'd cavalry from hurtling through on their two-wheeled chargers, and pad across a footbridge as the swollen, turbid current roiled and thundered below.

Then home, slowing to a walk around the schoolyard and back along the park, critical inner voices now finally still as the gushing Thames faded from earshot.

"So how come there's all this trouble over it?" I asked, as Kevin passed me his draft of an emailed reply to a constituent. Quick shower and change then I'd popped upstairs to the maisonette, in answer to his summons, to assume my role of part-time assistant.

Two designer velvet easy chairs in dusky olive-green were neatly arranged around a coffee table and teakwood TV cabinet in the double-aspect sitting room. For some reason, Kevin's place always makes me lapse into estate-agent-speak. Probably because it's so smart. Dove-grey Venetian blinds obscured the famous park view, daylight having long gone. The unforgiving hours of a people's champion.

"Well, land freeing up that close to the city centre should all be for housing. But the university has designs on it. And there are quite a few jobs down there." He stood and walked over to his deep-blue aquarium, shimmering against the far wall.

"Hm. What about the taxi drivers?"

"Sure, that's the odd thing." He rolled up a sleeve of his trademark striped shirt and plunged an arm into the water, causing an iridescent burst of tropical fish. "Officers ended up recommending the scheme with the access road. So there'll be a new bridge coming out from the end of the estate over the river to Oxpens, by the ice rink. Should take some heat off us over the LTNs."

"Low Traffic Neighbourhoods?"

"Yeah – y'know, we're not just closing roads, we're building 'em too."

Turning back after repositioning one of the plants in the tank, the Councillor flashed me a twinkle from those still-piercing blue eyes. Many a doorstep encounter, come election time, would swing his way through a winning combination with a snowy-white tonsure and matching Van Dyke beard.

His computer wallpaper was a sequence of dissolves: the Seven Ages of Kevin. At that moment, a picture of him clean-shaven, from the leaving do when he quit investment banking, just before the global financial crisis. In the City, "homos were just about acceptable" by then, as he put it; "facial hair, never." He dried himself off, rolled the sleeve back down and resumed his seat.

"You can't write this to Mr and Mrs Bowen, by the way." Householders were aghast at rubbish strewn across their street from parcels left on doorsteps by delivery riders – including food. Apparently, crows were opening them and snaffling the contents: a scene the elderly couple had witnessed "with our own eyes," as their email put it.

Kevin's draft response was short on diplomacy: "Suggest you grin and bear it." I had him promise to write to the companies concerned, reminding them of their responsibilities; inserted a few commas in the Councillor's stream-of-consciousness and handed back the laptop.

"What I rely on you for. Anyway, this bridge'll have bollards either end, that are supposed to retract if you point a dongle at them. They'll be for residents, emergency services – and taxis."

I took a deep draft of kombucha tea – Kevin's elixir, as he called it. "But the environmentalists are against it?"

"Yep. I mean, they have a point, we shouldn't be encouraging more cars. But they live in the wrong places."

"How d'you mean?"

"Where Greenies tend to live, they're all safe seats, like here. The LTN disputes are in the marginals, over in Cowley and Marston. More… how shall I put it? Multi-cultural."

"Ah – the Mosque." Daniel and I had briefly shacked up in Temple Cowley, a micro 'burb just inside the eastern city bypass, in the fraught years following the 9/11 attacks. Our Muslim neighbours were coming under heavy pressure from discrimination and – at times – official harassment. We'd highlighted cases in the paper of communities rallying round to defend them. But would they now be on different sides?

"Got it in one. The Regal Cars boys are all regulars there, of course. Mind, they make odd bedfellows – Muslims aligned with the far Right." The gravel in his Lowland accent edged up a notch at the expense of the honey.

"Didn't know we had a far Right in Oxford."

"They're not from here. Those demos against traffic calming, you get a shitstorm on social media and a load of thugs bussed in from God-knows-where. But then it makes a big splash in the paper, and of course the sitting members for those areas get the wind up."

CHAPTER
FOUR

First thing I noticed on coming back down: dirty washing staring back reproachfully from its basket by the machine. You'd think moving it there would be enough to get it clean, but no.

Letters addressed to me, set aside when sorting earlier, unopened on the kitchen table. Fish oil and vitamins on a plate beside the sink from that morning when I'd forgotten to pop 'em in. Late to rise, loath to leave the warmth of bed. Turn the heating up? Bills these days made for scary reading, so probably better not. Have to zip up the old fleece instead.

Time to open my own MacBook. Taking stock of the client emails waiting unforgivingly for replies, I noticed the WhatsApp icon flashing in a corner of the screen. I'd missed two video calls from Jem.

I'd thought of him that morning when listening to a strangely addictive radio show, One Good Thing, giving tips for health and weight loss. Apparently: snack on nuts instead of cake, read novels, take regular exercise. Who knew? Anyway, so my train of thought went – yes, and there's just One Good Thing in my life from my first marriage. Actually, very good.

"Hi Mum." At the sound of his voice, a mind's-eye gallery

instantly flashed up, of my boy on his first bike, off to school for the first time and so on; only to be pushed into the background. Little Jem had long gone, the space he'd previously occupied now full – very full – of Big Jem.

"Are you remembering about Sunday?" *Sunday? What?* "I'm drumming at Isis Farmhouse."

"Yep, it's in my calendar – really looking forward to it!" *Good cover, Mum.*

Spinney Comprehensive (later, 'Academy') had offered music lessons, but images of junior violin or flute were rudely dispelled when Jem discovered rhythm. Now, the years practising percussion for end-of-term musicals – straining the soundproofing in our little mid-terrace and the neighbours' patience alike – were seemingly paying off.

"Heard from Dad?" Meeting Callum had settled me down, no question. On the rebound from Daniel, stolid respectability was suddenly attractive – for a while.

"Yeah, but he can't come." Busy with his new family, no doubt (what did I mean, 'new'? His oldest must be a teenager by now).

"And how are things at the plant?"

"They've put me with one of the senior managers. I have to go to Board meetings." Now in his placement year of a course in Engineering and Motorsport at Oxford Brookes, Jem was gaining experience at BMW Cowley, the Mini factory. Could be why he was beginning to look and sound more like his dad. He'd got a shorter haircut, I noticed – dark and sober-corporate.

"Sounds fab. And have they said any more about the trainee scheme?"

"Nothing specific. But they wouldn't at this stage – it's about giving me people to approach next year, who'll know me and have seen what I can do."

"Learning both the how and the why?"

"You've been listening! OK, great, see you Sunday."

A client who'd cried off several attempts to arrange an initial session had emailed profound apologies for standing me up. He was in danger of being declared a Bolter. I replied offering to reschedule for noon tomorrow, Friday (last chance to avoid paying the fee for a no-show, under my seven-day cancellation policy).

I was just about to close the lid, put the computer on to charge, fix a liquorice tea and start winding down for the night, when WhatsApp twinkled again.

"I've got something, could be something big." Daniel, of course. No-one else would call that late or open a conversation without so much as a greeting.

"I'm well, thanks for asking – and you?" He gave a thin humourless smile, marshalling scant reserves of patience to engage with the mere mortal on the other end.

"Glad to hear. Look, I haven't got long. Expecting a call from LA." Of course he was – and they were, what, eight hours behind us? A respectable time of day, unlike here now.

"If something happens to me, I'll need you to pick this up."

"*Happens* to you? Sure you're not being a bit… melo-dramatic?"

"Probably." He sighed. "Look, Jan, I really don't have long, I can't miss this call. Just promise me – if needs be, you'll pick this up."

"OK." Deep breath. "If – IF – it makes any sense in my life at all, and you really, really need me to do something, I'll think about it. That do?"

"Have to, I guess." The set of his features adjusted, momentarily exposing the vulnerable boy within. Which I'd never been able to resist.

"So what is this big thing and where is it?"

"A leak. Something that could blow wide open. And somewhere only we know. Just remember that."

"I'll try, but…" There was a beep from his end, and, sure enough, his American call.

"Gotta go. You're a star. Laters."

I rubbed in rose and frankincense night cream with more than usual vigour. "Laters"?! When did he start saying "Laters"? And what could blow wide open?

I bent down with a piece of loo roll to rub a splodge of the lotion off the grey woollen mat: essential kit until temperatures rose to the point where the tiles could be trodden on barefooted.

The space felt cramped unless you knew the exact spot to stand – and from there, you could catch yourself in perfect profile through the reflection of one mirror image in the other. From the corner of an eye, I glimpsed my own cross-looking pursed lips and slightly flared nostrils and suppressed a snort.

It used to be enjoyably comedic, his mysterious, I-know-more-than-I-can-tell-you act. But it seemed to have dissolved what remained of his previous personality. I put it down as a cautionary tale, of what can happen when someone starts to believe their own publicity.

CHAPTER
FIVE

Ensconced under the duvet, coffee-stained cover and all, I finally warmed up and had little difficulty nodding off. But then, in the small hours, I was abruptly wide awake.

The sudden, intense feeling of something amiss, on taking leave of Cara that afternoon, came sharply into focus. Of course: Adrian couldn't be going fishing when Hewsons' closed early on Friday. Why? Because it was the close season.

I groped for my iPhone and looked it up to check. Yep. Fishing in rivers had stopped a fortnight ago and wouldn't be allowed again till June.

Back in the *Oxford Mail* days, I'd done a story about the big chub that gathered to spawn on the shallow gravel beds of Osney Brook – and the threat to their habitat from interference with water flows. The photographer had captured some vivid pictures to go with it. I remembered the plump, yard-long, green-and-gold creatures hovering on the swift current without apparent exertion.

So if Cara's husband wasn't playing the proverbial fool on one end with a worm on the other, what *was* he doing? I recognised the old itch, to delve deeper and find out what was afoot. Which would need very careful handling indeed.

Sleep eventually returned, through a miasma of Daniel and his leak, Adrian and his fishing rod, Kevin and his bridge, Jem and his drums.

Waking up groggy, with a difficult client, Sophie, due online at half past eight, I resolved to take myself in hand.

With a bit of minor rearrangement, the space between living room furniture could just take a yoga mat, so I spent twenty minutes bending, stretching and saluting the sun.

Grumpy old so-and-so, it still wouldn't come out from behind the cloud, I noticed as I stood in the kitchen waiting for the coffee to steam through. An extra cup of espresso would sharpen the senses, at the cost of having to cross my legs towards the end of that first hour.

Relieved at having both improved Sophie's mood and lasted out for the loo, I helped myself to nuts and a banana for breakfast. As the rain had abated, I drew the string around the top of the rubbish bag and took it out to the bin. Hanging baskets sat heaped up forlornly. Not worth replenishing them before a turn in the weather.

Back indoors, the dwarf ficus would appreciate the dust being wiped off its leaves – but did it need watering, or would that kill it? I was never quite sure.

Another client was due online at ten-thirty, followed by a half-hour break then, at twelve, Adam, the Bolter. Inevitably, halfway through that second session, as the twin magenta blobs of the Bilateral Base online EMDR platform zipped back and forth across the screen to stimulate eye movements, an email from him came in – crying off again.

So I took time from midday to draft a suitably sensitive response. After that, despite all efforts at prevarication, there was no way to avoid noticing that lunchtime, early closing at one o'clock, was approaching. And Hewsons' yard lay just a few minutes away by bike.

From the park opposite, a crow cawed disapprovingly as I strapped on my helmet. Could be the one bothering the Bowens.

I fastened up the coat around my chin, planning to hunch down in it to avoid being recognised. If there was the faintest glimmer of sunshine, I could put on the dark Ray-Bans from my pocket – but the cloud cover was complete.

I'd know my quarry by sight, having spotted him, from a discreet distance, out in town with Cara. When discussing him in therapy sessions, she'd occasionally mentioned Adrian's luxuriant dark hair and beard. On the latter, feelings were mixed, since it tended to reveal the ginger component of his colouring. But he'd never clapped eyes on me, that I knew of.

I headed straight for the best bargain in West Oxford. At Burger World, a van on the trading estate, Fat Les would serve you coffee in a polystyrene cup for a quid (cash only). You could probably strip paint with it, but hey, it was hot and came with free sugar – and what could you expect for a quid?

Sure enough, the coat pocket contained my small brass portrait of Her (late) Maj, which saw regular service in the slot release mechanism of an Aldi trolley. Have to be the basket on wheels next time. I handed it over, got my drink and sat down.

A perch on the wooden table-and-bench set gave a good view of Hewsons' yard as the top of the hour drew nigh. A giant poster, attached to the railings, assured passers-by: "We'll beat any project quote – guaranteed." Its neighbour promised: "All your timber needs – met." Next time I had timber needs, I'd be sure to call in.

The customer-end gate was shut, and through the grey bars I could make out the attendant locking up the on-site shop. Then, a four-wheeled Mercedes flatbed truck in dark red came cruising along Lamarsh Road and drew up outside the other gate, which was open.

It backed in, whereupon a forklift truck appeared from somewhere behind, and started to load pallets onto the vehicle. And the man operating the forklift was, unmistakably, Cara's husband, Adrian – ginger-tinged beard and all. Not a fishing rod in sight.

He and the truck driver secured the goods using those thick canvas straps that tighten with metal buckles. Then he parked up, walked across the yard and climbed into the Mercedes' passenger seat.

What really tickled that itch of mine was the look Adrian quickly shot around him as they set off. It could only be described as furtive.

CHAPTER
SIX

What to do with my shiny new nugget of knowledge? Just to give myself time to think, I walked the long way homewards, pushing my bike along the pavement of Botley Road.

Passed Carpet Warehouse on my right and looked opposite to Osney Court, a squat red-brick block dating from the early 2000s. Cara and Adrian rented one of the apartments, I remembered.

Should I find her and report what I'd seen? She would either be there or – come to think of it – probably on a shift behind the tills, a little further away at Dutchelm: Home of Household Tat (if I'd got that right).

In either case, I couldn't imagine that little vignette with any kind of ending that was not cross, embarrassing, or both.

Then, what *had* I seen? Adrian, er, doing his job as a forklift driver at Hewsons'. "I caught your husband, not fishing." It somehow seemed to lack moral force. Simultaneous pangs of hunger, indecision, and regret that Burger World was now far behind firmed into a resolve. I would seek tea and sympathy from Miri.

Sympathy assumed solid form in the last of that day's freshly baked sausage rolls, left over from the lunchtime rush. As for tea? I perused the list of speciality brews from the blackboard beside the door. Not the Rooibos today – how about the Lemon and Ginger? Surely too wet without something to soak it up. A matching piece of lemon cake somehow jumped onto my order all by itself.

"I bring it over," she said. There were deep red tulips in a vase on the counter and next to them some even more splendid blooms (chrysanthemums?) in complementary shades. Jars of spices on shelves behind – and, beyond that, a glimpse of the famous kitchen, where the magic happened.

On the wall was a framed black-and-white print of that strange Picasso war picture, with a row of pot plants above that were certainly better cared for than mine.

Was this right? I had a supervision session lined up next week, but that felt a long way off. And, in any case, my information had not arisen in therapy. I'd have to be careful not to say anything that could point to who was involved. So I silently rehearsed a pronoun-neutral account of the essential facts.

Miri set down my treats with a "back soon" before bustling off, in her invariable black mini-skirt, tights, and boots, to see to other customers.

Knives and forks nestled in a golden syrup tin, brought to my table, but a sausage roll is only fun with fingers. I'd just poured out the tea from its little red pot and taken a sip when she returned. "What is up, my dear?"

"OK, so I have this client, whose partner I've found out is lying to them." Her brown eyes opened a little wider, with a murmur of concern. "The partner pretends to be doing one thing, which means they're not available to do something else – something I think they *should* do."

"This husband-wife?" I nodded, mouth full of lemon cake.

"Bad, bad idea. Never come between." She saw my raised eyebrows. "If you are sure, you speak. But be very careful, Janna. You do not know – how to say – half of it."

"What if speaking out would be for the good of one, if not both?" Sun found a chink in the grey and sent intermittent rays through the big glass door to the terrace behind us. A few hardy customers were now trying coffee al fresco. I surreptitiously gathered up lemony crumbs between forefinger and thumb.

"How you know good?! This like – like dry sticks. You light, you set fire, can burn both. Better leave alone." Sage advice, no doubt, but it felt like an anticlimax after the detective work earlier. I tried a different tack.

"If I keep quiet, am I not helping the second partner to deceive the first? She might have a right to know." And there, I'd let the pronoun thing slip. Damn. Miri rocked back on the metal stool she had drawn up, pursed her lips, and shook her head.

"Is other lady?" I was forced to admit, not. "In such case, I think, leave alone. They find out by themselves in the end. If is right."

The woman came in through the terrace door who owned the sister and mother of Miri's whippet, so of course the creature was brought out from its lair in the back and pretty soon they were ooh-ing and aah-ing like it was some whippet convention. Three emaciated hounds felt like too much throbbing gristle in a confined space, so I took my leave and went home to prepare for the last client of the week.

CHAPTER
SEVEN

Finally, as the weekend dawned, Spring realised the year was passing her by. Clouds parted. Primulas sent pale yellow reinforcements to the gallant, battered garrison of snowdrops holding the line in the park. Assorted pipits and warblers chimed in with season's greetings.

Then, on Sunday afternoon, I cycled along the river towards Iffley to watch my son play the drums. Downstream from Donnington Bridge, willows and chestnuts had started to unfurl foliage whose green would deepen as the days lengthened.

The railings around the pub's garden were already parked up with bikes, so I lifted old Bertha over the other side to attach her to some solid metal. Nice thing about Isis Farmhouse – it could only be reached from the path, so no cars.

I'd always assumed the Thames at Oxford being called Isis was some Egyptian connection, but a client who's a Uni don put me right: it's Celtic, apparently. Little did those ancient Britons know they'd be lending their name to the plumbers, roofers and electricians whose vans go pottering around the city streets, thousands of years on.

I followed signs round the back to the barn, guided by the music already underway, then entered a large, low-ceilinged building, crowded with tables and chairs to the left, and – ahead of me – a dancefloor, marked out in black and white tiled squares, with couples swaying to the infectious Cuban beat.

Jem flashed a smile over his drumkit as I made my way to the bar. Suitably equipped with a bottle of beer, I scanned the tables for a familiar face. Sure enough, his housemate, Chris, was there, with partner Kerryn. I sashayed over to take a seat at their table.

"They're on good form," I said as the band reached a crescendo and the dancers paused to applaud.

"Yeah, sick. Everyone's movin' and groovin'. You OK?" I nodded with a smile as the band leader, holding a saxophone and suitably decked out in a Caribbean-style cream suit, announced the next number. A grey-haired activist from the Oxford Cuban Solidarity Campaign moved among us, rattling a collecting bucket. If only I still had that pound coin.

Was I above snaffling a few of the couple's fat chips that lolled temptingly in a bowl in front of them? I was not.

"How are things on The Leys?" The couple rented a room in my mum's old two-bed terrace. A lifelong Leftie and firm believer in public housing, Cathy Rose (née Tucker) had reluctantly exercised her Right to Buy when the New Labour government that got in from the late nineties showed no sign of reversing the policy.

She'd hung on till after Jem went to Spinney Comp, then fulfilled her own prophecy that "they'll have to carry me out of here feet-first." The Big C, of course. As only child and sole heir, I simply moved back in.

"All good," Chris reported. "We got that cupboard door put back on in the kitchen."

The couples gyrated as Jem and his bandmates – how many were there? At least a dozen – struck up another catchy number. Some had evidently come as a dance class, with the women sporting long twirly skirts for the purpose.

So – Blackbird Leys. At some point, Oxford planners decided to name council estates after rural idylls. See also Wood Farm and Rose Hill. You don't simply go *to* Blackbird Leys but 'on to The Leys.' It was reluctance by paying clients to do just that, when in-person appointments resumed after Covid, that led me to rent in leafy West Oxford instead.

The band signed off their first set with a triumphant "cha-cha-cha," and the man of the moment headed our way.

Anyway, so Jem now had Mum's old place on Falcon Crescent and lived off the rent from Chris and partner. Saved him getting too far into debt, what with his student loan and all.

"You came!" Was it just growing confidence that made him look suddenly broader and taller? The mantra from his childhood: eat up your dinner/sandwich/fruit "and you'll grow up big and strong." So here he was. Not sure about the shirt, though. A Hawai'ian number in – what was it? – mauve and off-white. *Don't say anything, Mum, might cross a line.*

"Of course." I resisted the temptation to reach up and ruffle his hair. "Quite a job, drumming for all those musos."

"Ah, it's easy. Same beat for each number." A young woman from the band came across from the bar and handed him a drink. We all chinked bottles and toasted his prowess. "Funny thing – I was in the toilets earlier and someone spoke to me about you." I raised my eyebrows. "He mentioned Daniel – said you were a nice lady and you should stay away from him."

"Really? Who was this?"

"Oh, just some guy. I didn't know him, he was at the next… urinal, you know. Or perhaps you don't. Anyway, I agreed with him of course."

"Seriously, Jem, you've got me worried." A haunting image dispelled the pleasant Sunday-afternoon fugue. Still fresh despite the years: Jem aged eleven, getting out of a police car, little face creasing into tears, rushing over to my arms. "What did he look like, this guy?"

"Er – not sure. He was gone the next moment. But Mum, seriously, he was right. Daniel's never caused you anything but heartache."

That summer – what was it? Nine years ago now – there'd been Facebook scares about child abductions in Oxford. Two years further back, when I'd still been on the *Mail*, a schoolgirl was snatched and assaulted; an episode that tended to prey on parents' minds.

"Can you see him now?" We all looked around the bar area, tables and dancefloor, but to no avail. Jem shook his head.

"Must've gone."

Distracted, I listened to the second set chatting on and off with Kerryn. Pretty in pink loose-fit linen shirt, longish dark hair tied with hippy-ish string 'n' beads, earnest manner. Thinking of changing degree courses to study Psychology. She got a rather perfunctory account of how I'd retrained as a therapist after leaving journalism.

On that past occasion, piecing the story together through his sobs, Jem and a friend had wandered off and got lost. They were just about to get into a strange car when a couple, who knew the other lad through their grandson, passed by through sheer fluke, intervened to stop them and called the cops.

Back at the Isis, as we parted with hugs, I tried not to let him see I was frazzled. Whoever spoke to Jem obviously knew who he was, who I was, and who Daniel was. And Jem, at least, hadn't known him. Maybe I would have done, if I'd set eyes on him – and that would have explained it.

Then, what could the mystery man have meant, that I should stay away from Daniel? Heck, I DID stay away from Daniel. Last time we'd parted was with a shared sense of finality. Our paths hadn't crossed for months – before the other day at the Community Centre. Then there'd been that bizarre chat on WhatsApp, where he'd been muttering about some big secret.

The ride home calmed me down a bit, though a cold wind had

begun to blow up. I'd left Jem with instructions to look after himself.

After The Incident, the next upset had come when school put on a talk about Stranger Danger, I recalled. But it had seemed to fade over time. He promised to let me know if he remembered anything else about his encounter in the lavvy.

It was near dusk when I got back to find a trade van parked in the street. Isis Electricals? No – Bracebridge, and a sparky at work, installing some kind of box thingy next door. "Mind if I ask what you're doing?" The neighbours, Tim and Wendy, were away for a few weeks, so I'd promised to keep an eye.

"New internet," he said, with a grin. "Booked in a few weeks ago. Should be up and running when they get back." I thanked him and went inside. He must have been on a decent whack, turning out on a Sunday for a non-urgent job.

Only when I took out my iPhone from the bike bag did I see two missed calls from Kevin, which could only mean something in his world WAS urgent. Listening to his message, he sounded "up a height," as Mum used to say.

"You'd think I'd have learned by now," the Councillor reproached himself. He'd spoken "off the cuff" to a reporter about shopkeepers displaying election posters in their windows urging support for independent candidates in the upcoming elections, opposed to the Low Traffic Neighbourhoods.

One of the shops rejoiced in the name of The Goldfish Bowl and – since Kevin's hobby of keeping tropical fish was reasonably well-known – he'd been asked specifically about it. His comment: "That will be a sure way to stop me supporting that shop and move to buying all my aquarium supplies much more cheaply online."

Reasonable enough perhaps, but, as he well knew, it crossed

a line. Elected reps were supposed to be in favour of local trade, political affiliations or not.

As the fish in question gulped and shimmered at us from their backlit midnight-blue tank, I helped him to draft an emollient statement, qualifying his earlier reaction, in time for the reporter's deadline. It would not prevent a set of pearl-clutching horrified responses from his rivals, but it would limit the damage.

CHAPTER
EIGHT

Emma turned up for her second session in a much more positive mood. She yearned for approval from her boss, Lindsey, as she'd done from her father years earlier. When it was withheld, she was miserable – only now, it had apparently been switched back on.

She shucked her coat and sat down with a smile. "He's like a different person. And everyone's really excited about the launch tomorrow night." The problem, of course, was that it could equally be switched off.

"That sounds great. But we need to find you a safe space, somewhere you can go when things get tough."

"OK."

"So let me invite you to picture somewhere calm and peaceful, where you feel protected. It could be real or imagined. What does it look like? What does it feel like?"

"I just love being on my own in my little sitting room, in my flat. Everything's the way I want it. I can sit with a nice cup of tea and just be myself."

"Great. Now, we're going to build you a team of nurturers, protectors and wise beings to be with you in that safe space. We begin by naming nurturers, who can comfort you.

Normally, we think of three: a real person, a mythical being and an animal."

She opened with Prue Leith, from *Bake-Off*, and Wonder Woman, then someone called Kayla Harrison.

"Who's that?"

"She's in UFC." Registering my blank look: "Ultimate Fighting Championship. It's on ESPN. She came in off winning the Olympics for judo."

"Ah." Surprise often lies in store when we judge by appearances, as I found I'd done with Emma, in her sober business suit and discreet make-up. Still, what does a fan of televised unarmed combat look like?

At that point, the doorbell rang. I suggested we ignore it, but it rang again. I knew Kevin was out, so I had to answer.

On the step was a rider in a black helmet, with a nose-mouth covering and tinted goggles, who mutely held out a brown paper carrier bag with takeaway food from Courieroo. "I haven't ordered anything." I looked at the receipt and instructions stapled to the bag. "No, this is for number 32. We're 42."

He looked again at the paper, and our door, where the number was clearly displayed, raised a hand by way of wordless apology, mounted his e-bike and went on his way. I went back inside to Emma.

"Right, so now you've got your resources of a safe space and your team, you're ready for Eye Movement Desensitisation and Reprocessing."

"Bit of a mouthful!"

"Indeed. Hence EMDR for short." She made a quizzical expression.

"We all live with early life memories that affect our responses in the present day."

"Right."

"Some of them get lodged in sections of the brain that are pre-verbal. So we can't access them just by talking. So pick up the paddles." I'd placed them on the desk beside her.

"These?" She gave one of them an experimental squeeze. "What do they do?"

"When I switch them on, they'll buzz alternately, left and right. That's BLS, or bilateral stimulation. That's how we open up those traumatic memories to be reprocessed."

We first installed the resources Emma had named, then dug deeper into the origins of her fragile self-esteem. By the end of the session, I was getting Prue, Wonder Woman, Kayla and the pony she'd ridden in childhood to help with scenarios when she'd sought approval and got upset when it wasn't forthcoming. We ranged over instances at the office, but also further back.

"What happened in the end, by the way, to your dad's firm?" At this, her confident demeanour faltered for the first time.

"It… failed. It wasn't nice."

"And how was that for you?"

"I was away at college. But my brother, Giles, took it hard. He was helping to run the business by then."

I looked closely at her, trying to read the layers of meaning in her face. "OK. Let's pick that up next time. Good session today."

∾

Checking emails before going out for my run, I found one from Kevin, booking me for media-minder duty at the Osney Mead development launch the following night. His careless remark about the aquarium shop had caused a row that was still rumbling on, apparently, in the fraught atmosphere of the impending election.

I looked again at the invitation. It was catered, so I'd get fed, though I'd have to go easy on the vino. OK – I could make that, being, as it was, only ten minutes' walk away. Have to knock another few quid off the next rent.

After the dry, sunny weekend, we'd had two days of relentless drizzle, thankfully abated but leaving behind rising floodwaters that would make the path across the park one for wellies, not trainers. So I jogged off the other way, up the road.

And blow me if I wasn't just in time to catch naughty old Joe Crow, picking at a morsel on the pavement, fixing me with an insouciant stare then flapping away with his prize. I had only to follow the line of debris to Number 32, where the food bag – what was left of it – sat on the doorstep. Bits of chicken and rice were strewn across the path.

For some reason, repeated doorbell-ringing failed to yield any response, so I picked up the mess as best I could and parked it in their bin. Have to have words later. The Bowens were right all along, then. Must admit I'd assumed the old dears were either seeing things or, at best, exaggerating.

∽

Back at the Community Centre the next day, I noticed Cara had been shopping. "Nice coat." Practical too: a natty zippered waterproof number in navy, with contrasting white drawstrings for the hood.

She beamed. "Eighty-nine ninety-five from Next." I craned across to see the label: Joules Portwell. Fancy. "Adrian took us to the Westgate, Saturday."

"He got that bonus at work then?" She nodded, still smiling. I'd been wondering whether and how to reveal that her husband had not been straight with her. However, Dr Des, my supervisor, when we Zoomed on Monday, had been categorical: "Keep it in the therapy room, Janna."

That supported Miri's advice, of course. Then, as a tale to tell a wife, it was the wrong way round. Snitch on a chap for fishing when he should be working, OK. But working when he should be fishing?

I set the thought aside and steered the session towards a hardy perennial topic: Cara's fraught relationship with her mother.

CHAPTER
NINE

It was gratifying to find myself expected at the Queen's Centre as it meant that, on the table by reception, there was a dinky little badge with my name on it. I could use it to cover the immovable stain on the lapel of my one good suit.

As I moved through to the presentation room, display boards of blue felt were showing posters with artists' impressions of the new development.

Pausing to snag a glass of chardonnay, I recognised a couple of Regal Cars men, looking uncomfortable in jacket and tie. Guests numbered about forty, I estimated – but, of the protesters I'd seen at the Community Centre, there was no sign; and no Daniel.

Kevin bore down on me, trim and dapper in a grey suit and open-necked blue stripey shirt. "Janna – let me introduce you. Lindsey Miles, Chief Exec of Brayford Construction." I took the opportunity to size up Emma's boss. She was somewhere in the background, no doubt dotting i's and crossing t's for the launch.

Not tall – I'd say about five-nine – but quite powerfully built. Intense-looking, slightly pale blue eyes. The most prominent feature was a luxuriant beard – dark blond, with nary a ginger hair in sight.

"So Kevin tells me you're a therapist?" he boomed. As I gave my standard brief explanation, he mentally worked the room, eyes darting this way and that. I could have told him I was seeing Bugs Bunny for a phallic carrot fixation, and Lindsey would have nodded politely. Still, it was his big night. I let him go and concentrated on the canapés.

We sat in rows for Lindsey's shtick. PowerPoints supplied images, from the same artist it seemed, of happy workers frolicking on manicured lawns between carbon-neutral offices "fit for the 21st-Century." Residents parked their cars among new-build high-density housing.

"I know many of you here from our development and construction community, of course. And I know you'll share my concerns about site security." There was a murmur of agreement. "We at Brayford are pioneers of the very latest technology: remote-controlled micro-cameras, invisible to the naked eye."

He turned to signal to Emma, behind him, and she switched the source of the presentation. Not graphics now but live video, the screen divided into eight squares. And what was this? The audience were suddenly looking at images from this very room – of themselves. But where were the cameras?! Gasps at the stunt were matched by a ripple of applause. The reporter from regional TV news, resplendent in a teal jacket, told her cameraman to get rolling.

"Gone are the days when intruders can see where the pictures are coming from, due to old-fashioned CCTV systems – and, more importantly, see how to get round them," Lindsey continued. "With the Brayford system…"

There was a sudden crash from behind him. Smoke started pouring into the conference room from a door now flung open to one side of the dais. Through it sprang protesters in matching white t-shirts with the words, "Lethal Cars" on the front, imitating the Regal Cars logo.

The fumes emanated from a portable smoke machine, carried by one of them at the front. Gas masks covered their faces to protect against inhalation. Behind them, two more protesters emerged, carrying the banner depicting the coughing planet Earth that they'd been creating at the WOCC – and, bringing up the rear, Daniel, the only one whose face was visible.

Guests stood up and began retreating, some holding handkerchiefs over their noses and mouths. Lindsey stalked off to one side and stood, glowering, with Emma in tow.

Daniel's clear, strong voice cut through the hubbub. "Your attention please! This development brings us closer to extinction. This road bridge sets up our city to be dominated by cars for years ahead. We're being manipulated into accepting it – so ask yourself why and how."

One of the Regal Cars men broke ranks, spitting fury. "You don't know what you're talking about! You Greenies – you just want to ruin our business! This is because we're Muslims!" Others from the audience moved to hold him back, and his tone shifted to one of quiet menace. "Just don't go crossing any roads after dark."

Daniel held his gaze with a neutral expression then, as the smoke swirled and the taxi man allowed himself to be ushered away, gave a signal to his crew to pack up and go.

With the air cleared and masked protesters dispersed, the TV journo was recording interviews in the Queen's Centre foyer. She'd leave with a better story than would have seemed likely in prospect. Kevin turned to me for a whispered conflab.

"I'd emphasise their right to have their say, but Council has to consider all points of view. Don't take sides, stay above the fray."

"Makes my point," Lindsey was telling the reporter. "Site security is uppermost. Of course, we'll be talking to the people here at Queen's about their system. I'm sure we can help."

I was allowing myself four squares of dark choccy with my bedtime tea instead of the usual two. Buoyed by my advice, Kevin had played the grown-up in the room with trademark panache. Still, Daniel, eh?! Always a source of surprises. Then my mobile rang. A gruff male voice.

"Miss Rose?"

"Y-yes...?" No-one calls me that.

"It's Thames Valley Police, Miss. I'm afraid there's been an incident. Can you come down to the station at St Aldates? We'll send a car."

"What sort of incident?"

"Sorry to have to tell you, there's been a fatality. A gentleman. Family's all abroad, apparently. From our inquiries, we've been told you're the person who knew him best, locally. We'd like you to identify the body."

∼

So it was final now. A cloth up to his chin and, above it, the still, slightly battered features of the man who had been, if we were facing facts, the love of my life.

"WPC Richards is here if you need anything, Miss." Family liaison.

"I'll be alright thanks." I'd never imagined Daniel dead. Well, you don't, do you? I'd have to stop thinking of those early days at the *Mail*, or I'd lose it big-time. And I really, really didn't want to do that in St Aldates nick.

CHAPTER
TEN

WPC Richards carried on liaising alongside me on the back seat. "I'm Denise. I grew up on The Leys, we lived in Windrush Tower. My sister Pearl was at school with you. She's the oldest, I was the youngest. Of five."

The BMW saloon turned off the orbital and smoothly back into the city along Botley Road, intermittent wipers seeming to take up the rhythm of my inner laments. "Ah – Pearl! How is she?"

"Yeah, good. Still there." I cranked the memory bank into gear.

"And still… nursing?"

"Yep, at Sanctuary Care now."

"In Iffley village?"

"That's the one." We fell into a more comfortable silence on the rest of the journey. "Anyway, let me know if there's anything you need."

"Will do, thanks." I let myself in and felt suddenly hungry. There was still half a packet of salted cashews at the back of the cupboard: slightly stale but OK.

So, Pearl. Wow. A name I hadn't heard in a long, long time. My childhood playmate through the stormy last months when

Dad was still around. Then, one morning, when I came down to breakfast, he was gone.

A few days later, when he still hadn't turned up, I had it out with Mum. She told me he'd left us because "there were other things he had to do." When I was judged old enough, some of the starker details got filled in. Gambling addiction meant he'd owed money to the wrong people and had to make himself scarce.

So my later life had been steered by conflicting tendencies. Seeking a stable replacement father figure almost certainly accounted for two ill-advised marriages.

At the same time, I'd wanted to forge an identity separated as far as possible from the one I'd grown up with. Now here it was, back again. Pearl. Must catch up. Sometime soon. Getting to Uni and into journalism was supposed to help – though it brought me back home. Then there'd been Daniel.

I popped in the last cashew, took a swig from the liquorice tea, sitting cold on the side where I'd left it earlier, and tried to calm my too-active brain into sleepiness. No dice.

"Knocked down, looks like," the desk sergeant had said tersely, harassed amid a backlog of incoming cases. Questions bubbled up that I should have asked. By a car, presumably?

Daniel, campaigner for Low Traffic Neighbourhoods and against the new road bridge from Osney Mead. What was that, deadly irony? Where, and how?

Inconveniently, it was too late to call anyone. I didn't want to disturb Jem since he was keeping office hours at the Cowley plant.

So I lulled myself with a tried and trusted self-care method: tapping on pressure points around the body while intoning a soothing mantra.

"Even though I screwed up with Daniel, I love and accept myself." Tap, tap, tap. Eyebrow, side of the eye, under the eye. Tap, tap, tap.

I should put those half-dozen or so books back on the shelf, not leave them untidily heaped on the table. The reeds still poked out of the air freshener bottle but the liquid had long since evaporated. Details that would have driven Callum to distraction.

∼

The turbulence of my formative years on the Leys had taught me one trick, at least: how to put on a brave face to the outside world and pretend nothing was amiss. So, come morning, I reached for the tools of my trade.

Hair slightly long and billowy? Simples: nail scissors to trim it back. I clipped off the scraggy ends from the back and sides, brushed the top over my eyes, leant forwards while peering in the mirror through the dangling strands, and shortened the fringe.

Shadowy eye sockets from a sleepless night? Time for the most expensive item in my bathroom cabinet: a golden tube of camouflage goo that rejoiced in the name, "Touche Éclat." How they think of these things… Problem: hardly any left.

I just about squeezed enough into the brush to apply a "natural, luminous finish" to the tell-tale dark strip under each eye, then smoothed it in.

Judging by the previous night, I'd need more soon, which would mean a trip into the city and the Elysian Fields – final resting place of the souls of the virtuous – otherwise known as Boots' Premium Beauty Counter. First, though, clients.

Friday morning brought poor Sophie back to my door – or, at least, my screen. And what did she want help with that day? The loss of a close friend, some years ago. She preferred to get bilateral stimulation manually, so I had her do butterfly hugs – wrists crossed over her chest, each hand tapping on the front of the opposite shoulder.

As her story unfolded, it transpired that she'd been left with regrets over unfinished business with the friend, which left her feeling unsafe whenever the memory popped back up. And, of course, another part – a critical manager – would scold her for that same feeling.

"I don't want to feel this anymore, I don't want to be affected in this way. I don't want to have this huge barrier." The BLS would help her come to terms with the upset and continued grieving.

Then she could respond by taking a vulnerable part of herself to her safe place and tapping in images of her nurturers, protectors and wise beings. For Sophie, Aslan, the lion from Narnia, loomed large.

So, that old timing – capricious? Or propitious? How do you regulate a therapist? Put a client in front of her. Inside, I felt my own parts churning away, echoing and mirroring the client's at every stage.

Overnight, whenever I'd been about to nod off, a critic would barge back in, taking me to task for not being this or not doing that, dooming my relationship with Daniel. That same voice seemed quieter after the session, at least.

I got through the rest of the morning on autopilot then headed for the shops – along the riverbank and up St Aldates. At the junction with Oxpens Road, as I waited in the bike box next to the bus lane for the red light to change, I had a sudden foreboding that someone or something was creeping up on me – and nearly jumped out of my skin when I turned round to see a massive looming double-decker about two feet away. Those new electric ones were so bloody *silent*. At least the driver got a good laugh.

The bike lock cable stretched both around stand and crossbar and through helmet straps, but my hair was now too short to stay up in the scrunchy, so I'd have to put up with it flapping around at neck level.

I braced my olfactory glands and headed into Boots'. Surreptitiously looking around to make sure no-one who knew me would see me handing over twenty-five quid in the cause of vanity, I stuffed the goods in my coat pocket, held my breath through the floral waft of the perfume section and scuttled back out.

Just around the corner on The Broad was Inkwell's bookshop, whose first-floor café offered free Wi-Fi. I climbed the stairs and checked emails on my iPhone for the first time that day – having sworn off after too much doom-scrolling in the sleepless small hours.

Straight ahead were the nonfiction books, with current titles arranged on a table to entice you up a small flight of stairs to the main section. The more abstruse the subject matter, the gaudier the cover, it seemed. You'd need sunglasses for the one about micro-nutrients (what were they?)

The café was to the right – with an enticing wave of sugary aromas, from all-too-tempting pastries, dismissed with difficulty. Nothing micro about them, unfortunately.

Babble on the Psychmail listserv (Linking the EMDR Community) about new courses and gadgets could be safely ignored – as could, for the moment, supervisees wanting forms filled in and accreditation points validated.

Then, amid the dross, three interesting messages. Now it had turned out to be worth sticking around, I ordered a macchiato and grabbed one of the comfy seats by the window, overlooking the Ashmolean Theatre.

One was from old friends, Mark and Celia, who'd heard about Daniel. How was I? Bearing up, hopefully. And – better – inviting me to join them for an evening out on Sunday. Movie and dinner on the Cowley Road.

A second was from Pearl. Denise had filled her in. Good to hear of me after all this time but sorry about the circumstances. Why didn't I come to the Church of the Holy Family on The Leys this Sunday? We could catch up over coffee after the service at the Communi-Tea café behind, run by her parents, Marvin and Mirlande.

She appended her mobile number. Maybe, but not this

weekend – and not the Church. I did have fond memories of the M and Ms, as we called them.

And the third was from Andy Singh. Using his personal email address, but explaining that he'd like to talk to me about police business. "Hi Janna." At least he wouldn't address me as Miss.

I'd seen Andy for a dozen or so sessions of EMDR through Police Care, a charity providing therapeutic support for serving officers. As a beat bobby a few years back, he'd witnessed someone burn to death in a car, without being able to reach them for fear of putting others at risk. Classic case of PTSD.

Now, apparently, Andy had made Detective Sergeant. He didn't specify – just gave his number, which I had in my system anyway – but I had to assume it was about Daniel. OMG. A jolt as I realised the police might be treating his death as suspicious, bringing back those questions I'd conveniently shelved since switching back into work mode that morning.

I sat and sobbed quietly (I hoped), rocking back and forth in the leather armchair, the stone statues on the railings around the Ashmolean opposite blurring into smudges. Inner critics now back – rampant in fact.

Sure, I'd call Andy, as soon as I could trust myself to stay calm. Even if it meant hearing that Daniel had been – what? Murdered?! It felt outlandish. His face, motionless on the slab, forced its way back into my mind's eye. Had there been one or two unexplained bruises and scratches? Probably, now I came to think about it.

~

I caught Miri in her last hour before closing on the Saturday afternoon. Chairs stacked and kitchen powered down, she brought out a bottle of plum brandy.

"Is always in the heart, Janna. Once you have loved. Never leaves."

"I keep going over it, thinking we could have tried harder at the time, or given it another go." She shrugged.

The flood on Botley Park had receded just far enough to dry out the children's play area. Absently, through the big window, I watched a boy and girl of about ten quarrelling over a swing.

"You can only keep moving forward, my dear. Never back." She conveyed with a slight shudder the particular relevance of this maxim to her own life story. There was always someone worse off.

Outside, the girl had given up and was now clambering across the curved yellow ladder. Miri and I exchanged wishes for a peaceful and quiet weekend.

On the way out of the Centre, a notice caught my eye from a local rock band, The Osney Ones, looking for a stand-in drummer for a forthcoming gig. I snapped it with my iPhone and sent it to Jem, in case he was free.

"Sorry Mum. I know he was a big deal for you. I didn't want you to have anything more to do with him, but not like this."

On the phone that evening, before going to the pub with Chris and Kerryn, there was some time for his old mum. He was very sweet – and grateful for the lead on the gig. Should he come over? No, don't worry, I'd be OK.

CHAPTER
ELEVEN

Sunday, I went to meet Mark and Celia outside the Ultimate Picture Palace on a corner of the Cowley Road. A young Chinese-looking woman, presumably a student, serenaded the ticket queue with a violin and piped accompaniment from a small beatbox.

Even I recognised it as the Spring bit from Vivaldi's *Four Seasons*. Well, I'd held to it, waiting on the phone for the GP. (Or was it the Wi-Fi company?) We might eventually get some decent weather to go with it, then the poor girl could do without her fingerless woollen gloves.

Next door to the white Art Deco cinema building was a frontage of spiky steel palisade fencing, on which was attached a canvas poster with a stylised yellow illustration of a house roof and the legend: "Canwick Builders and Timber: quality materials, best prices."

I always seemed to be hanging around outside builders' yards these days. OK, it was Sunday afternoon, but from the empty forecourt and locked sheds it didn't look as though much business had been done there for a while. Perhaps Hewsons was squeezing it out, beating the project quotes of the little guy.

The couple turned up wearing sympathetic expressions, just as the fiddler finished with a flourish. I'd found some coins amid the fluff in a corner of my handbag and slipped them into her violin case, open on the pavement.

"So Janna, poor Daniel – and poor you!" Celia looked particularly well-preserved in a deep red designer dress and matching woollen jacket.

"Thanks, yeah, bit of a shock. So, when did you hear?"

Mark, in tow, was debonair with a navy tweed peacoat and grey cords. "Police called me on Friday, asked if I'd seen him recently. But we lost touch years ago." He'd been News Editor at the *Mail* when we both joined, but soon left for a career in corporate communications. Always fondly remembered his regime, mind – in contrast to some of the rank idiocy that followed.

In the film, a painfully shy office worker had a series of vivid and extended visions of her own death (hence the title: *Sometimes I Think About Dying*.) Lying on a beach while bugs crawled over her, or hanging insensate from a crane.

Seemed to me she needed to add nurturers, protectors and wise beings; then those places might start to appear a bit more hospitable.

It felt a bit odd that the central character, the office worker, had no lines until nearly half an hour in. And then only to confide to her workmates that her favourite food was cottage cheese. Instead, she would bite her lip or shift her feet awkwardly under the desk – moments the director showed in lingering close-up.

Life changed when a confident new guy arrived at work and took a shine to her. The barriers gradually broke down. Coming on top of Sophie's session the other day, that's when I really began to believe the universe was tuning in to my – what? – grief, yes, but also a yearning for some kind of elusive sense of completion.

The food on offer at the UPP did not appeal, so I confined myself to a cup of builder's tea. Which meant that, when we rocked up at Shiraz, the Persian restaurant a few minutes' walk towards town, I was starving.

A big picture on the wall by the counter showed the back view of a dancer, clad in all black, plucking up skirts while pirouetting on tippy-toes in front of red-patterned carpets and windows. A broad swathe of turquoise ceramic tiling, fragmented like crazy paving, bisected the white walls a bit like a dado rail.

So to the menu. *Kashk-Bademjan* was, apparently, "fried aubergine mixed with dried mint and whey garnished with fried onions and walnuts." Sounded good as a starter. To be followed by *Joojeh Kebab*: "A skewer of grilled marinated chicken breast," with rice and pitta.

The aubergine turned out to come in a little bowl, best smeared on the chicken as a side. Whatever. Better than cottage cheese anyway. As Mark enjoyed his *Fensenjan Ba Morgh* ("traditional sweet and sour stew with chicken"), Celia leaned in. "So when did you last see Daniel?"

"I was there that night, when he led the demo at the launch event for the redevelopment."

"Ah, really?! Over at Osney Mead? We saw the report on BBC South. Clever, with the smoke."

"Yeah, but annoying to Brayfords, the developer – and my Councillor of course."

"Doesn't Kevin basically agree with the Greenies?"

"In private, sure. But he says the Council has to be seen to build roads as well as close 'em. They were his exact words." I seized the opportunity for another chow down on my kebab. Juicy and aromatic, with just enough spicy undertones.

Mark and Celia exchanged glances. "Yes, we've had all that over here," he said. "Lots of roads now have barriers to block through traffic, but it stirs up strong feelings." He picked up our bottle of Bordeaux and enquired with raised eyebrows. I nodded, and he poured.

"I do think they could have brought it in more… gradually,"

Celia said. "There's the Mosque just round the back of here, they hate the LTNs. 'Why aren't they in North Oxford?', that's the cry."

Well, it was a point. Commuters from the city's posh streets, driving to the station car park and catching trains to highly paid jobs in London? They could always cycle instead. OK, maybe not all the way.

"So did you talk to him?"

"Not there. We had a very brief call on WhatsApp, about a week earlier. Said he was working on something big, a leak that could come out. You know Daniel."

"Indeed."

I remembered the conversation with a sudden rush of recognition, combined with embarrassment that I had not made the connection before. "Oh shit, you don't suppose that's got anything to do with it, do you?"

Mark made a sceptical mouth gesture and waggled his head to and fro. "Sounds a bit vague. He always had some mystery on the go, even when he was at the paper – didn't often amount to much."

"But the police seem to think he could have been killed! There's a Detective Sergeant who wants me to call him – they must be treating it as suspicious."

Celia chipped in: "You've not spoken to them yet, then?"

"No… not since that night, when I had to identify the body." One of the framed golden discs displayed on the restaurant's wall featured a stylised eye with a grotesque grin-shaped black crescent below. Seemed an appropriate backdrop, somehow.

"Oh god, Janna, I had no idea, poor you. Couldn't they get someone from his family to do it?"

"All overseas, apparently." I munched on, as though swallowing the food would aid digestion of the bad memories. Did I manage to avoid spilling some on my good Smedley jumper? Just about.

Mark took a deep draft of the Bordeaux and mused: "You know, of all your intake of Newsquest trainees, I only know of one who stayed in the industry – old Jules Chapman, he's in Lincoln now. News Ed on the *Echo*, I think."

Above the surface: a sympathetic murmur for the crisis in local journalism. Below it, another "oh, shit" moment. Hadn't I promised Daniel I'd pick up whatever he was working on, if anything happened to him? For all the world as if we were still sharing the Investigations Desk at the *Mail*.

The shock of his death had put that conversation into deep freeze. But since it had warmed up, it suddenly felt very relevant indeed. I'd even scolded him for being melodramatic – and now look.

"It's getting late," Celia said, sounding just the right note once again. "Shall we get the bill?"

I returned to my bike and a nasty surprise. The padded cover I use to keep the torn saddle casing from chafing me down below – some sod had nicked it. I ask you! It had been tied round underneath and all. So, having taken leave of my friends, I set off in some discomfort, both without and within.

What was it Daniel had said, exactly? I pieced it together as best I could, on the cycle home. He was working on something big, a leak that could "blow wide open." He'd got the most grudging agreement from me to take it on. I'd been annoyed at him asking.

I let myself in and put the kettle on for a late brew. We hadn't had dessert at the restaurant, so I gulped down a couple of spoonfuls of Greek yogurt from the fridge while the peppermint infused.

Could a 'leak' be connected with his death? It seemed farfetched. It was movies that were supposed to present big adventures, while real life stuck to the level of the mundane. Mind you, judging by the film we'd just seen, Hollywood was not keeping up its side of the bargain, so who knew?

I'd see what Andy Singh had to say, then decide whether and how to "pick up" Daniel's leak. If it came to that, how would I start? And where? Some place only he and I would know, he'd said. Didn't narrow it down much. Another brainworm to keep me awake – just what I needed.

CHAPTER
TWELVE

While I made coffee, the radio man with the free health advice was burbling about the supposed benefits of green tea, which I'd always found insipid, yucky stuff. Plus, with no caffeine, what use would that be in the morning? I could think of *one thing* he could do with that idea, and it wasn't *good*.

Dr Des tilted our Monday Zoom session more towards therapy than supervision – a sure sign that he was worried about me. "You've had a massive shock."

We summoned up my safe place: the garden of a farm stay centre in mid-Wales, where I'd twice taken teenaged Jem on a Green World single-parent holiday and found support and understanding that often seemed in short supply at home. "What's it like there?"

"Quiet. Warm and dry. Sun filtered by green glades. Birds singing. Completely sure Jem's being looked after."

"OK, begin to tap that in."

I ramped up the butterfly hugs and proceeded to tell Des my troubles. Blossom, the gorgeous little bay mare I'd ridden on days out from the centre, saw service as a protector. "I had to leave her behind when we went home." Since it was my session and I was paying, I could indulge in outright self-pity. "Daniel and Callum both left me behind. Everyone I care about seems to bugger off."

"So I'm hearing there's a part of you that feels those you love tend to leave. Ask that part to look at you. How old does it believe you to be?"

It seemed an odd question, but I tapped obediently, closed my eyes and waited to see what popped up. Once that happened, the answer was obvious. "Oh my God, it thinks I'm seven. It's when Dad left."

"So what about now, it's so many years later, you're a successful therapist, with lots of colleagues and clients who look up to you, friends who like you. And you've got Jem. You care about him, don't you?" Of course.

"He could go anywhere, in the future. But he chose to study for his degree in Oxford – near you."

I thought of the odd episode at Isis Farmhouse and the scare when he'd gone missing at eleven. But Des was right – Jem showed no inclination to leave. And I was sure we'd somehow manage to stay close, wherever life took him. I tapped that in and emerged from the session feeling reinforced for the rigours of the week ahead.

A peanut ball from my secret stash was a perfect match for the rest of that morning's coffee from the stovetop moka pot – warmed for half a minute in the microwave – before the next client, Ben. Gentle soul, working part-time at a farm in Binsey, the village just up the lane on the other side of Botley Road, while caring for his eighteen-month-old daughter.

Ben's partner, a high-powered medic at the John Radcliffe Hospital, was a *shocker*. Frustrated with him and not shy with scornful invective. Poor lad. I should be seeing her too, really, but that would not do – so I sent him away with as much spring in his step as we could muster between us.

With no more bookings till the end of the afternoon, I'd run out of excuses not to call Andy Singh. As I picked up the phone, Dr Des's words of warning echoed in my inner ear.

He'd been concerned to hear that Daniel, my ex, had turned up shortly before he died at an event put on by Emma, my client. "I've got alarm bells ringing over boundaries, here, Janna." With former clients, there was more leeway – but even so, I'd have to tread carefully.

"Ah, Janna, thanks for calling, how are you?"

"OK thanks, yes. Still doing the butterfly hugs and the tapping?" I heard the grin in his voice. He'd been in a sorry state when first sitting in my office, two years or so earlier. Even, on his own account, making moves towards putting a cord round his neck, when providentially a friend rang his doorbell.

"Yeah, sometimes, when the need arises. Look, it's good to talk to you, sorry for the circumstances, you probably realised, it's about Daniel Kerr."

"Indeed."

"They dragged you in to identify the body, I believe. Can't have been pleasant." Anyway, the crucial moment in his EMDR came with forgiveness from the woman in the burning car. Not literally, of course, but in his own mind.

"Seems his family were all overseas. So how can I help you?"

"We're collecting witness statements from that event in the Queen's Centre on Osney Mead. That's the last time we've got anyone who saw him alive, so far at least. I understand you were there?"

"Yeah, with Councillor Munro. I help him with comms." *And the assignment in question was supposed to be a free feed and an easy little earner. So much for that.*

"OK. 'Scuse me a moment." He broke off to speak to someone else. I pictured a busy investigations room. "Could you come back into St Aldates at all?"

"Sure – I could come now, actually, if that works?"

He sounded relieved. "That would be great. See you in, what, half an hour? Ask for me at the desk."

I strapped on my helmet, refreshed my lippy, zipped up my Gore-Tex against the drizzle and Bertha carried me along the riverbank and back towards the cop shop.

On the way, my eye was caught by a set of A4 coloured posters attached to a tree beside the path. Encased in plastic covers against the elements, they flagged up the "horrendous damage" the new road bridge would cause to the park. Another even warned would-be lumberjacks they'd be "committing a criminal offence" if they disturbed any nesting birds. I scanned the QR code to investigate later.

~

Andy looked good. In your average telly 'tec drama of recent vintage, he'd find himself serving under a female DI, character defined by a rumpled, cheap grey suit and hangdog expression. But fact parted company with fiction. A navy blazer, well-cut, over an open-necked plum shirt. He'd lost a little weight.

He swiped us through at the front desk, and we headed down a corridor behind to find an interview room. "You made it to CID then?"

"Yep. Got an attachment, six months, worked on that stabbing in Walton Manor last year. The Inspector got bumped up to Acting Super when the old man retired and took me with him. So here I am."

"Well, congratulations. Long hours though, I should think? Must be tricky with Julia."

Before setting off, I'd glanced back over the notes from our sessions to be reminded that Andy's struggles with the fire trauma had put his relationship under strain. He grimaced. "We're separated at the moment. Not sure how long for. Anyway, you haven't come to hear about me."

He looked through the glass window of a door off the passageway to check the room was vacant. We went in and sat down. Plain formica-topped table with orange plastic chairs on metal legs. No lavish use of taxpayers' money on interior décor, clearly. "So how well did you know Mr Kerr?"

"Daniel?" What to say? Settle for neutral. "We met through work, originally, over 20 years ago now. Lived together for a while, then split up."

"As a couple?" An "mm" and nod from me. "Sorry for your loss, in that case. Had you seen him much recently?"

I recounted the glimpse amid the row at the Community Centre, then the launch – missing out the WhatsApp call. How come? It would take more explanation than I felt ready to give at that point.

"So you saw the argument, then, at the Queen's Centre?" I nodded. "And heard what was said?"

"I think so. Anything specific?"

"One of the guests, an Iqbal Hussain, was there from the Regal Cars taxi firm. He addressed Mr Kerr directly, it seems."

"Yeah, he was cross." I dredged up the memory. "Said the Greenies wanted to ruin their business because they're Muslims. Seemed unlikely to me."

"Anything else?"

Was there? I thought again. "He might have told him not to go out on the road, something like that. Could be the new bridge, I suppose, if it does get built."

"We've been told by other witnesses that what Mr Hussain actually said was, 'don't go crossing any roads after dark.' Could that have been it?"

"Yep. Yes, that was it. Sounds like a threat, now you say it."

Andy put down his notebook and looked me directly in the eye. "Cause of death hasn't been confirmed. Waiting to hear back from forensics, there's a backlog. But the fact is, Mr Kerr's body *was* found on a road. He'd been run over. Pretty clear he was crushed to death."

It took what felt like an age for those words to sink in. After that, they carried on sinking and took me with them. "Crushed"?!

Next thing I knew, WPC Richards was back, in the adjacent chair. "Janna? Miss Rose? Are you alright? Andy's got them to fetch you some tea."

"God, I'm sorry, what happened?"

"You passed out, I'm afraid," Andy said. He put down a steaming mug on the desk, with a plate. "Thought you could do with a biccie to go with it."

I drew deeply on the sweetened hot fluid and, on autopilot, broke a digestive in half, dunked one of the bits, and popped it in. The conversation from before my blackout came lurching back. "So where was this?"

"Near the launch event, on Osney Island. Right by that pub on South Street, you know? The Boater."

Now the words were actually meshing with familiar places and images, I felt another downswing. Clutching at the tabletop for steadiness, I slopped in some more of the tea. "So you reckon someone from Regal Cars ran him over? To kill him?"

"Can't say. We've questioned Mr Hussain, of course. He left the launch in a hurry, but he can account for all his movements after that. We're looking into it, but it seems he's in the clear, personally. Still, those words could indicate motive. And, as he runs the firm…"

"He could have got one of his drivers to do it."

"Again, we've no evidence of that so far. Inquiries are ongoing, as they say. And this is all in confidence, mind. Since you were… close to him."

He produced a brief printed version of the main bits from my statement, which I duly signed. Encouraged to stay and finish my tea and biscuits, I was parked in a comfy seat in a waiting room. With a twinkle and a "keep your chin up," Detective Sergeant Singh was off to on-go his inquiries.

WPC Richards watched over me till she was sure I'd recovered enough to cycle home. I got a nifty little booklet, "Giving a witness statement to the police – what happens next?," from the

Criminal Justice System as a souvenir of my visit. Assured that yes, I'd read it, and I'd take care, she waved me off.

In fact, with each push of the pedals, I felt a surge of energy. Righteous anger, probably. How could anyone do that to Daniel? At least Andy was on the case.

Plus, it had finally dried up. I seemed to recall from the radio that was yet another One Good Thing – positive ions after rain were supposed to make it the best time to be outdoors. Strange: a pleasurable feeling of excitement mingled in with the grief and outrage. Had to be them. Not just any old ions.

CHAPTER
THIRTEEN

The digestives at St Aldates had been so comforting that I popped in at Waitrose on the way home and snagged another packet.

Having seen off a late-afternoon Zoom taking a supervisee through the dreaded application form for consultant status, I tucked myself up on the sofa and opened my Precious Box.

Not a euphemism, honest – a literal box, made of dark old wood with a carved lid, which I'd been given in childhood and used to keep a collection of odds and ends from down the years that once had meaning, and in some cases still did.

Buried deep: both wedding rings. A badge from Brownies (Water Safety). A commemorative Crown coin that Gran Tucker had given me from the Queen's Coronation, in a dark red leather case. A whistle on a rainbow shoelace from the Notting Hill Carnival.

I supped more tea (builder's) and made a most satisfying mess with soggy biccies while lifting out and looking through memorabilia from the early days with Daniel.

A picture of us from an *Oxford Mail* fancy dress do, as Beatrice and Benedick from *Much Ado About Nothing*. Not everyone got that. The sports editor thought we were Tweedledum and

Tweedledee, which, to be honest, might have been nearer the mark.

What really got to me were the little notes he would leave on yellow stickies, on our shared desk at the office, in our own private shared code to let me know where and when to meet him.

RD's was The Van – after the Roddy Doyle novel. To us, that meant the food truck outside the Cash and Carry, just down the Mead from the *Mail* office. Yup, we hung out at all the romantic places.

SL (Secret Life) 7 was a reference to the James Thurber story about Walter Mitty, whose name was adopted by the pub on Osney Island in those days, before it reverted to The Holly Bush. So we'd sup there at seven o'clock before going on into town.

For some reason, the letters and numbers tended to blur before my eyes, for all I dabbed at them. The good Marksies' tissues would be lucky to last the evening at this rate.

I scrolled through old photos, long ago digitised onto my MacBook. People often used to get us to pose side by side. Being of similar height, build and colouring, there was something faintly twinny about us. Some of the snaps caught us playing up to it with synchronised expressions or hand gestures.

Then it was online for a scroll through Daniel's Twitter. I supposed the account would just remain, subsiding gradually beneath the sheer accumulated mass of posts from millions of users worldwide. Even I was still on there, it seemed, despite being virtually inactive in the ten years-plus since I left journalism.

I could upgrade to a subscription service and go ad-free, but where else would I get to hear about great deals on flue gas monitors, or options for realising my digital strategy?

Daniel, by contrast, had been busy. There were links to environmental reports, UN resolutions, direct actions, exposés on independent media sites of politicians' links to lobbyists for polluting industries.

He really had become a full-on eco-warrior. Me? Probably more of a worrier. In fact, now I was there, I recalled Kevin's explanation of how protests against Oxford's Low Traffic Neighbourhoods had formed an unholy alliance with right-wing online activists.

Now, if I could figure out how this worked, since it had mutated into X… I clicked on "home", then switched settings from "Following" to "For you." Then searched Low Traffic and Oxford.

Straight away, "The Wolverine" (@Wolverine65443982) jumped out and seized my attention, by the throat if necessary. "LTNs Low Traffic Neighbourhoods Cycling Campaign & Sustrans lobby groups have had their fun. Big street party over – LTNs need to go, roads returned to their intended use. Our towns & cities were never designed around a million cul-de-sacs."

Then, @Togethernov had tweeted in triumph, a couple of days earlier: "WIN: 3rd LTN in Newcastle bites the dust Heaton 'Low Traffic Neighbourhood' roadblocks to go. Hot on heels of Fenham and Jesmond LTN axings."

He (I presumed – not sure why) was self-described in profile as a "conspiracy realist/coincidence analyst." Both had followers well into the tens of thousands.

There were so many, most with equally opaque Twitter handles (or were they now X handles?). One chimed in with: "LTN madness must STOP. Council elites divide communities so already quiet roads become dead zones while those around suffer bottleneck congestion. #StopLTNs."

The latter provided a link to a website called Transport Watch. I clicked through to find a picture of a protest in Cowley, two years ago, over the east Oxford scheme. Sure enough, some of the demonstrators held up placards (or adverts) for Regal Cars: Keeping Oxford Moving Since 1995.

According to the article: "Hatred of cars is often based on the idea that they create inequality. But this viewpoint is marked by a high degree of hypocrisy. The main reason low-income households struggle to afford a vehicle is precisely because anti-car policymakers have imposed huge additional costs on car ownership."

Yet another source of agitation, it seemed, was the World Economic Forum and its backing for the concept of "15-minute cities," which contributors tended to see as evidence of a plot by elites to deny common people's freedom.

Throw in claims of religious or even racial discrimination, as in Oxford, and the contortions of fury on the faces at the Community Centre began to make more sense – even if, I was sure, they were entirely misplaced in attribution to Daniel and his fellow Greenies. But as a motive for murder?

The taxi man at the launch had issued what sounded like a direct threat, as Andy reminded me. But wasn't that just the kind of stuff people say, in the heat of the moment?

I had to snap out of it so I splashed my face with cold water and went for a quick walk along the park and back, then put on a lively online playlist as I fixed myself something proper to eat. Sliced cooked chicken from the same supermarket trip fitted nicely between wholemeal sourdough, as Coldplay reminisced about global rulership. A splurge of mayo would convince the lettuce and tomato they were still just the right side of their use-by dates.

For a naughty extra portion of carbs, I topped off the stack with a layer of ready-salted. There's a reason why that rhymes with can't-be-faulted. Honeybabes (could that be right?) were Pressin' the Button, or some such, and I was movin' and groovin' around my small living room, sarnie in one hand, plate in the other, when WhatsApp trilled out from the MacBook.

I paused the music and picked up. With that gesture that looks like wafting air on your face but is meant to signal to the other person that you have a mouthful of food. And the slight nodding motion as you finish chewing? That too.

Jem had heard back from The Osney Ones. "I've got to do a

rehearsal with them on Thursday at five. They're putting their kit in the hall at that little school near your place. Easter hols start on Good Friday apparently, so they can leave it in there. Could I stay over?" I swallowed, finally.

"Of course! That would be great. Next day we could do that walk to Binsey church, if you like, have a proper catch-up. We could get lunch at The Pike on the way back."

"Well, actually Mum, I've got to get a train the next morning, that's why it'll be good to be in West Oxford. Dad's invited me for the Easter weekend, he's got match tickets for Arsenal." Of course he had.

"Ah, that'll be so exciting. Well, OK, sure, let me look after you that night, and we'll send you off in good time on the Friday morning to Newbury."

The music could go back on now, but somehow the moment had passed. The silence was broken only by munching and crunching.

CHAPTER
FOURTEEN

Even with the bathroom cabinet light still off, it was clear the old Barnet was in need of attention. With some misgivings, I switched it on. Yep, sure enough: scratch that and substitute "outright resuscitation."

I'd reckoned on leaving it till later that day when I would shampoo and blow-dry at the pool after my swim. But that had clearly been over-optimistic. The words 'lank' and 'mousy' sprang to mind. It would have to be given emergency treatment.

I grasped a clump and vigorously pulled a comb through it several times backwards, then repeated with different bits around the sides. The back-combing at least gave it a bit more body, but that still left the unappetising dull sheen of the surface.

So I sprinkled a bit of talcum powder onto my fingers and rubbed some in here and there to disguise the grease. OK, that was better, though sudden head movements would have to be avoided, lest the client suspect dandruff. Or snow.

So then, to the perennial question: hair up or down? In the end, I hunted down the elastic band I'd used to keep the cashews fresh in the open packet, from its hiding place at the back of the kitchen worktop, and gave myself a mini-ponytail by way of compromise.

On the way out of the bathroom, I glimpsed my profile in reflection. A bit Alpine. Or was it Alp-like? Still, could be worse. At least it would make sense of the snow.

Vague intentions to book in with the stylist would have to be brought forward. Maybe I'd finally bow to the inevitable and get it cut in a bob.

Come to think of it, the TV reporter at the Osney Mead launch had worn one. Lots of on-screen women did. Easier to keep neat in tricky situations.

And come to think of it again, I realised I hadn't watched her report. It should still be available on the programme's website, presumably. But that would have to wait, as the day's early appointment was nigh.

I flipped my iPhone camera and propped it on the desk to use as a mirror, hurried through make-up, smoothed myself down a bit and opened the session.

I'm sure therapists are not supposed to have labelled categories for clients. Kind of thing that gets frowned on in the pages of *Therapy Tomorrow*. But I've always found it helpful. Or at least, difficult to resist.

As well as Sobbers, Bolters and occasional Shockers, at any given time my list tends to contain one or two reps of The Worried Well. Susie, online that morning, was a case in point.

So what, in her enviably comfortable and pleasant life, did she want to work on now?

"I'm inclined to feel that I have to fix things for other people, especially people I care about."

I was suddenly aware of how big my head was on the screen inset, showing the picture Susie would be looking at from the other end. Her disclosure called for a sympathetic nod, but I'd have to be careful not to dislodge any of the talc.

"Has it ever backfired?"

"I've had the feedback from Max (her son, 27) that when I do that, he gets the message that he's not capable, and that has backfired at times, when I stand back and see him behaving in a way that it's clear he doesn't trust himself to do what I am doing for him."

My critical parts were straight in with *God almighty, woman, is that the most you've got to worry about?* but I kept that to myself.

"When he commented on what was wrong about the workplace, I would come back with comments like, 'you can't think that way.' I'm aware I'm trying to fix him."

In keeping my head still, I suddenly noticed a reflection on the desktop computer screen: the frame around one of my certificates, displayed on the wall to reassure clients they were in good hands, had come apart at the corner. Another job for the list.

"OK, my parts detector is telling me there's a scared part, a guilty part, a fix-it part. Can you just be aware of those parts in you? Where's that anxious, guilty feeling in your body?"

"In my chest. Even now, just being able to talk about it is a little bit of relief." *I should think so too, you're getting my best sympathetic voice.*

"Just put that hand on your chest to let that part know you're here for it. We're doing some unblending here. How do you feel towards those parts?"

"I feel compassion, I feel warmth."

And that was how it was done. Give me a gold star. We ended the session on a positive note. She was still Well, just less Worried. I even got away with the hair – or at least she was too polite to mention it.

I warmed up coffee, grabbed a few spoonfuls of dry granola and a banana for brekkie, and flipped through on the MacBook to search up BBC Oxford. Sure enough, last Thursday's late-night episode of *South Today* was still available on the iPlayer.

The smoke trick by Daniel and his crew made one of the headline shots: "… and protesters disrupt the launch of a major redevelopment plan for Oxford's West."

The lead was a voice-over about a triple-fatal motorway crash in that morning's rush-hour, followed by a half-minute recorded piece from a male reporter outside a hospital in

Reading where the injured had been taken. But the bulk of the bulletin was on the launch. That was the new story from their time slot, after all.

The cameraman had been rolling on Lindsey when the Greenies entered, so just panned across and refocused to catch it in real time. Daniel's voice rang out, off-mic but still intelligible. Then the recorded interviews, with Lindsey himself and Kevin, and the reporter's piece to camera, speculating about the possible influence on Council elections of the scheme and opposition to it.

No more Daniel, though, which struck me as odd. Surely she would have wanted to put some questions to him? And it would be unlike him to miss the chance of more exposure. I didn't remember seeing him in the wash-up afterwards, but then I wasn't looking for him.

The studio presenter wrapped up with a brief account of some football club appointing a new coach, and a farmyard goose riding a skateboard, before wishing us goodnight and handing over to the regional weather forecast.

I made a note of the reporter's name: Lauren Kemp. I could call her, to ask whether she'd got an interview she hadn't used. Andy must have contacted her, I supposed. As it was, though, my viewing had only deepened the mystery.

Still, I could head off for my swim with a clear conscience. The cycle route took me through from riverbank to canal – remembering to duck underneath the railway bridge – along the towpath then up past some of the august Victorian red-brick mansions of central North Oxford.

Suffice to say, the council leisure centre, tucked away behind Summertown shops to the north, did not aspire to the same architectural standard. At least a couple of life hacks could improve the user's experience.

Public swimming was scheduled to begin at 12.30, directly after the schools session. You were supposed to wait in the corridor, then enter a changing room filmed with grubby water from dozens of damp teenaged feet.

Nup. Those of us in the know went next-door to the dry changing room, officially reserved for gym users, instead; then swaddled in towels and scuttled out, round and through at the last moment.

So I could pop straight in and enjoy a brief interlude of quiet pool time before it started to fill up. I used the fast lane since that was the widest, right up against the far end.

A few minutes in, when others joined, I'd have to duck under the rope and go medium. Else run the gauntlet of flying feet from racing turns, and the trail of destruction from Butterfly Man, a regular who seemed to insist on ploughing through the pool like a hydrofoil.

With cool water gliding past me, I mellowed towards Susie and her high-class problems. And wondered whether Lauren Kemp had seen Daniel that night.

CHAPTER
FIFTEEN

"He's been really taking it out on me this week. Well, since the launch. You were there, you saw what happened."

"You mean the protest?" Emma nodded. "Sure, I could tell he was angry. Understandably, of course. But that's just one of those things, surely? No-one could hold it against him. And he seemed quite sanguine afterwards."

"You don't know what he's like when he's crossed. He's clever, he knows to put on a smooth appearance in public, but when it's just me and him, it's different."

I recalled the restless energy and questing gaze from my brief encounter with Lindsey at the Queen's Centre. He'd been tense, for obvious reasons. And that response was probably what made him such a success in business. But it would most likely be an uncomfortable personality to be around for any length of time.

"That sounds hard. So run the scene like a movie, pressing pause at the moment when you were most upset." She closed her eyes, and her breathing noticeably quickened.

"We had to spend a morning at the site office in town on Monday, and he got me to fetch him a sandwich from Pret. But they didn't have the one he wanted, so I got him another, similar. Then, when I brought it back, he shouted at me?"

When she was in distress, her voice tended to go up at the end of a sentence, as if she were asking a question. "So what are you noticing in your body, as you remember that?"

"I've got a real churning in my stomach. I feel really stupid?"

"Just pick up the buzzers, go with that." I flicked the switch to pulse. After a bit of BLS, I was about to prompt her, but before I could ask, she threw in something else.

"He's been calling me 'woman.' Y'know, 'where's that report, woman,' just to wind me up. He knows I hate that."

"I don't blame you." I could tell there was more. "Go on."

"I dunno, the stuff he gets me to do sometimes. I mean, it can't be part of my job, but I have to do it?"

"What, like?"

She licked her lips and adjusted her feet, I noticed – as though bracing, perhaps, to summon up a disagreeable image. "Delivering stuff, picking stuff up. Getting me to take rubbish out."

"And what's your job title, Office Manager?" She nodded. "Well, I'm sure you're right; they're not things you should be asked to do. How do you feel, when you're being asked to do these things, and he's shouting at you and calling you woman?"

"Totally overwhelmed and unable to cope." This turned on the waterworks – confirming her status as a Sobber. Poor lass.

"And what's the image, where are you and what's happening?"

"I'm sitting at my desk in my office, crying. Annoyed with myself for not being able to deal with things."

She shook her head, dabbed at her eyes, and pushed her hair back behind her ears. It was fresh outside: a welcome change from mist and moist. A breeze combined with the sunshine and some early leaves to throw a few syncopated shadows through the slats of the blind on to my office wall.

"Stay with those thoughts and feelings. What's coming up now?"

"I'm not good enough. I feel sad, upset. Overwhelmed?"

"And where are you feeling that, in your body?"

"My chest is all tight, my head's pounding, feels like it's going to explode?" She looked frozen and terrified: a clue, and a cue to dig deeper into where this stuff was coming from.

"Holding those feelings, drop back in time, as far as you can. Very first place you land. How old are you? Where are you?" A faraway look came into Emma's eyes along with an inexpressible sadness around her mouth.

"I'm four, I think, or five. In the kitchen at home over dinner. Mum and Dad arguing, him complaining about having to work so hard and her always letting him down." I made a sympathetic murmur. "It was me. I was the problem. Her daughter, not turning out the way he wanted."

I got her to pick the buzzers back up and unfold the child's ordeal several more times. Huge waves of emotion, different insights and recollections. Gave me writer's cramp just keeping up with the notes. Half a box of tissues later, I had to find a way to get her out of there in time to end the session in reasonable shape.

"What does that child need? Who could do that?" She did one of those sobs-cum-deep-breaths that signal the person is getting a bit of control back.

"Kayla."

"And what would she do?"

Once again, the lip-licking and foot-adjustment, before she came back with surprising vehemence. "Kayla would get him in a chokehold." Yes. This was not going in *quite* the right direction.

"Is that what she does?"

"Yeah, that's how she won her first fight on UFC, got the other woman in a chokehold, from judo?"

I didn't want Emma to get the idea that putting people into chokeholds could represent a practical solution, though I sympathised with the feeling that her father, in that scene, deserved it. Lindsey too probably, for that matter.

I tried to bring her back to her own resources. "And what does it make you feel, to have Kayla on your side? About yourself?"

"I'm good, I've got this, I can cope."

She visibly calmed down over another minute or two of BLS, so I took her back to her safe space and team. That used up the rest of the session, whereupon I was able to send her away fit to face the outside world.

Hopefully, Lindsey would calm down a bit, too. His behaviour of late, judging from Emma's account, would qualify him as a Shocker. Hosing down the week's upsets had still left us no time to go over the failure of her father's business, I noticed, as I wrote up my notes. Have to be next time.

Over lunch, I clicked on 'Contact the BBC', only to be directed to the 'Have Your Say' section of its news website. No, I did not want to share my questions, stories, pictures and videos, thank you very much – just speak to a person.

By some miracle, the newsdesk number in my old journalist contacts book did still work, however, and I left a message to ring me back. The call came through between mouthfuls this time, thankfully. "Janna, hi, it's Lauren Kemp here from BBC Oxford."

"I saw that excellent piece you filed from the Osney Mead launch the other day." Bit of flattery never does any harm.

"Thanks! And for lining up the Councillor for us. Saved a bit of time when we were up against a tight deadline. So, how can I help?"

"I was wondering about Daniel Kerr."

"Oh God, yes, I heard he'd died. Someone from the police called me about it."

"Yeah, they're treating it as suspicious. Seems he was run over on purpose."

"Right." This took a moment to register. "What, it could be murder, you mean?"

"Well, they're not saying that yet, but it looks that way. They've been interviewing people who were there, so maybe we'll get something soon."

"Blimey. Weren't you on the *Oxford Mail* with him, a while back?" *Steady, Janna old girl.*

"I was. But that's a long time ago. I saw his little speech in your report, but not a separate interview with him. I was just wondering – did you record one, and not use it, or just decide not to?"

"Neither. No, we looked for him, but couldn't find him. I assumed he must've skedaddled with the rest of his crew – maybe worried about getting arrested. I wanted to put some questions to him, of course. And they'd asked me to sound him out as a guest for local radio that weekend."

Even on the phone, her voice had that enviable BBC authority. Good intonation – all too rare these days. "Ah right, so you didn't see him?"

"Not after the demo. We were getting shots in the foyer as guests milled about, then set up to interview the Chief Exec. By the time we got to Munro, Kerr had gone, I'm sure of it. Of course, in the old days, I'd have had a producer with me, who could have got him to wait. But that really *is* a long time ago."

"Indeed," I mouthed absently, thanked her for calling and took her mobile number, promising to update her as soon as I heard any more from Andy Singh. I should have asked her where she got her bob, but remembered too late. As for Daniel? Well – curiouser and curiouser.

CHAPTER
SIXTEEN

Tense encounter with the bathroom scales the next morning. I tried standing on one side instead of the middle, but those pesky electronic digits were unmoved. Blame fell chiefly on the biccies.

At the WOCC, Miri was reluctantly persuaded to bring soup without bread. A yummy concoction involving chicken and mixed beans. The Cake Resistance Front just about held out, reinforced by strong coffee and a pear smuggled in from the fruit bowl at home. I felt ready for the worst Cara could throw at me – good thing too, as it turned out.

She slumped down in the chair with a heavy sigh. What sort of week had she had?

A shake of the head. "I wouldn't know where to start, Janna, to be honest with you. I'm at my wits' end."

I made suitably sympathetic noises and encouraged her to go on. "Me and Adrian have never had such rows. He's lost the plot. If he's not shouting, he's sulking. It's doing my head in."

"I'm sorry to hear that, Cara, truly. What's brought this on?"

"Kyle swallowed his key the other day, the key to his lockbox." *Eeh, the little sod.*

"His lockbox?"

"Yeah, the one he keeps his cash in, from his special overtime."

Gosh. I remembered Adrian's furtive glance as he climbed into the truck at Hewsons'. Surely there was only one reason people got cash-in-hand these days – to keep it off the books? It took quite an effort to keep a flicker of interest and – what? surprise? excitement? – from registering in my expression.

"I'm sure that must have caused him a lot of frustration. But he shouldn't be taking it out on you." I shifted slightly on the vinyl-padded chair to lean towards her.

"Says it's my fault, for not keeping an eye on him. I had to keep Kyle off school, Tuesday, and spend all day going through his Number Twos. Told work I was sick. Well, I felt it, after that."

"Oh my God, that sounds terrible, poor you. Did you find it?"

She nodded. "In the end. Christ, what a day I had with him." She teared up, turned her head partly away from me and leant her chin on her hand for a moment, on the chair's wooden arm. "Three times, it took. Least I had my washing-up gloves. Chucked 'em out now."

That was a relief, anyway. "Adrian must be grateful to have it back, though?"

"You'd think!" She shook her head again. "Now he says he can't trust me with it, he's hidden it. He's not eating with us, he's getting his dinners brought round, by that – what's it called? – Courieroo."

"And this is all from Kyle losing his key?"

"Yep. Least, that's what set him off." Now we were getting somewhere.

"Ah, so he's upset about something else?"

"It's ever since he started working them Friday afternoons. He's… not himself."

"He's not fishing, then?"

She snorted. "Fishing for something. Not fish, that's for sure. He wants to try fishing in the lavvy after his son's been in there."

So Adrian was agitated since his cash-in-hand extra work had begun. Interesting. "And Kyle? How was he yesterday?"

"Don't ask. Played up at school again. I did get him to the Doctor's last week, he's got a referral to a specialist now. So we're on the way to getting his diagnosis. Reckoned to take months, mind, from this point." *That's progress, I guess. Gran Tucker would have clipped him round the ear.*

"OK, well done, I can imagine how tough that's been. Anyway, look, this is your session, and all we've talked about so far is the men in your life! Let's get you to take up the buzzers and do some processing."

~

On the way back to the flat, I shopped for dinner with Jem, due in at seven from his rehearsal with The Osney Ones. Tinned tomatoes, tomato purée, veg stock, garlic, onion, spiral pasta, parmesan and – lentils. Of the dried red variety. I remembered a bunch of broccolini to steam on the side. We could have lemon curd yogurt for afters.

I lifted clean spoons, bowls and glasses straight out of the dinky little drawer dishwasher. One of the clever space-saving touches that got added with the renovation.

A last look, before pulling the blind, at the blinking red light in the sky away to our east. Disembodied by darkness, it appeared as some celestial phenomenon. In fact it sat on top of a crane working on the new power station across the river. Presumably to ward off low-flying buses.

So – lentil pasta. A favourite from the old days with Mum. Trick was, to build in as much concentrated flavour as possible to complement the pleasant texture – but bland taste – of the lentils themselves. As I fried the onions and garlic, my mind ran back over Cara's session and Adrian's strange mood.

Hewsons' was a well-known national chain, so it would be very odd if they were involved in anything under the table.

Then, there was the unmarked truck that turned up to take away the goods, as I'd watched from Burger World – not one of their own.

If it was just hush-hush, that might be enough to make him – what was Cara's phrase? – lose the plot. I really, really hoped he hadn't got drawn into anything criminal. That would be all they needed.

The lentils had to soften and inculcate gradually in the tomatoes and stock. Pinch of dried oregano, splash of balsamic, regular stirring and an occasional top-up of water or glug of oil. Must be a metaphor in there for therapy sessions with tough clients, but my tired brain gave up. Add the right juices, allow to stew. Brings out the flavours.

I took his jacket on the way in, the BMW name badge – Mr Jeremy Hodgson – bringing a tear to my eye. We polished off the lentils with a bottle of Merlot and mulled over The Osney Ones and their forthcoming gig at Tap Social. So what did they play?

"Cover versions, mainly, and one or two of their own songs. Quite a few from your era, actually. Y'know, the olden days."

"Cheeky young pup! What like?"

"Oasis, *Cigarettes and Alcohol*. Some by James, Keane."

"Keane?! That's ambitious. Must have good vocals, then?"

"Yeah, they're on the level. Matt's got good range. And pitch."

He helped himself to another few squares of Dairy Milk. He'd even brought some Easter choccy to share. The sleeve around the big purple bar displayed the words, 'Love you, Mum.' Have to stay off the scales for a day or two, mind.

"So what have they got you doing now, at the plant?"

"Online stuff mostly. I'm working to a manager in their social media team, Beate, she's based in Munich at Head Office."

Wow, that sounded grand. My boy at the centre – nay, epicentre – of a global operation. He enjoyed downplaying it, so I disguised my feelings with a joke. Avoidant coping mechanisms: good habit, or bad? And was I wondering as a therapist, or a mum?

"Social media?! What, do cars have likes and dislikes these days? Post pictures from each other's leaving dos?"

He gave me a slightly reproachful look. "It's a massive marketing channel. Point is, there's a lot of competition, lots of envy and badmouthing that goes with it. That's the bit they've got me on."

"What, badmouthing?"

"No, silly! We're trawling social media to pick up negatives: attacks, false rumours, that kind of stuff. It's a big company, lots of people want to have a pop. But it's the organised stuff that we try to counter."

"Organised stuff?"

"Trolls, bot farms and stuff." He sighed at my blank look. "OK, if you want to damage BMW Mini, for any reason, anyone can post criticisms online, that's free speech. But if you're a competitor, or you have an axe to grind, and you've got resources, you can set up fake accounts, called bots – or get someone to do it for you. There are firms that specialise in all this. Anyway, those accounts can then be programmed to like and repost each other's posts, promote each other's feeds and so on."

"I see. I think. So that can grow into a big problem?"

"Sure – if we don't counter it. We can go bot-spotting and report them to the media companies, but by the time they do anything, *if* they do, the damage is done. We can also do our own stuff to tilt the algorithms back in our favour."

"Right. Well, good for you, sounds exciting." *I have literally no idea what you're talking about. Hey-ho.*

"It is, kind of. Also, they asked me to try it and decided I was good at it, so it's nice to get some recognition, you know? I mean, this is only over the last couple of weeks, so I'm still learning. But Beate's pleased."

"Great. You'll have to tell Dad, he'll be impressed. Might

want to recruit you." What different worlds we'd inhabited all this time, with our son as the only crossover point. And what a funny old world that would be, if Jem ended up working for him.

"Ha-ha. Different game, Mum – they're not consumer-facing. Well, not *public*-facing, anyway. You know what he says: 'Humdrum Aggregates – we're everywhere, but no-one's ever heard of us.' Anyway, the motor industry is my degree, remember."

"Of course." I took a swig of the red wine. "What is Dad now, by the way? Regional Director, isn't it?"

"Managing Director."

"Is he really?! Good for him. So, he's got everything he wanted – the big boss in the big house with the Dolly Bird."

"You shouldn't keep calling her that, Mum, she's a very nice lady."

"I'm sure." *Got her hooks into you too now then, has she?* "She's certainly very blonde. And she committed the cardinal sin of being prettier than me."

"Well, you know, beauty is in the eye of the beholder."

"Bless you." Now I *did* reach across to ruffle his hair. "What about you? Have you beheld any beauties lately? Anyone caught your eye?"

"Maybe!"

"C'mon, you've got to give your old mum something to go on." He'd had a couple of girlfriends before, but none that lasted. Not that I was worried. Yet.

"OK, we met on The Leys. Denise, she's called. She's in the police."

"Not Denise Richards?!"

"That's her. How come you know her?" Ah – so there was another reason for that smart new haircut. Not just work. Perhaps the mauve and white shirt too, come to think of it. Good job I'd kept shtum.

"I've just met her. She was the family liaison officer when I went in to be interviewed about Daniel." And wow, hadn't she kept that quiet?

"Ah, right. When was that?"

"Er… last Friday."

"Yeah, I've not seen her since then, she's been on duty the last few weekends. We'll go out Monday, the bank holiday, we're both off work then."

"I was at school with her sister, Pearl, she reminded me. And her mum and dad run the café behind the church."

"Yeah, we've hung out there. Communi-Tea. They do great jerk chicken."

"That's it." I couldn't help turning a fond gaze on him. Young'uns, eh? Plus, in the short time I'd known Denise, impressions were favourable. If he could hang on in there, she'd be good for him.

"OK, I'd better turn in, Mum. Early start, we'll have to be on the road to north London by mid-morning."

"Sure. Jump up and I'll pull out the sofa bed." I set out the clean bedding.

"Great dinner, thanks."

"Glad you enjoyed it. You probably don't get time to do much cooking?"

"Not much. Must admit we've been ordering a lot of Courieroo recently. By the way, that reminds me: you said to let you know if I remembered any more about that chap at Isis Farmhouse. Y'know, the one who talked to me in the loos?"

"Yeah?"

"He was wearing a Courieroo jacket. Had the logo on it, here." He pointed to his chest. "I mean, there must be thousands of them out there. But still – for what it's worth."

CHAPTER
SEVENTEEN

Kitchen cupboards got the shock of their lives as I bore down on them with a full-on chemical onslaught and elbow grease. It'd be the Long Good Friday for them, alright. If only from the sight of me wearing my broadest headband—the one I reserve for serious cleaning. Fit to shock an East End gangster.

The washing machine had not quite healed up through disuse, so I laundered bedding along with shirts and smalls. There was just about space to put up the clothes horse in the bedroom, so—with mizzle in the air outside—I stuck all the damp stuff in there. The duvet cover, stain now removed, would drape over the bedroom door.

When the rain finally eased, I set off running, down Osney Mead as usual, past the Queen's Centre and along the riverbank. At the trees, a new notice had joined the others, announcing: "Easter Monday Action: Link Arms Against the Link Road."

I paused and read on. "In a climate emergency, our city is poised to take a wrong turning. The first new road purpose-built for cars in a generation. Tell Council: think of the planet, think of our children's future. Say no to the Osney Mead redevelopment."

Activists would gather on Monday at midday to form a symbolic human chain along the path, around the sliver of woodland due to be removed to make way for the bridge.

On another trunk, there was a separate poster with Daniel's picture and a heading: "In Memoriam: Daniel Kerr," and underneath, in smaller letters: "A great leader of the climate action movement."

The text noted that his death was "thought to have been caused by a car—as he was leading our campaign against the new road bridge." There would be a space for activists to pay tribute at Monday's demo.

I jogged on, diverting past the ongoing works at the footbridge and between walls layered with graffiti of successive eras, in which the words "Free Palestine" were the most legible. Along the brickwork, a big yellow cat perched with a sardonic facial expression aboard a red kayak.

What did I know about what had happened that night? Not enough. He'd been deliberately run over and crushed to death. It seemed that had not been made public, however—or it would surely have appeared on the poster.

Strange that I hadn't heard again from Andy Singh. Days had zipped by. Maybe the police had someone in the frame. Or were they at least—what was the phrase they used to use in press releases?—close to making an arrest?

Lauren Kemp would have interviewed Daniel for the BBC if she could, but missed him. So he must have left the Brayford event without speaking to her. How come? He was comfortable on camera and generally keen to get his message across.

Then, I kept circling back to that strange WhatsApp call—the one where he'd got me to agree to "pick up" whatever he was working on, if anything happened to him. Well, something had, so here I was. There was a "leak," which I could find in some place only he and I would know.

Ideas of where that could be had half-formed in my mind's eye now and again, in the intervening days, only to be instantly dismissed as implausible. That was why I hadn't mentioned it when questioned. Hopefully, I would never have to later rely on it in court. The whole exchange felt so vague and insubstantial as to be of no practical relevance.

I touched the railing on the slope up to the road at the end for luck, then turned, giving myself a couple of minutes' walk to get some breath back.

The taxi man at the launch had seemed threatening, and I'd seen how cross the other drivers were at the Community Centre. They were clearly riled up over Low Traffic Neighbourhoods. Social media would see to that, as I'd found out.

Hence the political pressure Kevin had mentioned, leading the Council to opt for the redevelopment scheme that would make more space for cars. But, again, would that lead any of them to murder him?

There was one final meeting coming up, I recalled, breaking back into a jog, where Councillors would consider objections—but from what he'd said, it was basically a foregone conclusion. Whatever the demonstrators had planned for Monday, Brayford and Regal Cars would get their way.

As I ran, I glanced across at the Greylag geese, honking and gaggling on the sodden, vivid grass by the far bank. Quite a few of them paired up in same-sex couples, I remembered reading.

Jem had got off in good time that morning for his trip to the football, a couple of nights as a guest in Callum's Newbury mansion, then back for a hot date with Denise. Pretty much a young man's dream.

The WPC was off duty on Easter Monday, apparently, but would be working today and over the weekend—the last of a set before her shifts changed. What about Andy? Surely detectives had to detect on a Good Friday? It wasn't a bank holiday, after all. If my incoming number appeared on his phone, he might pick up.

I could have been patient and waited till I got home, but patience is an overrated virtue, I've always thought. And I'd had the idea now. I slowed back down to a walk, paused the music and dialled, picking my way past discarded plastic water bottles and an empty box of Crunchie Blast choc-ices on the path.

"Janna! How's things?"

It was a bit outdoorsy in the background at his end, so I had to speak up. I was under the railway bridge at that point, compressing the sound, so a passing dog-walker looked at me askance.

"I'm just wondering how the investigation's going?"

"Into Daniel Kerr? It's not, really." Not? Had I heard aright?

"How d'you mean?"

"Well, the case is very much still open, of course, but we've finished the investigation for now. Your interview was just about the last bit." *But that was nearly a whole bloody week ago.*

A tendril of smoke from the stove on a grimy beige narrowboat wisped upwards into the damp air.

"So... do you know who did it?"

A chuckle. "Not yet. I mean, there's nothing else to do *on* it, as things stand."

"I thought you were tracking down taxi drivers and suchlike."

"Yeah, Regal Cars handed over the electronic logs for all their units for that night. None of them went anywhere near the location where Mr Kerr was found, though."

The path diverged onto the springy surface installed the previous year to link to the industrial estate. Could I, a mere member of the public, be expected to make any sense of what he was saying?

"So what are you doing now?"

"Today? Burglaries in Risinghurst."

"Right. So that's it then?"

"For now. Look, we're appealing for more witnesses, we've got posters up at that pub, The Boater. I've put in to the brass for permission to do a presser next week. Someone'll come forward who heard or saw something. It's often just a matter of waiting."

"But there are no other leads?"

"'Scuse me a sec."

He evidently cupped the phone to speak to someone else – perhaps explaining that he was still on a call. I passed the low dome-shaped brushed-steel sheds of the Oxford Uni Institute for Thermo-fluids. Brief mental image of white-coated boffins boiling giant kettles. Must be more to it, surely? Outside was a heap of massive sandstone blocks, which might have been a sculpture or perhaps just where someone left them one day, absent-mindedly. As you do.

There was a 'thunk' of a car door, and when he spoke again, the background was quieter.

"Other leads? Not that I'm aware of. We interviewed everyone we could contact from the launch that night. That's the last time anyone saw him, that we can establish."

"Right."

Now he sounded as though he was going through his notes. "Customers at The Boater… we got the ones who'd booked for dinner; the pub had their details, so that was straightforward. Nothing of any help from them, though, that we can tell. That's about it."

I thought of the planned human chain protest, scheduled for Monday, and the space for tributes to Daniel. "What about the other Green activists, the ones who did the smoke demo?"

"You've got me there. We've not managed to speak to any of them. They were all masked up, so we couldn't face-match any of them from the security cameras. And, of course, people like that are a bit reluctant to contact police."

"How come?"

The seductive aromas of the Coffee Traders café beckoned, but I resolved to press on, save the money and make a drink when I got back. A couple of hardy souls were braving the slatted wooden seats outside.

"Issue of trust. I mean, strictly speaking, we could be after *them* for, ooh, let's see, aggravated trespass. Then we could look through the latest version of the Public Order Act and find something."

"Right. But they're the only people you still haven't talked to?"

"Yup, they're the last ones. From what we've been told, they high-tailed it pretty quickly, but they might have arranged to meet up somewhere, so they could have seen Mr Kerr later on, I s'pose."

"Mm." Right. Wrenching my gaze from the smeary white metal canisters of Quantum Cryogenics, with their tangle of pipework at ground level, I decided to roll my last dice. If not then, when? "I did speak to Daniel the week before, on WhatsApp. I didn't tell you when I came in."

"Really? When was this?"

"The previous Thursday night. Thing is, he said he was working on something big, a leak that could blow wide open. And – you know we used to work together on the *Mail* investigations desk?"

"Yeah?"

"Well, he asked me to pick it up if anything happened to him."

Andy let out a low whistle. "I see. And do you know what it was, this leak?"

"That's just it. I've no idea. He said it would be somewhere only he and I would know. I've thought and thought, but I just can't imagine where he meant."

"Got it. OK, look… I'll go back through the notes from the search of his computer, see if there's any hint on there. Mind, the DC who did it told me there was nothing that looked confidential, and she's a bit of a whizz."

"Thanks."

Drawing level with the primary school, it was time to head for home. When did pedestrian lights at crossings start taking so long to turn green? A banner slung from its railings picked out, in letters of yellow and pink, a message about clean air and car drivers switching off their engines. Which reminded me: "What if *I* could get some of the Green activists to come forward? I might go to their protest at the woods on Monday."

"Sure, if you're in contact with any of them, ask them to give me a ring. But tread carefully, yeah?"

"Sure will."

"There is one more thing, actually. We heard back from forensics. Again, this is in confidence?" I murmured assent. "Postmortem showed Mr Kerr – Daniel – was already unconscious when he was run over."

Good job I'd actually got across the road by then, as that stopped me in my tracks. "Right. So that means…?"

"Cause of death was multiple organ failure. It *was* the vehicle that killed him. But someone – or something – had put him out first. So it must've been murder. Inquest'll confirm, of course. But he probably didn't feel anything, you know. From the wheels."

"OK, thanks," I mouthed absently – and, with a promise to keep me "in the loop" on any further developments, he went back to his burglaries.

CHAPTER
EIGHTEEN

The wheels. Their impact, and the effect they would have had. On Daniel. Things, I now realised, that had lain unconsciously suppressed. Sure, there was a degree of compensatory psychic benefit from hearing that he wouldn't have felt them. Kind of Andy to point that out. But still, the wheels. Shit.

There was a meter at the far end of the car park as it converged with the footpath. Pretty sure it had never seen service as a leaning-post before, but there's a first time for everything. It took a few moments to shake off the dizziness.

Then, as the flock of terns that had made a temporary home on the park in its new seasonal role as a lake rose with a grey-and-white rustle, a sudden flush of indignation: *Blimey, is that all we get for our taxes?!* Completely unfair, of course – he was just following procedure. And hadn't he said he was planning a press conference about it? That might yield something.

I let myself in, slumped on the sofa and sought distractions till I could muster up the energy to go and shower.

Through the door had arrived the first rival leaflets from parties seeking support in the forthcoming Council election. They seemed to be vying to display their environmental credentials. One sitting member had voted through funds to maintain the flowerbeds in Frideswide Square, by the station. A challenger dwelt on the outrage over tree-felling.

Even at half-attention, I began to intuit the Green protesters' point. How did a development scheme in Oxford, of all places, end up including a new road – one that would destroy ancient woodland and bring more traffic?

Maybe, as Kevin said, we simply lived in the wrong place. Voters to the east, where anger was bubbling over the LTNs, were doubtless being appealed to in very different terms.

~

Time to get back to my list of jobs. It had stayed dry, just about, so I unlocked Bertha, strapped on my helmet, and headed out up the Botley Road towards Heptathlon. A sports warehouse that big would have to stock saddle-covers, surely? The ripped casing on my bike seat had begun to rub a hole in my warm woollen leggings. Couldn't afford to lose those, as there still seemed to be plenty of chilly weather in store.

Looking behind to make sure it was safe to cross the main carriageway, I glimpsed one of those e-bikes, barrelling along the cycle lane, some distance back. Another delivery rider. Hang on, though, as a powered vehicle, shouldn't it be on the road? It did look pretty chunky.

You don't wander in lightly to these labyrinths of retail. Among rows of hiking, running, football and tennis gear, there were kites, canoes and miniature goalposts.

A RadBug bodyboard could be mine for sixty-odd quid. Back on the beach, I could enjoy a game of pétanque with a set of plastic boules for the special offer price of a fiver.

Enough with the water sports? Why not try horse riding? I knew of colleagues who specialised in equine therapy. (Opening line: "Why the long face?") Unlike a paddleboard, the nag inconveniently wants feeding, of course. Hey, no problem at

Heptathlon, where you could snag a bag of horsey muesli and some berry-flavoured biscuits.

In a still-befuddled state, of course I missed the bike section right by the entrance, so completed a full tour before finding what I'd come in for. The kiddy seats sent me a bit gooey, remembering Jem and his little hands snuggling for warmth on Mum's back as we zipped along on cold days when he was tiny.

So finally to the seat-covers. Another "blimey" at the price: eight ninety-five. Made from memory foam, it said. I'd assumed that was just for mattresses. What was the old joke? Don't have an affair, your bed can now blackmail you. Boom-boom. So I paid up, cursing the Cowley Road thief, and walked out.

The e-bike was parked by the cycle racks, so maybe two-wheelers just stuck together, whatever their source of propulsion. No sign of the rider. Or riders – it had a double seat, I noticed. Sit-up-and-beg handlebars, fat tyres and sprung suspension. Rack on the back with the familiar turquoise Courieroo padded delivery box. It seemed quite a heavy-duty machine to be sharing lane-space with us poor pedal-pushers.

Opposite on the trading estate was a drive-through branch of Costo Coffee. As I fitted the new cover on to Bertha's saddle, whom should I espy – unmistakable, even from a distance – but Emma Kesteven? Driving off in her pearl-white Tesla and sipping from a big cup, probably an oat milk latte or some such. At least it was for her and not Lindsey. And Mr Musk was doubtless better at cars than he seemed to be with social media (judging by my foray on to X, formerly Twitter).

Restored at last, comfort down below inspired me to add a couple of bike-bound errands on the way home. I popped into the post office for stamps, and, on an impulse, scoped out the fridges in the Co-op supermarket behind. Yes: tomato juice.

This was the latest tip from One Good Thing man – way to get a substantial gulp of savoury taste with low calorie count. Plus, tomatoes were actually better for you processed than fresh, he reckoned. Lots of nutrients got released. I looked forward to spending the evening suffused with lycopene.

∼

I returned to find a pleasant surprise in my email inbox. To mark the turn of the financial year next week, my accountant, Derek, was offering an early bird discount for business clients who could send him their duly summarised turnover and expenses by the end of April. As I generally kept mine up to date, that should knock a hundred quid off his services for the next tax return.

I had to guess he'd mentioned it to his partner, Faith, whom I knew from classes at the Mindful Mat yoga studio on Osney Island, because there was one from her, too. Would I like to meet up with her and another friend, Barbara, to visit the art exhibition at the Community Centre tomorrow afternoon, then go for a walk and (perhaps) a drink?

She'd attached the brochure, from Oxfordshire Artweeks. We'd be able to see ceramics, drawing, glassware, jewellery, painting, photography and textiles, it seemed, in "an exciting medley of styles and techniques." Local artists would be on hand to discuss their work.

Easter was a tricky one, I always found. People tended to go to family. Miri had packed up the café for the week and was off with cousins from the old days in Banja Luka, now settled in Godalming.

Jem had gone to his dad, of course – which left me at a bit of a loose end. So I pounced on Faith's kind invitation and started to look forward to an afternoon to take me out of myself.

CHAPTER
NINETEEN

On the way into the WOCC, I paused to sign the Expressions of Interest sheet, pinned to the noticeboard, for the Centre to purchase a communal cargo bike. In recognition of the semi-permanent flooding that had extended across the early months of the year, someone had added, in felt-tip: "how about a communal paddleboard?!"

The exhibits were all on display in the Centre's smaller room, opposite the hall. The others had not yet arrived, so I browsed.

Textiles took the form of cushion covers decorated with faces of multi-coloured cats. Photography reminded us of nature's promise: at some point, it would finally warm up, and the hedgerows would be speckled with vivid mauve campions and delicate pink wild roses. Then, later, we'd enjoy the gentle shades of autumn.

In the Ceramics section, there were curious little three-legged figures whose bodies formed small bowls, with lids decorated by slightly sinister humanoid features. But what really took my eye, on the table in the middle, was a collection of jewellery made from glass beads, mainly in a range of blues. Just my colours, in fact.

Faith and Barbara entered as the artist embarked on a little talk, so we exchanged smiles and waves across the room and listened to her story.

"The aim is to be completely sustainable with jewellery," she began. "The glass is all recycled, so it's come from bottle banks – in Ghana. I do fair trade with a producer, Oklah Tetteh."

She'd certainly gone to some lengths to tread lightly on the earth. Not sure about the air miles, though.

"Okah's oven, where he melts the glass down, is made of clay from disused termite mounds. And the metal stands are all reclaimed springs from lorries, which are just the right size apparently."

I suddenly felt like doing something for myself for a change, so, when she'd finished and the women and I had exchanged greeting hugs, I bought myself a necklace and matching earrings for a total of forty quid.

Barbara had a sticky red dot fixed on to the cardboard mounting of a cat cushion cover, indicating it was sold. Their old family moggy had just expired, it seemed, causing gloom and despondency to her kids. It would be some kind of kitty memorial.

"So I heard about that man being found dead the other week, on the island," Faith said, as we strolled along the riverside path. Her cornflower-blue eyes misted with concern. "Did someone tell me you knew him?"

We passed the tall old Georgian houses near the bridge, greyer and grander than the Victorian terrace that followed. On the other side, the pointy yellow crane hung still and silent over the great red-brick hulk, once and future power plant for Oxford West.

How close now was the Thames to bursting its banks? A bit below peak. Must have been a few nerves behind those neatly painted front doors a month or so back, mind.

"We were together, for a while. Twice actually – last time a few years ago now, though."

"Oh, I'm so sorry." Barbara joined in with sympathetic murmurs. "And is that right, the police are investigating it?"

"Yes – well actually it seems he was killed. On purpose, I mean." I could still hardly credit the words coming out of my own mouth. The oh-my-Gods of the others caught the mood.

"I don't think they've got far with finding out who. They interviewed me because I was at the development launch that night, on the Mead. That's where he was last seen."

"Well, I'm sure it's come as a big shock. Let us know if there's anything you need."

"Thanks."

"It's always seemed such a safe place, I must say, West Oxford," Faith mused, mounting the steps up from street to riverside path in expensive-looking burgundy leather boots. "In fact, that's one of the reasons we're sorry to be leaving."

We crossed the footbridge over the Osney rapids, funnelling floodwater towards the hydropower screw in its glass-and-wood housing.

"Ah – I didn't know?" Too late, I realised I must have sounded like Emma Kesteven, inflecting upwards at the end of a sentence. Put it down to the Daniel-related collywobbles of the previous moments. *Catch yourself on, Janna.*

"Yes, Derek's just working from home now, we don't need to be close to an office in Oxford. We've found a place in Islip. So – village life. It'll give us much more space. And it'll be nice for the children."

I could have lamented the Curse of Rose – yet another who was leaving just as I thought we could grow close. But in my new catchy-onny mode, I forbore.

In any case, there was Barbara's lamentation to listen to. The family pet had expired shortly after her father-in-law moved in.

"I'm sure that was coincidence." His wife, Barbara's mother, was now in a care home up Cumnor Hill being nursed for dementia, but here was the thing – his distressing habits included watching porn on his phone. "Openly, in the living room." We tutted. "I did eventually pluck up the courage to ask him to stop, but he just sort of laughed it off. I mean, am I being unreasonable?" *She should send the old goat to see me, I'd buck his ideas up. Six sessions, tops.*

So we arrived at The Boater in a state of three-way sympathetic righteousness. Another Artweeks venue, as it turned out. Someone had painted impressions of arched bridges over Oxford waterways in the style of Monet with his garden of waterlilies. Clever. I recognised the one by the marina at Binsey, and another from the upstream side of Iffley Lock.

We ordered large glasses of chardonnay, but while Faith waited at the bar, my eye was drawn to the other image adorning the pub's stuccoed walls: two Thames Valley Police posters, on opposite sides, appealing for information on Daniel. Complete with his picture, which must have been fairly recent.

"Found dead on South Street. Did you see anything? Did you hear anything?" It gave the date and time of the incident, and a hotline number to call.

A row of blackboards above the bar displayed the pub's Instagram handle and Wi-Fi password: VeganVeggie. Blue-and-white square Delftware tiles on the wooden frontage combined with distressed floorboards, exposed brickwork and solid-looking antique furniture to create a vibe that was both smart and chilled. *They should get me to write the brochure.*

We could sit at one of the tables by the window until half past five, when the kitchen would open and they'd be needed for diners. It was shaping up to be a busy evening: each one had a Reserved sign perched on the board.

"How's the move going?" Barbara asked Faith.

"Well, we thought. But our buyers are wanting us to move out a bit earlier, so we have to hurry up. They're Chinese, apparently. We thought maybe they're used to things moving faster." We took a swig and shook heads over people's lack of patience in today's world. What? We're all allowed to contradict ourselves sometimes.

"So I've just realised, Janna, your son. Derek mentioned him the other day. He's lost his dad, poor guy. Is he all right?"

"No, he's Callum's son." They looked confused. OK, with deep inward sigh... "When Daniel and I split up, I had a massive rebound, met and married someone else within a year. I was expecting by then."

Sympathetic noises, swigs of the Chardonnay all round. Barbara took up the interrogation. "Right, so is Callum still around, then?"

I had to report that he was living with his second family in Newbury. And the words, "Dolly Bird" never passed my lips. Honest. "We didn't last all that long. Basically, when Jem was born, he wanted me to just stay at home. Not go back to work."

"Really?! Bloody hell, where did he think you were living, some nineteen-fifties time warp?!"

"I mean, we've got wombs and kitchens, so why do we need rights, eh?!"

In the middle of the coming night, clocks would go forward for British Summer Time (Summer? Hah!) and it would still be light at that hour, but as it was, on leaving the pub we stepped out into darkness. Darker than it should have been, in fact: the streetlight opposite, on the corner of South and East Streets, was out. I went over to it and used the torch from my iPhone to read two stickers, both from the council, affixed to the metal pole. The upper one said: "Don't be in the dark! Help us fix faults fast."

There was a freephone number for the public. Below it was another, however, which glumly added: "This unit is not working due to an electricity supply fault. It has been reported to the local electricity supply company for repair."

So – the posters inside appealed for anyone who'd seen anything, on the night of Daniel's death, to contact police. But it would have been quite late then: it was already well after dusk when the reception at the Queen's Centre got underway.

We went back into the pub and I summoned a somewhat harassed bar manager for a quick word. When had the streetlight stopped working? "Erm, a few weeks ago, now. We've been in touch with a Councillor about it. Sophie, what was his name?"

The bartender beside him didn't look up from the pint she was pulling.

"Kevin Munro." Of course. Kevin would know when the report had come in, and when the stickers had gone up. Or he could find out.

If those notices weren't already on display by the time Andy Singh had called in – and presuming that was in daylight – he might not have realised it. But it was extremely unlikely that anyone in The Boater would have been able, on the night in question, to see anything on the road outside at all.

CHAPTER
TWENTY

On Easter Sunday, Kevin and I convened the Curmudgeons' Club. An only child like me, childless himself, and long ago exiled from his parents' family, he earmarked holiday weekends as an opportunity for progress on long-term work projects.

I was proofreading (and surreptitiously editing) the cover letter to go to prospective publishers of his autobiography – "probably never see light of day, but still, it's for me" – when he offered kombucha tea. I took a swig, enjoying the astringent quality. One I was busy trying to inculcate into his prose.

"I hadn't realised you were already stirring up trouble when you were at uni. That was before AIDS, wasn't it?"

"Sure was. Stirring up trouble was the only way to get anywhere. We put on the first Lesbian and Gay Awareness Week at Stirling student union." Having finished off by correcting grammar and punctuation, I passed back the MacBook.

"How did it go?" Through Kevin's picture window, I watched as a pair of brown-and-white Greylag geese made splashdown on the now-shrunken Oatlands Park lake. Might be checking out a new home in case the new road bridge took away their riverbank field. And, come to think of it, they might be a same-sex couple. How did they raise awareness, I wondered?

"Well, you know that thing from Schopenhauer? Every new idea undergoes three stages of response – ridicule, then violent opposition, before being finally accepted as self-evident? We were in the ridicule stage."

"At least you didn't get violent opposition."

"Oh, there was plenty of that, too. You had to be careful where to go and when. There were some pubs that were off limits."

"Sure. Talking of pubs, I was at The Boater yesterday. They had posters up about Daniel." Kevin's walls – painted a classy shade of dark blue-green – were adorned, in contrast, with original abstracts, slabs and blobs of bright colours mainly. Photos from his activist and political career were framed and propped up on the bookcase.

"Sure, yes, we haven't talked about that. Are you OK?"

"Will be, thanks. Anyway, the police are appealing for people to come forward if they saw anything, outside there on the night."

"Right."

"Only it would have been dark, of course, then, and when we were there the streetlight was out. People at the pub said they'd complained to you about it."

"Yes, I remember." He bent over the screen on his lap and looked through his email line-up. "Yep – message came in at the start of last month. I just passed it on to the department."

"OK, so it would have been out on the night of the launch. And there were stickers on the lamp-post, one saying to report faults, the other that the electrics were out. Do you know when they went up?"

"Let's see, I should have got notification… yes, that was just last week. Took 'em a while."

Probably waiting for communication from the electricity company referred to in the second sticker. Nothing the council could do about that, unfortunately. "Right, that's what I thought. The police would have gone round there, presumably during the day, to ask for any witnesses. So they wouldn't have known the light was out."

"'T'would appear not."

"Thanks."

He took off his reading glasses and peered across at me. "Are you plotting something, Janna Rose?!"

"Not sure. Probably! I mean… OK. I spoke to Andy Singh, he's the detective who's looking into it. I know him slightly, he was a client for a while. Only he said the police have no more leads." And a full week had gone by since I went into St Aldates to be interviewed, I realised, putting down my empty cup on a coaster to protect the polished cherrywood side-table.

"Mm. So now you're planning to investigate it yourself, is that it?" Was I? Suddenly, now the question had cropped up – yes, I probably was.

"Well, I'm going to the Greenies' protest tomorrow, against the new bridge, on the riverbank path. The police haven't managed to speak to them – you know, the ones with the smoke from the launch – so I'll try to find them. Maybe they know something we don't."

They might have seen Daniel later, as Andy had said. Or even, if they'd had a rendezvous fixed for a certain time and he hadn't turned up, that could narrow down the window for his murder. Any snippet of extra information could help, I supposed.

"Right. Well, tread carefully, is all I can say. If someone killed him, and you're off sleuthing, they won't take it kindly."

"Mm. The police said that too. But I've got to find some way of stirring up trouble – as you did."

"Touché. Just let me know you're back safely, OK?"

Back downstairs, I scrolled through the online petition posted by the groups opposing the Osney Mead redevelopment. It would "destroy mature trees and hedgerows," apparently – on top of the concerns over increased car traffic. Could that be right, that there had been "no environmental impact assessment"? And "zero consideration of the unresolved flooding issues in the area," as the activists claimed?

The plan, as I recalled from the map displayed at the launch, was for the road to cross the river then come down at the far end on the green space next to the ice rink – but old Isis might have other ideas. The heavy rains of winter had signalled the dangers all too clearly. Not to mention the geese.

I sliced mature cheddar into cubes to stir into my jambalaya shredded chicken broth from the microwave. It did seem as though quite a few loose ends had been left dangling – and not just in the soup.

Lindsey had appeared completely confident at the Queen's Centre event – until the protest, of course. But none of these aspects had been mentioned. Daniel might've pointed them out to the BBC – if he'd been interviewed.

A smoky aftertaste of paprika and red peppers was fun to rock back and forth across my tongue to cool, as the sharp tang of the cheese melted in. I took a swig of weak elderflower cordial in between each spoonful, enjoying its mild fragrance by way of contrast.

So – Kevin and his autobiography, eh? I'd sure as hell never write one. But it made me wonder how accounts of my own doings must sound to others. Always squirmed slightly when explaining how little time spanned the breakup with one boyfriend, finding another and falling pregnant, marriage, then divorce. Faith and Barbara were agog.

I'd enjoyed a fairly easy time carrying and delivering Jem. I was looking forward to getting back to work. There were stories I'd been developing for the *Mail*. But then obstacles started to crop up.

Help with childcare, from husband or in-laws, would go missing at crucial moments. Mum could juggle her shifts at the school kitchen, but only with enough notice. Felt I'd been led up the garden path, not just the aisle. Efforts to forge compromise would be thwarted. So, sure, supportive responses still helped.

Coffee puffed and chuffed its way through as I popped the soup bowl into the dishwasher. I'd enjoyed the mix of different flavours and textures. Combine the best of Daniel and Callum in one vessel and you'd have a promising blend. But life, unlike lunch, doesn't work like that. Not mine, anyway.

CHAPTER
TWENTY-ONE

Easter Monday brought a change in the weather. Over the past few days, the air had been still and damp, treating us to clammy, through mizzle, to occasional drizzle. Now, a stiff breeze chased clouds across the blue horizon, varying in shades of grey, from off-white to ominous charcoal. Alternate sunshine and showers were forecast.

I'd woken before dawn, tried lying on one side then the other to no avail. Sleep only returned once the pillows were propped up, at the cost of stiff shoulders and a cricked neck. So I pushed back the sofa and venerable armchair in the living room and set out my yoga mat for half an hour of flexing and stretching.

As I was off to the tree-hugging protest later, I would get in the mood with a suitably themed soundscape from the online Mindful Mat Noise Generator. Sure enough, there was one called Woodland Atmosphere.

Leaves rustled in a gentle breeze, with the odd buzzing bumblebee. Then came assorted birdsongs, which proved pleasant accompaniment to my Downward Dogs. What dogs might be doing downwards in among those trees could be ignored for present purposes. Then, in the background, came a distinct cawing, as if the recording wallah had disturbed a colony of rooks. Or perhaps crows.

I suddenly remembered the Courieroo delivery during Emma's session and the absent residents a few doors along. If rogue corvids were feasting on takeaways and making a mess, we'd all need to be careful not to encourage them.

The yoga helped with my aches and pains. I treated myself to a long, warm shower and took my own sweet time with such preparations as face cream and nail file.

Outfit for the outing: white t-shirt; reliable old blue floral frock; almost-matching cardie; woollen leggings for warmth; waterproof coat in case of showers, and tough outback boots. Practical, and flexible to match the new supple me.

So first, I popped out up the road and rang the bell at number 32, where this time the door was opened almost straight away. Ah, so that was where the chap lived, slightly reminiscent of Louis Theroux, whom I'd glimpsed a few times coming and going. "Hi, I'm Janna, I live at number 42."

"Morning! Colin." Did he already seem a tad full of himself with that smile, or was it just the resemblance to Louis? I rehearsed the story of the food bag, the mistaken address, the marauding crow, and the debris, but his slightly smug expression was now replaced by a mystified frown.

"Can't have been for us; we never get food deliveries. Allergies, you see."

Right. So how come the rider had his number? "Can't imagine, sorry."

We bade each other good day, he closed the door, and that was that. Maybe the courier had been way off, even on the wrong street. Someone at some other number 32 had gone hungry. Mysterious.

It was still an hour or so till action time, so I let myself back in and pored over emails while the light levels in the apartment dipped and rose with the scudding clouds outside.

A supervisee applying to a residential course somewhere in

Suffolk had a fiendish form to fill in. No, I couldn't (wouldn't) do it – that was a job for her. A couple more clients taking it upon themselves to cancel sessions got reminders of my seven-day notice policy. And no, there was no exception for a school holiday.

∽

In my coat pocket when readying to leave, my fingers brushed against an unfamiliar object. Of course – the new blue necklace. Distracted by the Boater/streetlight episode, I'd forgotten all about it.

It wasn't a day for the earrings, but the range of hues in the Ghanaian glass beads would go nicely with the ensemble. So I slipped them on, let myself out, and unlocked my trusty steed to go off and join the demo against Kevin's new bridge.

Bertha and I cruised along the park, then through the industrial estate, to a nondescript office building by the river which was, apparently, something to do with the Bodleian Library. Breezeblocks and steel frame visible through plain glass cladding, amid some drab institutional brickwork. Bit of an architectural contrast with the original. Deserted today, so I ignored the No Cycling sign, rode right up to the front doors, and locked the bike to some railings, looping the cord through helmet straps and all.

I fell into step with a couple a few yards in front who looked like they might be heading for the protest. The matching scuffed boots, probably. From the graffiti wall under the railway line, a faded cartoon of a monkey's face grinned maniacally.

We turned off the riverbank up a slope to the parallel path through the woods. A minute or two further on, the crowd duly appeared.

There were folk of all ages, from parents with young children to quite a few in the veteran stage. One, who'd come on a mobility scooter, wore a blue quilted jacket with the words

Williams Racing on the sleeve. All milling around chatting, waiting for the arm-linking and speeches to begin.

A girl of about ten, in a pink quilted anorak, gazed up at me with mute appeal from beneath untidy blonde hair. She waved a giant homemade cardboard sign whose text, in green and black felt-tip, read: "Keep our city car-free! There is no Planet B!"

It looked a decent turnout, perhaps a hundred and fifty or so all up. Predominant fashion items: woolly hats, jeans, and fluorescent bibs. I began to feel a bit overdressed, so when no-one was looking, I slipped the necklace off and stuffed it back in my pocket.

The trees themselves seemed keen to live up to expectations and were now sprouting forth in abundance, lest they appear underdressed. There were even a few hardy bluebells beginning to peep out.

From somewhere further down the path, the howl of a megaphone being tested, then an amplified female voice: "Thanks for coming, everyone. We'll have the speakout in a few minutes. First, let's all link arms against the link road!"

In good humour, the protesters started to spread out and join at hand or elbow to form a human chain around the endangered trees.

I walked along to the far end to see if I could recognise anyone who might have been at the smoke demo at the launch. With no faces to go on, though, it was hopeless.

I took the outstretched palm of the woman next to me – grey hair, benevolent smile – and people started stepping out of the line to take pictures, presumably to post on social media.

Now there was an idea. If I could capture a few images of protesters even remotely likely to have been in the group that night, I could send them to Andy. Some similarity of hair, dress, or build – coupled with police facial recognition, now they were not masked – could help to identify them.

A chant went up: "Keep our city car-free! There is no Planet B!"

The megaphone crackled into life again: "OK, thanks everyone, let's all gather by the footbridge for the speakout."

As the demonstrators reassembled, I whipped out my iPhone and looked around for any possibles. Snap, snap.

Megaphone Woman was revealed as young and slight, belying the big voice. She stepped onto an upturned plastic milk-crate. Earnest expression surmounted by hennaed curls escaping from under a green headscarf; two-toned magenta puffa, faded jeans, and blue trainers.

"So we've come here today because we're all *outraged* at the Council building a new road bridge in the middle of Oxford!" Pausing for cries of "Shame!", she continued: "These woods have been here on this planet for longer than humans. These trees have the right to be here, not be chopped down to make way for roads and traffic."

We'd formed a phalanx on a wide section of tarmac where two paths converged, overlapping onto the grass. Waiting alongside the speaker were a tall, thin middle-aged chap with doleful expression in a grubby light-blue woollen hat, hands buried in the pockets of a donkey jacket, and a younger woman whose tightly curled hair, brown with blonder ends, mopped out above strikingly pretty, regular features of café-latte complexion.

"We've lost a great friend and ally in the climate protest movement," the speaker went on. "Daniel Kerr led us in opposing the new road bridge that would destroy these woods. He spoke out at the launch on Osney Mead last month. Then later he was found run over. Killed by a car on a road." She spaced out the last few words for effect. The crowd raised an answering murmur of consternation.

"Anyone who wants to pay tribute to Daniel can come to the front and speak for two minutes. First up, we've got Mick and Wiz from Extinction Rebellion."

Keeping the megaphone slung over her shoulder, she passed the hand-held mic unit to Mick. "Thanks, Amelia. Comrades, what we're actually seeing here today is anger. Anger at the planet being trashed for profit and greed."

More cries of "Shame!" from some near the front. Among the banners and placards, a few brandished, above their heads, those U-shaped solid metal bike locks. Curious. Maybe to advocate two-wheeled transport instead of four.

Surely these were my most likely candidates? Amelia had referred to Daniel leading "us" – and she was clearly part of the same group as the other two. I got some good close-ups of all three as the speeches went on.

"Daniel never thought of himself or his own, only the cause," Wiz was saying, in an accent from somewhere in the southern hemisphere (New Zealand? South Africa?)

And that was one of the problems, ultimately, when we'd been together. Always off chasing excitement, not enough attention left over for me. Did I detect a wistful undertone in her voice? Had Wiz been close to him and had a similar experience?

Once the speeches were declared over, there was more of the same chanting, then – as if at some subliminal signal – a collective decision seemed to follow, that we'd done enough for the day. The crowd began to disperse.

CHAPTER
TWENTY-TWO

I could circumvent the groups still standing around blocking the path by taking a narrow diagonal sloping track down through undergrowth to the riverbank, where I could stride out for home.

Two men were on the way up, so I caught the eye of the one in front, smiled, and stepped to one side. Instead of going the other way to let me pass, however, with a return smile, he moved in front of me. Then the second came up alongside him.

I turned, only to find Mick bearing down on me, with Wiz and Amelia close behind.

"We want a word with you," he said. Oh shit.

"Yup, she was definitely at the launch," Wiz piped up. "With that Councillor."

So these were my peeps after all. And they now had me pretty well trapped. Mud and nettles either side. In mounting panic, I looked around for help, but the other demonstrators were either moving off or preoccupied with their own conversations, some way away on the tarmac path.

"You've been taking pictures of us." Up close, Mick was fierce and gruff. "That's why Tat and Squirrel stopped you from disappearing off."

I'd turned again, in search of a way down, but sure enough, the two men were still in the way. One small, with prominent front teeth, wispy stubble and long frizzy hair secured untidily in a brush-like tail. The other, an Asian guy with a smile showing very good teeth but giving, as it turned out, a misleading impression of good intentions.

"So come on, what are you really doing here? Spying or something?" Even without the megaphone, Amelia projected her Received Pronunciation with impressive tone and confidence.

"Show us the pictures you've taken," Mick demanded. "Come on – hand over your phone."

No, this wasn't going to happen. I took a deep breath. These people would see reason, surely, if I explained. "Look, I'm not going to publish them or anything; they're just for the police." It was out of my mouth before I realised how it would come across.

"She's admitting it!" This from Squirrel, in exactly the squeaky timbre to match his appearance. The others issued various noises of supportive outrage.

"That's not what it sounds like, OK? I know the detective who's looking into Daniel's murder." Wiz gasped. "Fuck. He was *murdered*? But the police haven't said that."

From their expressions, Mick and Amelia were equally taken aback. "We thought death by dangerous driving or something, but *murder*?!"

"They've just had it confirmed. They're going to announce it in a press conference this week." I didn't know that for sure, but Andy had said he would try to put one on. Mick's expression changed, the set of his shoulders announcing that he'd reached a decision.

"Right, I reckon we'd better talk. Look, sorry to scare you an' all that. We were planning to go for a quick bevvy. If you can join us?"

It was an obvious chance to piece together whatever they knew about Daniel and his movements on the night of his death.

I released a deep breath, trying to keep it quiet. "OK, thanks. I'm Janna, by the way."

The Extinction Rebels led us down a tarmac path back to the riverbank, brambles brooding sullenly either side in dark green, poised to billow out as the days lengthened. From the bottom, Tom Tower, on the facing side of Christ Church College, jutted briefly into view above low-rise apartment blocks across the water.

Mick's short ponytail, poking out from beneath his beanie, waggled with agitation as he strode along. "You work with that Councillor, Kevin Munro, yeah?" I nodded. "I've been on marches with him. He's a campaigner from way back, always been solid."

"Yeah, respect, man," Tat put in.

"So how come he's now in favour of building a road through the middle of Oxford?"

"Well – I'm not sure he is, really. When he spoke to the BBC that night, he said both sides should be heard."

There was a collective snort at the mention of the mainstream media.

"Of course, they wouldn't interview Daniel," Amelia cut in.

I told them about Lauren Kemp and her attempts to find him that night, which produced shrugs. We diverged around a venerable tabby cat, paws tucked in as it hunkered down in the middle of the path.

"Anyway," Mick continued, "we all know it's going through, this development. But what about Kevin? What's he afraid of? Why doesn't he speak out against it?"

I gave a brief version of his explanation, that opposition to Low Traffic Neighbourhoods, mobilised in marginal seats, had left his council colleagues looking to prove they could build roads as well as close them.

"That's Oxford for you," Amelia said. "It's got this right-on rep, but it's selling out to developers all over."

As the river split into two channels, we passed an overflowing council litter bin, bearing the legend, No Fly-tipping. Across on the island, a Union Jack on a flagpole was defending a well-tended back garden, presumably against any stragglers from the Spanish Armada. We turned left at Folly Bridge and crossed the road to the Top of the River, signboard marked with crossed oars rampant.

The grand old three-storeyed inn, honeyed limestone walls fetchingly offset by woodwork in dove grey, stood outlined against a clearing sky. "Dogs and wellies welcome," a blackboard, propped at the entrance to the beer garden, announced.

"Let's take this table," Mick said. By moving a few chairs out from under a square blue awning, we could enjoy some all-too-rare spring sunshine.

Indeed, we could hire a steamboat, according to a venerable painted wooden sign on the tall, weathered-brick building beyond the marina, and "travel through miles of glorious Thames scenery." As it was, we'd make do with a downstream view past Christ Church meadow and the college rowing clubs on the left bank.

Flower baskets, hanging from an Olde Worlde lamp-post, added splashes of colour. A crane shaped like a crooked elbow, lovingly restored and painted white with black trim, stood ready to hoik out boats – or, perhaps, over-enthusiastic drinkers – from the water.

Squirrel would get a round in. Mick and Tat ordered beers, Amelia would have a snakebite-and-black – presumably to match her hair – and Wiz a spritzer. He looked a question at me.

"I'll have a beer too then, thanks. Just a half."

"So how come you're out taking pictures of a demo for the police?" Mick asked.

I explained what I knew of the investigation. At the news that Daniel had been rendered unconscious before being deliberately run over, there were hushed oaths and a shaking of heads.

"So they have no idea, as things stand, how Daniel got from

that demo at the launch to being found dead just round the corner, an hour or so later."

"Well, we never saw him after that," Amelia said, pausing as she lifted the dark-red concoction to her lips. "We were supposed to meet up again the next day."

"We got clear before the cops turned up," Tat put in. "We weren't invited, so…"

"Yeah, that'd put us in line for Crap Arrest of the Week," Squirrel said.

So they couldn't shed any light on what happened next, seemingly. Even if they did come forward, they would be of no help to Andy's inquiries.

"How did you lot get in to begin with?" The rebels exchanged glances.

"That was me," Wiz said. "I got a casual hire as part of the catering team and opened the back door to the place. Round by the wheelie bins."

"Mm. And someone might even have snuck along earlier," Mick added drily, "and snipped through the padlock on the gate by those bins, with bolt-cutters."

"Right. All sounds so simple when you say it."

"My bit, yeah. People take no notice of the staff putting on the food and drink," Wiz said. "Too busy hobnobbing and being important. They just look past you. So you can get up to all sorts of stuff."

I took a sip of beer and turned to Amelia. "You were saying, Osney Mead is not the only case where green space is threatened?"

"Right. Every time there's land up for grabs, the council gets proposals that respect the environment. But there's always one with stuff like new office blocks, industrial units, access roads – and that's always the one that wins."

"Where else?"

Through Kevin, as well as picking up stuff locally myself, I reckoned I knew everything that was going on in West Oxford.

When I was on the *Mail*, I'd have been across the rest of the city too, but I'd since lost track.

"The meadows up at Wolvercote," Wiz said. "Sold off for private housing a few years back. Crazy prices, great for the rich." Well, expensive houses were a fact of life in north Oxford – even that far from the city centre.

"We've been trying to stop 'em at Cowley Marsh Rec," Squirrel chimed in.

Now this I did used to know, being very close to where Daniel and I had rented in Temple Cowley. "What's happening there, then?"

As he explained, he fiddled with the zip of the dark grey fleece he wore under his waterproof, cradling what was left of his pint in the other hand. "Well, on the Cowley Road side, there's a pay and display car park, then behind that, the old sports pavilion, and some more parking." I nodded. "So they're building over all that, knocking down the pavilion, and grabbing half the playing fields in with it."

Surely not? A sudden vivid recollection – Daniel and I taking a picnic there one summer's evening. Setting the world to rights, we suddenly realised everyone else had gone, and it was dark. Which was when the fun had really started…

"Tat locked on for that one," Wiz said.

The man himself nodded and smiled his smile, only this time with more of an ambivalent Mona Lisa vibe. He dug inside his russet-coloured herringbone peacoat and pulled out a small U-shaped bike lock.

"Ah, so that's what they're for! I saw people holding them up at the demo."

"Used that to lock himself to a digger, didn't you, mate?" Mick knocked back the last of his beer.

"Yeah, put a chain through it and looped it round myself and the mechanism. They called the cops, though, and I didn't fancy the cells, so I undid it. Needed the loo, anyway." The others chuckled.

The beer went right through me, of course. By the washbasins in the ladies', I found myself standing next to Wiz. "I heard you talking about Daniel. Were you seeing him, then?" No point beating about the bush.

"For a while." She gazed in the mirror and made some minor adjustment to her lippy. Not that she needed it. "He wasn't the easiest man to *keep* seeing. But I'm guessing you know that – from experience?"

"Got it in one."

"So this is the last thing you can do for him, then, eh? Find out who killed him."

Again, it took me aback to hear it put in quite that way, as it had with Kevin. But what was I doing here, if not investigating? Seemed she'd got that in one, too.

Wiz left and I turned to follow, then paused, surveyed my own reflection, dug out the necklace from my pocket and put it back on.

CHAPTER
TWENTY-THREE

The rebels and I exchanged contacts, resolving to keep each other updated with any news. A bit of bilateral stimulation from the walk back along the riverbank helped to calm me down. Left-right-left-right.

I tootled through the industrial estate and across the park on Bertha, let myself in and decided to have a few minutes' sit down on the sofa before cracking on.

And gosh, where did two hours go? This demonstrating malarkey was seriously knackering. Or maybe it was the beer. Good job there were no clients waiting. I splashed my face with cold water and put a coffee on. Still time to settle down to the quiet jobs I'd allotted to the afternoon.

A campaign was underway to remount the bathroom scales, but it would take another few days at least. Sarnies-with-ready-salted, no matter how delicious, would have to go on hold. Instead, I dug out ingredients to cook myself a tuna, bean and tomato sauce.

The last onion was a bit woebegone. Outer layers stripped off, it would survive, with a bit of TLC. Might be a therapy metaphor in there somewhere. Celery and carrots were fine, so that was the sofrito sorted. Everything else was dried or tinned, plus chicken stock gel – unappetising when going in but a treat on the tongue. I could add some frozen peas for extra greens, making several portions to consume with quinoa, and have a week off the carbs.

Peel-chop-stir. No instant results from my sleuthing, then. Daniel's final movements remained obscure. It was interesting, though, to hear about other sites where green spaces were losing out to development. Presumably under similar political pressures, both in-person and online.

Once the sauce was ready, I left it to steep and opened my laptop, ready to watch presentations from the EMDR Association annual conference. I could have attended in person, but in the end decided to leave the delights of Daventry and its state-of-the-art meeting facilities to another year.

And hey, that was impressive. Not the speeches, but an email from Andy Singh, winking out from my inbox. An actual public servant, actually working on a bank holiday. Ah – now we were getting somewhere. The Chief Super would front a press conference, appealing for information about Daniel's murder, the next morning at St Aldates nick. Would I like to come along?

It so happened that one of my Tuesday regulars couldn't make her session, so I'd enforce my seven-day cancellation policy and she'd have to pay to miss it. "Family stuff," apparently. Chance for her to appreciate the therapeutic benefits of handing over the moolah. Salutary effects of self-sacrifice, something like that. "And let it go…" So yes, it would fit perfectly. I could attend.

Back to the conference page. First up was some lawyer trying to tell a room full of therapists there's no such thing as suppressed memories. Good luck with that. Then I browsed through "Strengths & difficulties in using EMDR in prison settings." Some interesting snippets, but definitely on the dull side. Guess you had to be there. Daventry, or prison? Whatever.

Another, on "Dialogue with Death: loss, grief and death anxiety," looked more original. It opened by noting reports of ghost sightings: "Might seem far-out, but bear with me," the presenter said. Seemed they'd always been there in human experience – the sightings, anyway, regardless of whether the ghosts were real. And, as part of the treatment for grief, why not go with that?

I'd assumed it might be helpful with clients, but, as she expanded on the theme, it started to feel closer to home. The presenter explained how she'd brought comfort to some poor old chap whose wife of decades had died of breast cancer.

"He was like a wounded animal in the first couple of sessions," she recalled – from the trauma of the deathbed scene. "Then I asked him to imagine where she is now."

Hey presto, the wife started to appear and even guide him. In response to instructions from her "ghost," he moved house to be closer to his grandchildren, which brought relief and happiness.

"I've come back from the darkness into the sunshine," he'd told her – this after only six sessions. So who cares if she was real or not? We could all do with a bit of that. I'd managed to miss the showers when I was out, but, as if on cue for some kind of pathetic fallacy, the all-too-familiar drizzle was now back. Roll on sunshine, I say.

∼

The next morning, I cycled the familiar riverside route to Police Central, gave my name at the front desk, flashed my driving licence as ID, collected a visitor tag and got shown into an anteroom.

Lauren Kemp was there with her cameraman, along with a rival crew from Central News and a couple of young chaps with notebooks, evidently for newspapers or wire services, whom I didn't recognise. I assumed one would be from the *Mail*.

"While since you were at one of these, then," Lauren said, with a sympathetic expression. She wore that kind of make-up some women seem able to carry off as though by instinct, at once flattering and unobtrusive. Must've been pricey.

Her smart brunette bob was set off by a jacket in dark plum, more fittingly sober to the story but just as well-cut as the teal number she'd sported at the launch.

"Sure is." I'd never been much of a one for police stories. Throughout my time, the paper had a couple of reporters who specialised. I'd been on the weekend desk for the odd city centre stabbing and suchlike. If we'd covered the original crime, we were expected to follow it through detection and prosecution. Old habits…

A constable in one of those new high-necked black t-shirts with epaulettes poked his head around the door. "Morning, ladies and gents. If you'd like to step this way?"

"Ooh – here we go. The uniformed leading the uninformed," one of the reporters said.

I tucked in near the back as we trundled off down a corridor, further into the building. In the conference room, two rows of blue-cushioned metal chairs and, at the front, a desk with name-plates: "Chief Superintendent Peter Yates" and, next to it, "Detective Sergeant Andrew Singh." A big Thames Valley Police logo on the wall behind.

The cameramen placed their tripods. Lauren and the other TV reporter held up notebooks in front of the respective lenses as the operators set a new white balance under the garish electric lights. One of the print journos put a small electronic recorder on the desk.

From the door at the back of the room, a shortish, plumpish woman in a navy skirt suit, with greying dark hair and a slightly anxious cast of countenance, emerged to take charge.

"Morning, everyone. I'm Anthea from the press office. OK, so the way we'll go today, you'll hear first from Chief Superintendent Yates, then there'll be a few minutes for questions. You can ask Detective Sergeant Singh about operational matters on this inquiry only, please. Anything on policy, it's Mr Yates. OK, everyone?"

To murmurs of assent, she popped out again, then reappeared a moment later with the two officers.

The Chief loomed large with a neatly pressed blue uniform. Andy had donned a Detective Sergeant's grey suit – though well-cut, I noticed – with plain white shirt and dark tie. He caught my gaze from a seat on the back row and widened his eyes slightly by way of acknowledgement.

A brief welcome and preamble from Yates was followed by his money line: "We now know Daniel Kerr was murdered. He sustained multiple organ failure, caused by pressure and impact from a motor vehicle that was deliberately driven over him. Before that, he'd been rendered unconscious."

Somehow, hearing it in the crisp, technical language of a top cop renewed the shiver down my spine.

Andy followed up: "We've received help from members of the public who were near the scene on Osney Island around the time we believe Mr Kerr was killed. I'd take this opportunity to appeal again – if anyone saw him on that Thursday night, please call the incident hotline. Even if it feels unimportant to you, it could help us to establish his movements, and that could be crucial to the inquiry."

Anthea handed out information sheets while the officers bade us good day and made themselves scarce. One of the print guys picked up his e-recorder and shot straight off, presumably to file copy, as the other phoned his newsdesk.

Lauren sidled over to me and asked, *sotto voce*: "Could *you* do us an interview, Janna?" Ah. I hadn't thought of that when I'd blithely accepted Andy's invitation to come along. And was that Daniel's ghost, listening in? Surely it would tell me to agree? But – on screen? Eek.

Mental checklist: hair, slightly uneven from previous ministrations with nail-scissors, but acceptable. Washed a couple of days ago. Lippy, I could replenish in my iPhone camera/mirror.

Good job I'd applied some of the new Touche Éclat that morning.

Outfit, not bad, though I said it myself. Plain grey silk shirt with a smart blue jumper, the new necklace, high-waisted jeggings. Matched my Gore-Tex, anyway. I'd pass muster. "What, just as someone who knew him, you mean?"

"That's right. Personal recollections." The Central crew had left by now, so she could speak more freely. "We've got such a lead on this story, with the pictures of Daniel from the launch. And of course, since we spoke, I know you were close to him."

"Right. And have you got any rellies?"

"We've tracked down a couple, but they're not in Oxford, and not keen to talk."

"I see." I took a deep breath. "OK then." There – done. No going back.

"Great, thanks. As long as the rain holds off, we'll do it outside, if that works? I thought we could walk to the riverbank path. Then we can do some establishing shots there too."

The cameraman picked up his kit, Lauren shouldering the tripod like a trooper. I followed them out through to the police station foyer, where we handed in our temporary ID tags, then up the road and back across Folly Bridge.

Must admit I'd got so carried away admiring her make-up, hair and fashion sense, I hadn't reckoned on her actually wanting anything from me. Then, when she pounced, I could think of no reason not to do as she asked. Mark of a good reporter.

"So tell me about how you met Daniel." I briefly recapped the tale of our time together on the *Mail*. "How did you feel when you heard about his death?"

Was that his ghost again, popping up to guide me? "I just couldn't believe he wouldn't be there anymore. I know he was controversial, he had strong views that lots of people didn't agree with. But he wouldn't hurt a soul. The thought of him being murdered – something doesn't add up."

Yes, that was it. Something didn't add up. I did my bit of acting, walking along the path three times while the cameraman got different shots, looking wistfully at the flowing water. With the new impetus in the police investigation, along with extra publicity from the BBC and others, surely the missing elements would surface before long?

CHAPTER
TWENTY-FOUR

As I warmed up my portion of tuna-bean-tomato sauce later, I wondered what I'd look like in Lauren's package for the BBC. I could take my dinner bowl to the sofa and tune in while I ate.

Watching telly in real time, how very 'Noughties'. At least I came across as relatively sane and appeared acceptably neat. Hair got caught a bit by a passing breeze in the middle of the clip they used, but that served to disguise any differences in length on either side.

Andy was suitably beseeching as he urged members of the public to come forward. The creases on the Chief – both the uniform and his craggy features – deserved a whole segment to themselves.

The hotline number was prominently displayed as Lauren, in her smart jacket and classic broadcasting voice, wrapped up with a piece-to-camera, shot on the corner of South Street. Bet they loved that in The Boater, which appeared in the background.

Detectives had renewed their appeal for witnesses, she said, to "what's now been confirmed as a brutal murder, here at the heart of a busy riverside neighbourhood close to the city centre, under the noses of diners at a local gastro pub."

Food there must be good to thrive amid tough competition. But I was willing to bet that nothing on the menu could be tastier than my own concoction at that particular moment. Went down a treat. And hey – more tomatoes. Surely they added up and made Two Good Things?

To celebrate, I scooped out the last spoonful of Greek yoghurt, dolloped it into a tall Pyrex jug, added a banana and some slightly wrinkly red grapes, and whizzed them all together with the food mixing wand.

Satisfying to watch the blades whirring through the glass sides, blending the ingredients. Even more satisfying to consume half a pint of sweet pinkish gloop with a clear conscience. Two more of my five-a-day, right there.

~

"It was just horrible," Emma was saying. "I went away to college that year, for my business course?" The upward inflection was back at the end of her sentences. "There was already some trouble that summer from the Credit Crunch, if you can remember that?" I nodded.

She'd dressed differently this time, in a knitted olive jardigan over a merino wool t-shirt, with jeans and trainers.

"Working from home this week," she explained. It suited her, and I told her so, bringing a brief smile. Still wore that gold chain, though. Still inclined to fiddle with it, too.

"So where was this, Oxford?" I'd tried to place her accent. There were occasional short northerly vowel sounds, especially when she was riled up and complaining about Lindsey and the indignities he inflicted. Still, in the melting-pot world of business, I had to guess many people would sound about the same these days.

"No, Lincoln." Ah. Brief mental picture of a big cathedral.

Next year's EMDR conference would be held there, I recalled from the Association's website. Had to be an improvement on Daventry.

"So what happened next?" The building firm owned and run by Emma's father had taken a hit, it seemed, when a major client ran out of cash and – in the rapid downward spiral of the Global Financial Crisis – couldn't get any from the banks. So the work ceased, with knock-on effects for suppliers.

"I got back at the end of that term, went to all the Christmas parties, it was… horrible," she said again. "I'd see friends from school, whose dads were sparkies, or joiners, or plumbers – all ruined. Dad had gone down and taken them with him." She picked up a tissue and dabbed absent-mindedly. "They all blamed him, but he wasn't there, so they took it out on me?"

"And how were things at home?" I wanted us to work on some of her deep stuff, where she'd developed, or at least reinforced, the default pattern of seeking approval and feeling miserable, beating up on herself when it was not forthcoming.

"We had a terrible row one night," she said, shaking her head at the recollection. "Dad was like a different person, shouting at us all. Told me I'd wasted money by going to college."

"How did it make you feel, being told that?"

"Like I didn't matter? It was back to me being useless, never being any good or amounting to anything."

"Right… so let's process this memory. It's probably being triggered by what's going on now at the office, so we're going to help you to find some distance."

"Sure." She shifted her weight in the chair from one buttock to another, pursed her lips slightly and leaned forward to signal attention.

"So pick up the buzzers, close your eyes and go back to that terrible row, when your dad shouted at you and said you'd wasted money. What can you see?" She drew a sharp intake of breath.

"Oh my god, it's scary, it's like he's breathing fire all over us."

"Where's that scary feeling in your body?"

"It's weird: I've got a real tingling feeling in my hands and feet. And my legs." Hmm, yes that *was* unusual. Might be an urge to run away, I supposed. The sobs were coming thick and fast now, so I nudged the box of tissues within reach.

"And the thought, the belief about yourself when you look at that scene?"

"I'm in danger, I'm going to die, but I'm not worth anything anyway, so no-one will care." Wow. So this was definitely the moment to switch on the current. She calmed down sufficiently over a minute or so of BLS for us to continue. But then she volunteered something interesting.

"You asked me what I could see? I'm really small, not a student, a little girl. With pigtails."

"Right. And how do you feel towards that little girl?"

"I feel really sorry for her."

"What kind of sorry? Open-hearted compassion kind?"

She nodded and, through sobs, just about came out with the affirmation I needed to hear. "Something like that." It meant I could send adult Emma into that scene to help the little girl, interweaving approaches from another form of therapy, Internal Family System.

"So can you imagine stepping into that scene with little Emma and comforting her? Let her tell you her story." Moments ticked by as the buzzers did their work. Left-right, left-right.

"She's telling me it's all her fault, she doesn't matter."

"How is it for you to hear that?"

"I just want to give her a big hug and make her feel better."

"Sure. Before you do that, is there any more she wants you to know?"

A great sob convulsed her shoulders, but she recovered her poise, disengaging one hand from the buzzers for a moment to tuck her hair back behind her ears. "She wants to tell 'em they're wrong, it's not fair, I'm good, I'm doing all the right things."

Interesting. Especially in light of previous sessions, where she'd told of being abused and exploited by her boss, Lindsey. We'd have to circle back to those episodes, but carefully. "Right. So did you? In that scene, or in other scenes like it, do you tell people that?" She shook her head.

"Why not?" Another big sob.

"I'm just afraid they'll tell me off and shout at me. That I won't get anywhere, it'll just make things worse." No wonder she was put-upon in the office.

"OK, we've been using concepts from another therapy, not just EMDR but Internal Family System." She raised her eyebrows. "In IFS terms, that little girl is an exile – a part of you that takes all the blame."

"Right. Makes sense."

"And what happens is that a protector part comes along. Not the same as your protectors, who you named last time – like Wonder Woman."

"And Kayla."

"That's right, Kayla too. But this is a different protector, it's a part that prevents the exile's emotions from being triggered, to shield it from the upset. It sometimes helps to visualise the protector part. What might it look like?"

"The Joker, from Batman Dark Knight." *Wow, she was straight in with that one.*

"Right, The Joker, scary guy. Wasn't he…"

"Heath Ledger, yeah. Died from drugs when the movie came out?"

She was obviously a fan. Quick guess: it would probably have been in cinemas at roughly the time she left for college – and the building firm's collapse. "OK, so we've got little Emma as the exile and Joker as the protector. What does Joker say to Emma when she wants to speak up for herself – for you – and tell everyone they're being unfair?"

"He just says it's not worth it, they're right, just keep quiet, then they'll forget about you and you can move away." *Hmm. Notable choice of words.*

"And is that what you did, move away? To Oxford, far away from family in Lincoln, from those horrible experiences?"

She licked her lips and adjusted her feet, so the left was resting on the right – and nodded. That would do for the day. Time to bank the gains.

"OK, good session today, well done. What we've been doing is helping you to unblend from these parts, so you can witness that traumatic scene, not be in it. Might it help you to draw them, little Emma and The Joker?"

She shook her head, with another brief little smile. "Alright. So next time, we'll try to figure out how to get these parts to relax back and give you some space. They might even start to do different things, take on different jobs. So when you're in these stressful situations in future, they can be on your side, as allies not problems."

I found a ball of old Blu-tak in the back of an office drawer, pinched out a bit from the middle where it wasn't too dry, and stuck the sagging picture frame around my certificate back into place.

As it was time for jobs, I might as well pop through to the kitchen and wipe the splash-tiles behind the hob, measled from my tomato-ey cooking exploits the other day. I even gave the house plants some water and detached a couple of dead leaves.

So – poor Emma, eh? If I didn't manage to turn her out, at the end of our sessions, better able to speak up for herself, I'd hang up my buzzers and declare the world a muddle. And that would never do.

CHAPTER
TWENTY-FIVE

Miri was still away in Godalming, her *ersatz* Banja Luka, so the café was closed. Probably a good thing, as I was under a self-imposed sausage roll embargo. I grabbed nuts, grapes and Wensleydale for lunch, before saddling up for the WOCC.

Cara's world had settled down a bit. She'd had a heart-to-heart with Adrian, and he'd agreed to stop his extra cash-in-hand jobs on a Friday afternoon. "It was stressing him out, Janna, doing that stuff on the sly. And he was taking it out on us."

As to exactly *what* he'd been doing, and for whom – still none the wiser.

"He won't tell me, but he's going to tell his boss he's not doing it no more."

The dwindling leftover cash was still kept in the lockbox, but without locking it. Key thrown away in case of any mishaps with Kyle. In any case, she was getting a break. "He's at Mum's this week, while school's off."

∽

Back home, I slipped into the old yoga pants, set the playlist on my earbuds to some cheerful girl band, and jogged off through the park and industrial estate to the riverbank as usual.

A stray lone scull had evidently made it through under Folly Bridge from the rowing clubs and was now sweeping back downstream. Oars grinding in the rowlocks, oarsman in a blue vest over a white long-sleeved t-shirt wearing a look of intense ginger-haired concentration.

Feeling a bit puffed out coming back, I slowed to a walk past Osney Lock, with its thundering hydro power plant, and The Boater. Looked in through the window just as a shaft of sunlight suddenly penetrated the cloud cover and picked out the cunning Monet-style painting on the wall, of the arched bridge at Iffley Lock.

Hm! Bloody locks everywhere. Thames locks. Extinction Rebellion, with their U-locks. Kyle and the lock on Adrian's cash hoard. Rowlocks to the lot of 'em, I'd say.

Then, walking along South Street, a tiny worm of memory began to burrow its way towards the surface. Aloud, I gave a sudden nervous laugh of dawning realisation. Couldn't be, surely?

Mind racing now. Yes – a lock. Daniel and I had once got a lockbox, one of those ones where you put keys for guests if you rent out your house. But it was when *we'd* been renting, in Temple Cowley.

There was an old-fashioned hardware store round the corner; it came from there. We were so happy in that house. Our heyday. But we had to move out after six months when the owner sold up.

So one night, with everything packed ready to go, we vowed to come back. Somehow save up to buy it for ourselves one day. We staged a romantic little ceremony, with a cheap bottle of bubbly from the Co-op, and buried one of the front-door keys, in the lockbox, under a paving stone in the back garden, right by the fence. Combination set to our two birthdays: 2-7-1-5.

In with it, as I recalled: one of the two-shots we took when horsing about with a passport photo machine at the local shopping centre. A way to leave something of our own and a promise to return.

That was somewhere only he and I would know. Right? Could that've been what he was on about? Might the secret, whatever it was, be hidden in that lockbox? Could he have gone back there, found it, opened it, and put something in? Then replaced it, to retrieve the thing later – or get me to?

I could go and find out. In fact, I could go now. No more thrupping that day; the afternoon client had cancelled. School holidays. Right, we were on. Sense of purpose renewed, I broke back into a jog.

∽

The shower brought a cascade of doubts and second thoughts. Daniel had been working on "something big." The lockbox was very small. Well… that could be explained. It was obviously information. I'd seen enough modern spy thrillers at the cinema, dealing with identity, supremacy, ultimatums and such, to realise that could be stored on a data chip. Which would fit nicely.

Andy had said the police found nothing on his computer, but computers could be hacked – remotely, the moment the user went online. Even I knew that, so he certainly would. If he'd been in possession of sensitive material, he'd have stored it somewhere else.

With the steam, less comfortable ideas came seeping in. If Daniel was seeing some luscious young babe like Wiz, wouldn't he have forgotten our love nest on Junction Road? What would have made him think of that? Then again, it was supposed to be somewhere no-one else would know, besides the two of us. It had to be worth trying.

So I dressed quickly in jeans, turtleneck, Gore-Tex and trainers. Grabbed a hefty screwdriver from the toolbox in the cupboard under the stairs and popped it in my handbag, which I slung in Bertha's basket; strapped on my helmet and pedalled off.

Near the foot of the Cowley Road, a traffic squabble led me to pull in at the kerb, to avoid a red hatchback vrooming aggressively as it veered over onto my side and sped off towards town.

I just glimpsed the angry expression of the man behind the wheel. Scowling, mouthing, and shaking his head. The object of his wrath was a dark blue saloon, stationary and blocking the lane, whose driver was chatting through his open window to two riders on a chunky e-bike, in the middle of the road, beside his door. He waved in airy apology to hatchback-man's rear-view mirror.

Drawing closer... yes, it was one of Regal Cars'. Logo proudly displayed on the panels. As if on cue, taxi guy looked straight at me, said something to the riders, and the lead one – sporting helmet and tinted goggles, nose-and-mouth mask pulled down over chin as he talked – turned and watched as I cycled past.

Hang on – hadn't I seen that bike before, recently? I steeled myself to keep looking straight ahead. You don't want to get into staring matches on the roads – not unless you can make that kind of noise, speeding away in a red hatchback. Lots of very touchy folk around these days.

But, from the corner of my eye, the machine looked remarkably similar to the one parked outside Heptathlon the week before. Down to the delivery box on the back-rack from Courieroo, whose logo was also visible on the riders' matching black puffa jackets.

I shook my head and pressed harder on the pedals. The mission beckoned. Shiraz Persian restaurant passed by, then the Ultimate Picture Palace, where I'd seen that strange film with Mark and Celia.

A little way further east, I turned off down Bartlemas Close, then through a chicane-type set of wooden railings on to the cycle path, the familiar track up the hill to our old haunts.

The route took in a short section of road alongside some allotments and a secondary school on the left, then dipped under some trees and came out to reveal a view on the right across Cowley Marsh Recreation Ground.

Except that view was now very different from my recollection of twenty years ago. I skidded to a halt and gawped. Barely a hundred metres away was a row of interlocking metal fence sections, and behind them, mixed-use sports ground no more. Instead, brown earth and grey concrete, where a yellow digger was parked.

I slipped the lock around wheel and frame, leant Bertha against a tree trunk and walked across the grass, at the cost of damp feet as rainwater soaked through my trainers.

Through the fencing, I saw for myself what Squirrel and the Extinction Rebellion activists were on about. The former sports pavilion and changing block had gone, with scaffolding up and new buildings starting to take shape.

Signs on the perimeter announced Birchwood Developments as the firm responsible. And there were several others apprising any would-be intruders of the CCTV camera system – provided by none other than Brayford Security.

So Birchwood, whoever they were, must have put in the bid for the development that bit off a chunk of precious green space. There was always one, Amelia had said, whenever a piece of land came up in the planning system. And it always seemed to win the tender.

I walked further round. On the corner facing the Cowley Road side, a white wooden board featured an artist's impression of the finished scheme, which would provide new business units, office space, and access road. Whoopie-doos.

CHAPTER
TWENTY-SIX

So all that would be left of our old picnic ground was an elongated triangle of turf, with a wildflower garden at one end. Not that it would have stopped us from sitting, eating and – more to the point – drinking. But having those new buildings so close would scarcely improve the vibe.

Then, there'd been many occasions when I'd passed by and seen the whole space in use. Footy games underway, either between teams with actual kit, or just dads and lads (and lasses, for that matter) kicking about, using the goalposts. Even cricket, in summer. No room for that now.

With a sigh, I set off back along the path and started to climb. The cycleway morphed into Barracks Lane, a cul-de-sac banking steeply up the side of the golf course. No development proposals there – just on shared or common land, woods or public playing fields. I pedalled and puffed.

Then it was a right turn past the old hardware shop – still going strong, it seemed. I pictured the assistants wearing their brown coats, delving into the labyrinthine storeroom behind the counter in search of fork handles (or was it four candles?) Lastly, I turned right again, onto Crescent Road, then into a lane to my left.

This was where I would have to get crafty. Away to either side were small blocks of flats, belonging to Brookes Uni. Mostly international students, I remembered Jem saying once, who could afford high rents to go with their exorbitant fees.

The Halls Office, a brick cabin that housed on-site admin and security, had a sign on the facing wall indicating that the area was under camera surveillance "monitored with immediate response." Brayford again.

Straight ahead was a row of four spike-topped wooden bollards, with interlocking temporary steel railing panels propped behind them. On the far side – yes, it was still the same. No building yet on the patch of ground directly behind 45, Junction Road, our old address. Weeds poking through asphalt. At the far end, a row of traffic cones, with a heap of tree cuttings beyond.

Old reporter's maxim: act fast and look confident. That way, I could reach my goal before anyone had time to respond, or simply deter challenge by radiating entitlement through appearance and demeanour.

I propped Bertha on her stand and shouldered my bag from out of the basket. Squeezing through the gap beside the right-hand steel panel was easy. Now I had to check the wooden fence at the back of our old garden, working my way along from the near end.

And lo – a couple of metres in, a plank I remembered being loose twenty years before was still not secured into place at the bottom.

I fished out the screwdriver and used it to lever the board away from its neighbour then, with a shove, managed to move it to one side, revealing the profile of a paving slab with soil below. And lo again – in a cavity in the middle of that band of earth was a small but perfectly formed black metal lockbox.

I lifted it out, knocked off the dirt with the screwdriver and hastily slipped them both into my bag. Resisting the urge to run – dead giveaway to any watching eyes – instead I walked back to the bike, giving every surface appearance of calm, purposeful authority while quivering with excitement beneath.

Before moving off, I couldn't wait to examine my booty. Bestriding the frame, I clicked the combination dials into place, 2-7-1-5; pushed the big grey plastic button downwards and sure enough, the door swung open. Inside: the key and photo as I'd remembered, and... that was all.

Oh. A close examination of the box revealed nothing more. It had just lain undisturbed throughout those two decades. Intense wave of anti-climax and disappointment. What to do? I kept hold of the key and just clicked the lockbox shut. No point re-scrambling the dials. I popped it back into the bag.

Surprisingly powerful urge: now I was here, might I as well check whether this key would still open the front door? Was that mad? I'd look for any signs of the current residents being at home, of course. And I could always just explain. "I used to live here over twenty years ago so I thought I'd let myself in." There – that didn't sound at all mad. If there was no-one in, I could have a quick sticky-beak for old times' sake, then just as quietly leave.

Round onto Junction Road itself, then, which turned out to be part of the East Oxford Low Traffic Neighbourhood scheme. Directly in front of me, blocking one lane: a big square wooden box, from which dense dark green vegetation sprouted. Jagged-edged triangular leaves and small white flowers. On the front of it: the instantly recognisable circular white road-sign with red edging around black silhouettes of car and motorbike, indicating it was closed to vehicles.

Alongside, a green rectangle with white lettering: "Road open to," and stylised outlines of pedestrians, a child on a pedal scooter, a wheelchair user and a bike. Next to the flowerbox, another bollard, set in its own patch of concrete, would prevent rogue drivers from slipping through regardless.

The whole area did seem very quiet. And there was no visible burglar alarm anywhere around the entrance to our little palace of yore.

I passed between flowerbox and bollard with clear conscience on my two wheels, leant them against the garden wall and – on the same bold reporter's principle as before – marched confidently through the gate and up to the portal of bliss, then inserted the key. Nope. It went in all the way, but wouldn't turn, no matter how much I tried to jiggle it. The lock had evidently been changed.

There was nothing for it, in that case, but to turn away in total defeat. Damn! I slipped the key into my pocket, went back to Bertha, put the bag in her basket, fixed to the back rack behind the saddle, and mounted up.

At least I could treat myself by taking a pleasant route home, around the edge of Florence Park and onto the riverside path at Donnington Bridge. Slightly further, but I was in no rush.

Turning to trundle off down the hill, I heard a buzzing sound, getting rapidly closer from behind. As I turned around to look for the source, there was a sudden, hard push on my right shoulder and Bertha and I toppled over to the left and came crashing down on the pavement.

Limned against the sky, a figure clad all in black, with helmet, tinted goggles and face-mask, bent down and snatched my handbag from where it lolled, half-in and half-out of the bike basket.

I was sure I caught a glimpse of the bugger's neck, as his puffa was unzipped over a black t-shirt. Was that a tattoo, cross-shaped with transverse stalks on the ends?

With lithe movements, he straightened up and resumed his seat on the passenger pillion of a chunky two-person e-bike, which then sped off down Junction Road.

Bloody *hell*. To haul myself to a sitting position was to become aware of a stabbing pain in my left ankle. Elbow wasn't much better. The side of my head had slammed down too, but luckily the impact was absorbed by the helmet. All I had to contend with there was a slight feeling of dizziness.

Hard on the heels of this physical self-assessment came a flush of fury. How dare they? In broad daylight?!

Plus, I was sure they must have followed me. Yes – imprinted on my mind's eye, the turquoise-coloured Courieroo delivery box on the back as they'd ridden away. They must have been the ones talking to the Regal Cars man on the Cowley Road. Very bloody telling.

Oh shit, oh shit. My phone was in that bag. And credit cards? No, thankfully. Purse in my coat pocket, now I came to check, along with the keys from my actual, present home.

Well even so, they weren't bloody getting away with it. Might have a head start, but I knew what they looked like, and I was determined to get my bag back. Old, but good quality – a calf-leather Radley in classy dark red, with famous little-dog logo and all.

Ignoring bumps and bruises, and despite the nagging ankle, I set off down Junction Road in hot pursuit. OK, lukewarm pursuit. Straight away, at the halfway point, a choice. Continue straight on down, or hang a right onto Temple Road?

I took the right, freewheeling on between the empty old limestone barracks building to one side, houses on the other, eagle eyes out for any sign of my quarry. As I approached the primary school – closed for the holidays, of course – I could swear… yes, as I got closer, there it was: a bag, lying side-down in the middle of the road. *My* bag.

Powder compact and ballpoint pen had spilled out, along with the nametag from the Osney Mead development launch. I leant Bertha on the school wall and scooped things up, then retreated to the pavement to find out what was gone. Ah – that was a relief, my phone was still there. Various bits and pieces, check, check, check. Hang on. Go through everything again. All seemed present and correct. So what had they actually pinched?

Nothing *at all*? Well. Tribute to my prudence, or a bit of an indictment, that I actually owned nothing worth taking?

Then I realised – the one thing missing was the lockbox. I sat down abruptly on the kerb, suddenly aware of just how achy the ankle and elbow now were and starting to feel distinctly nauseous.

There'd been a GP's surgery at the bottom of Junction Road when we lived there, I remembered. Somehow, I levered myself back into the saddle, laboured up the gradient to the intersection, turned right and then down again.

Sure enough, on the left at the end of a limestone wall, the blue NHS sign and squat ivy-covered brick premises of Temple Cowley Health Centre hove into view. The receptionist took one look at me as I limped in, bike helmet still on, I now dimly realised, and said, "I'll get help."

A motherly dark-haired nurse in blue uniform appeared and ushered me through, with suitably sympathetic noises, to a quiet consulting room beyond. "Looks like you've had a nasty shock."

I'd given a brief outline of my misfortunes. The words, "pushed me off my bike" and "bag stolen" drew the response I'd been hoping for.

They insisted I stay sat down for half an hour before heading off. The nurse put a cold compress on my ankle, held in place by a tight bandage, and dressed my elbow. There was bruising and a nasty graze, even through my jumper and coat. She took my temperature and blood pressure and had me swallow some ibuprofen. I gratefully accepted an NHS biscuit and cup of tea to help them down.

Should they report this to the police, the receptionist poked her head round the door to ask? No, don't worry. I was building momentum for another trip to St Aldates. I'd report it to the police, alright. I had a lead – one that would connect Daniel and his secret (whatever it was) to the original suspects. It was time to go and see Andy Singh.

CHAPTER
TWENTY-SEVEN

"They're obviously in cahoots," I said again. Gratification at catching the Detective Sergeant in the office – presumably between trips to crime scenes and whatnot – had rapidly given way to frustration that he didn't seem to invest more significance in my findings.

"Well… you say you saw these men talking to the taxi driver. They obviously knew each other, but…"

"And remember it's not the first time I've seen that e-bike. It was following me when I went out to Heptathlon last week."

"OK, you saw it that day, behind you, but we don't know it was following you. And it might not be the same one." He caught my eye. "Though, sure, there aren't many on the roads like that, from your description."

Denise had come in off patrol through reception as I waited after giving my name at the desk, listened politely to my tale of woe, and flipped back into family-liaison mode. "Could be stalking behaviour, guv." Andy nodded and made a "yeah-maybe" shape with his mouth.

"Have you counselled anyone recently for, let's say, something like partner abuse?" he asked. I looked blank. "I'm just thinking, if it *is* someone stalking you, it could be connected with your therapy."

"A partner might react badly if you've advised someone to end a relationship, or report them for something," Denise added. This only fuelled my exasperation.

"OK, but look, you've ruled out Regal Cars as responsible for Daniel's death…"

Andy did a double-click of his ballpoint, which I'd already decided was a sign he didn't believe me. Telling him I'd been trying to enter a stranger's house using a twenty-year-old key probably hadn't helped, to be fair. "Well, not ruled out, we just have no evidence so far to connect them."

"Right. But that was because their drivers hadn't been near the scene that night. What if a taxi ran over Daniel somewhere else, then the guy riding that big bike put his body on the back, strapped to the other seat, say; took it to Osney Island and dumped it? I mean, they're allowed to go anywhere, those things – cycle lanes, Low Traffic Neighbourhoods."

"Again, we can look into it. I'll certainly contact Courieroo and see if they can tell us who those two are. We've got your description, including the neck tattoo, we can put that through our database. And we'll keep an eye out for anything similar."

"What about the lockbox? How come they stole only that? They must have watched me getting it. Somehow." *Steady on, Janna, this could start to sound paranoid.*

"Well… if your purse wasn't in the bag, there possibly wasn't anything else in there they could easily shift. They might just have grabbed it as a souvenir. They do, sometimes, strange as it may seem."

Denise's radio crackled into life, and she spoke briefly to her shift captain on the other end. "Got it, skip. On way." She turned back to us. "Gotta go, I'm afraid, Janna. Take care, yeah?"

I was bursting to ask her about Jem, but that would have to wait. She left the interview room, with Andy clearly keen to wrap things up. At least there was the lead with the company; maybe he could track down my assailants.

"Look, if you're worried someone's following you, that's something we do take very seriously. Not to spread alarm, but stalking's been shown to lead to other offences. Keep an eye out, vary your routine, yeah? If you usually go out the house one way, try going another, if you can."

I nodded, suddenly feeling very weary.

"And if you see anything else, call in straight away, OK?"

∼

Morning: fresh coffee and an effervescent Vitamin C, dissolved in cold water, braced me for yoga. Legs up the wall and spinal twists. Felt a bit less like an ironing board.

I popped a slice of frozen sourdough in the toaster and lathered it with peanut butter, squashed banana and a squidge of runny honey. More caffeine got me back into some semblance of working order.

Today was Kevin's last on full Council business before going into election mode, which meant substantive issues would have to be shelved to give the good voters a chance to send in new reps who might make different decisions. Not that his own seat was in serious jeopardy, but we'd scheduled a session with his correspondence.

He noticed my bandaged ankle straight away, of course. A combination of snowy-haired, blue-eyed twinkle and the honeyed portion of that Scots burr soon extracted the whole story. "What have the police said?"

"Well, I actually got in to see that Detective Sergeant I told you about, the one who saw me for therapy, who's running the case. He sort of poured cold water on the connection with Daniel and his big secret. But he was going to contact Courieroo and ask about those two bikers."

"OK. So, promise me you'll leave it to them from now on?"

"Scout's honour." Right hand cradling kombucha tea, I tried not to wince at a stab from the sore elbow as I raised my left in mock salute.

"So happens *I've* heard from Courieroo," he said, opening the MacBook on his lap as we made ourselves comfortable on his lavish velvet armchairs. I raised my eyebrows for a reminder of the present connection. "About the Bowens."

"Ah yes, of course. Did I tell you I actually saw that happening, just up the road?"

His turn with the eyebrows. I briefly recounted the Case of the Wrong Address, the cheeky crow and the mess that ensued. "Right. Well there you are, I s'pose. Anyway, the message says they'll remind delivery riders of their code of conduct."

I couldn't help wondering whether it said anything about knocking people over and snatching their bags. He scanned on down the email.

"And members of the public who have concerns can ask to see rider ID, they're supposed to show a Courieroo photocard."

"Good, well that's something to tell the Bowens, I guess."

He leaned across to swivel the slats of the Venetian blind as the sun grudgingly decided to gleam in. "Sure. Mind, I've been looking into it, and of course it's not that simple. An old mate of mine runs a Uni institute on casual work. All those riders are self-employed. And he reckons a lot of them run around with branded gear from the big companies, when they're really working for smaller outfits that operate on the margins."

"I see. So a rider who turns up with a Courieroo box, or wearing a Courieroo coat…"

"Is not necessarily working for Courieroo, aye. They might have done once, then just kept the stuff. The merch is in some demand, apparently."

I'd heard that somewhere before recently. Of course – that's what Jem had said. The mystery stranger in the loos at Isis Farmhouse had worn a coat with a Courieroo logo. Yet another connection! And in yesterday's pell-mell, I'd clean forgotten to tell Andy about it. Damn. Still, Kevin's intel pointed to the same conclusion: there were probably thousands of them out there, with no ongoing involvement in the company itself.

CHAPTER
TWENTY-EIGHT

I descended from the Councillor's eyrie with a vague feeling I'd forgotten something. I clicked on to my own emails and, sure enough, there was one from Jem. His gig with The Osney Ones was tomorrow night at Tap Social, a bar-cum-nightclub just up the road. Of course! He wouldn't stay over because Denise would be there, and she'd drive them back to The Leys.

Well, that was something to look forward to. Some of the songs the band covered were from – how had the young shaver seen fit to put it? – "the olden days," meaning twenty years ago and therefore belonging to his ancient mum's era. Great.

And about him with Denise? What were my feelings? Pride, certainly. Mingled with admiration and, I had to admit, a certain degree of pleasant surprise that he'd managed to pull her. Especially as she must be a few years older than him. Would be very interesting to observe them as a couple.

First, I had to deal with the Bolter. Yes, Adam had finally appeared on my screen. One of the problems, apparently, was that he'd been trying to fit sessions into the lunch hour at work. That had been stymied by various issues. A disobliging boss, wanting him to delay his break at short notice.

His scheme had been to access the online Bilateral Base platform using his phone from the car, to get some privacy, but last week his usual parking space near the office was blocked.

We opened with space for his tales of woe. He could speak freely now because he'd booked the day off work. End of the holiday week and a more relaxed atmosphere, at least till Monday dawned. So he looked comfortable, sitting in a cream leather armchair at home.

Turned out his issues were pretty standard stuff. He'd not been able to sustain a relationship, through years of trying. Was this connected with traumatic incidents in his childhood? He'd been bullied, disbelieved when he reported it and punished for "causing trouble" when he spoke out again.

He chose blue star-shapes for the pulsing on-screen blobs to do the BLS. As his eyes followed them back and forth, Adam reported feeling, when reliving that experience, that he didn't matter and nobody would love him. Which, yes, would be a ready-made barrier for anyone in a relationship with him – like his recent girlfriend. It was the breakup with her that prompted him to seek therapy.

I sent him away with a few resources, based on his success at work and with other relationships. And a promise to work on the childhood trauma next time, with full-on EMDR.

That kind of testimony would always send a shiver down my spine, though. As Adam dredged up uncomfortable memories, I couldn't help thinking of Jem's childhood crisis, his near-abduction.

There was so much about that episode that felt unknown and uncertain, then and now. But at least we'd focused on his feelings, believed and supported him, and offered sympathy, not blame. Hopefully, that would help him with Denise – or whoever grew close to him in years to come.

Tap Social: pub, club, microbrewery, institution, icon? Or all of the above? Set up originally to give jobs and a start on rehabilitation to former prisoners, it positioned itself on the upside of every issue. Beer? Still brewed on site. Staff wages? Best in the trade. Furniture? Pre-loved, scrupulously recycled.

To pause a moment on the way in and scan the posters advertising future events was to be reminded of Tap's sheer range. You could go to live bands, variously-themed discos or a weekly comedy night. So far, so familiar. But there were also craft fun days for the kiddies, and women's wrestling tournaments (all-in). Maybe I should mention it to Emma.

Propping up one end of the bar as usual: old Bill. Not the cops, but an actual guy called Bill. Who was old. Propping up old Bill, his devoted black labrador, Charlie. Well OK, and a bar stool. And his iPhone, seemingly. He sat peaceably in his corner, tapping away one-fingered, hunched over in green zip-up fleece and blue jeans. By his other side, a half-empty glass of light-coloured beer. Or half-full? Yeah, he looked more that sort. And the beer? Probably the own-brewed lager, False Economy.

Matter of fact, I'd have one of those myself. Charlie lifted his head to give me the soulful eyes as I joined the queue to order, then rested it back down on his paws.

Seated with the crew from The Leys – Denise, Housemate Chris and his partner Kerryn – I took a deep sup of beer and soaked up the vibe.

High above us, the domed steel roof should give plenty of space for sound to echo as intended. Not now from the power tools of yore but electrical kit of a different kind. A couple of band members had come out on to the small stage away to our left and begun testing out the amps. "Two-two. Two-two."

"Always reminds me of the old joke," Chris said. "How long you been a sound engineer, then? Dunno, one-two-two-two-two years or so." And suddenly, there he was – Jem, adjusting the height of his seat behind the drum kit. He gave a small inconspicuous wave in our direction as the older guys checked he was on-page.

"Nice shirt," I said. Floral pattern, dark red on navy. Big improvement on the one from Isis Farmhouse. In pale contrast above it, the light momentarily caught his long, slender jawline, like a crescent moon.

"Hm! Yes, we chose it together," Denise said. Gratified chuckle with a slight edge. Perhaps he'd been left to order the other by himself, and she'd not approved. It was fun seeing her out of uniform. Her braided hair, gathered in a bun while on duty, now fell attractively to neck length. She wore a black V-neck mini dress in soft cotton with gold and cream small daisy pattern; leggings, tan leather ankle boots and faded brown cord jean jacket.

The Osney Ones opened with a rock classic, about fighting the law and the law winning. In the style of the great punk version, which even had a couple of their enthusiastic older fans pogo-ing over near Bill's corner. The man himself had wisely made tracks, taking Charlie with him. (Or perhaps it was the other way round.)

I couldn't help wondering whether some of the more recent recruits to the Tap Social staff felt a bit hot under the collar at the lyrics. Were there one or two nervous looks behind the bar, and a sudden involuntary moistening of lips?

Matt, the singer, sported a black leather jacket with steel-ringed detailing on the arms, which he pumped to the rhythm at the crescendo to ramp up the atmos.

The second set was more mellow, with more demanding vocal parts and, I had to guess, more difficult percussion too. Not like the insistent boom-boom-boom of the earlier numbers.

My lad kept a careful eye on the other band members as he combined cymbals and even a short tambourine break here and there with some slower drumming. Tongue slightly protruding from the corner of his mouth: sign of concentration, known and loved since childhood.

Matt shucked the jacket and stood, short-sleeved paisley shirt plastered to his torso, romancing the mic with close-cropped, wedge-shaped ginger head. Yeah, he was good.

We danced and, in my case, sang along to some of them. Lyrics from the olden days, word salad to the young'uns, fresh as lettuce to me. Jem popped over for a quick chat afterwards, blushing in the applause and raised glasses, quick hug and peck from a beaming Denise.

∽

Flowing and glowing homewards, I basked unabashed in old memories, attached to classics of the nineties and noughties in The Osney Ones' repertoire.

One in particular where a well-known pathway by a river led to a fallen tree.

When the Temple Cowley house went away, Daniel and I had seized the opportunity to rent closer to the office. A flat in Thames Wharf: no great shakes as living space, but just off the bankside path north of Osney Bridge. The summer of walking and talking had its moments. But, before the leaves turned, we'd begun to cool. We both sensed it.

That record was just out, I remembered now: *Somewhere Only We Know*. We adopted it and clung to it like driftwood.

And there really was a fallen tree, with a secret way round the back to a mini-clearing where we'd sit and hang out, whispering as walkers passed by, oblivious.

I suddenly hit the brakes and screeched to a halt. Flowy-glowy fugue over.

Oh. My. God. *Did you hear what you just said to yourself, Janna Rose?!* In that interior monologue thingy?!

Weren't they the very words Daniel had used, in the WhatsApp call the week before he died? That I'd spent so much time and attention puzzling over?

I should pick up whatever he was working on, if anything happened to him. And where would I find it? "Somewhere only we know." OMG. Again.

CHAPTER
TWENTY-NINE

The narrowboats pulled at their moorings, as Daniel had done, with ever greater force, over those few time-dimmed months. The *Oxford Mail*, local news in general and, ultimately, me. All holding him back from the great mission of his life, whatever that was going to be. Seemed to change week by week.

Probably why I hadn't thought of this before. Hurtling like a river in full spate towards our first break-up. Sad times I had no wish to revisit.

Night passed in a ding-dong battle with fevered excitement. I'd had half a mind to set off and explore our old haunt there and then, soon as I'd realised. I could use a bike light to see by. Only the floodwater put me off. That section of path was very low in places.

Of course, I then slept in. Four o'clock yoga, combined with ibuprofen to dull my aching ankle and elbow – and probably the peanut ball I'd washed down with cold liquorice tea, to make the painkillers kick in – combined to good effect. Waking with a start, the urge of wondering brooked no delay. Splash of cold water, quick black coffee and banana, then out.

I pedalled towards town then hung a left past the handsome

villas on Abbey Road. Thick end of a million gazing down impassively from each one.

Locked Bertha to some railings at the cheap end by the Victorian terrace, overlooking the confluence with Castle Mill Stream. One of the houses had a Sold sign up, I noticed. I briefly wondered how much these were going for now.

Across the arched footbridge, there was a "Path closed due to flooding" sign, which I duly ignored. I hate wellies, but I'd dug them out of the cupboard under the stairs and put them on as a special concession. Warnings be damned.

As it turned out, I did have to squelch along, up to ankle depth, for twenty or thirty metres. An actual moorhen broke from under my feet in a flurry of frazzled feathers. And those narrowboats, eh? Life on board might be fine and dandy in dry spells, through lazy evenings reclining on deck. But fast flows and taut ropes would do my head in.

I presently reached a small, concreted hump with wooden railings on either side, covering a drainage channel and, immediately after it to my right, the old tree. Yep – *our* tree. It stood just clear of the water.

I parted the soggy undergrowth with a wellied foot to reveal the secret path. As I distinctly recalled, one trunk of the giant willow had come away at the join with two others, just on ground level at the rear, and toppled over. Back then, it was newly fallen, sprouting green. Today: well-rotted and home, no doubt, to a whole ecosystem based on fungi, centipedes and suchlike.

Underfoot, where we'd sit and enjoy the quiet, just mud and dead twigs. I scanned the scene, left and right, then up and down. Completely hidden from the path, now as then. So what, precisely, should I be looking for at this point? Chief topic of those wakeful hours overnight.

OK… Daniel and I had been partial to the occasional spliff. Chilled us right out. That year, there'd been a row over cannabis being reclassified. Lots of people wrongly thought that meant decriminalised: something the local plods seemed to take as a personal affront. They responded by ramping up stop-and-search, in a boneheaded bid to increase arrest rates. We'd covered all this for the paper.

The wooden-tops were not above prowling the riverbank for easy pickings. So rather than stride out in possession and risk getting nicked, we found a hidey-hole in that tree to stash the gear. We could skin up on site. Rizlas, roaches, lighter and resin, all tucked into a bag of Cutter's Choice. Somewhere only we knew, in a fallen tree along a familiar pathway.

Come to think of it, the haze might have been another reason why I'd been slow to realise what he meant. Now, could I spot that same crook of a sub-branch with deep hollow at the axillary point, where it nestled away from prying eyes? Yes, that looked like it… bit thicker and higher up than I remembered, but that was to be expected. And still – just – within reach.

I stood on tippy-toes, as far as the wellies would permit, and felt inside. Braced for a bite from some indignant invertebrate resident. But no, and OMG again, could that be it? A bit of plastic, surely?

I gave a gentle tug and out popped one of those food sacs, fastened shut by pressing red and yellow tongue and groove together across the top, just a few centimetres across.

Inside it, a small, elongated rectangular parcel of clingfilm, layer upon layer. My hands were shaking too much to peel it, so I caught the wrapping in my teeth and pulled it away in stages.

And there, as I opened it up, was a black plastic case. I pulled it apart at the middle to reveal – sure enough, as I'd imagined – a data chip.

I almost dropped it in a puddle for trembling. OMG yet again. This was it! Had to be.

It was all I could do to keep my hands steady enough to unlock Bertha. Bit embarrassing. A gang of removalists were there by then, van open and ramp down as they began taking stuff out of the Sold house. At least I gave them a good laugh.

Back at the apartment, I stood and deliberately took a series of deep breaths. In through the nose for four; hold for four; out through the mouth for four. At least then I could trust my fingers to do the necessary.

Sitting at the office desk, I fired up the big computer, remembering to switch off the Wi-Fi. No point nixing Daniel's precautions at this point. They'd turned out to be quite elaborate, all things considered. So I didn't want to be online for the next stage, just in case.

I inserted the metal plug-in bit to a USB port. An icon winked into view on the desktop: "DKerr." Steadied my hand again, took a couple more of those breaths, moved the cursor over it and clicked.

Right. No password, just one file, an Excel spreadsheet, called Connections_2.xls. Opening that revealed the familiar gridwork layout. Sheet 1, each column headed by two letters: BFD, BWD, BBG, Cash, COU, CWK, GNet, HEW. Dates, seemingly, down the left-hand side.

And in the squares, as I looked across the rows? Figures, running into thousands and in some cases tens or even hundreds of thousands. Simple stuff, if you could understand it, with a key to its meaning, I supposed. Trouble was, I didn't have one.

OK. Sheet 2, more figures, in two columns, for just one of the initial entities: BFD. Sheet 3, same for BWD.

I wondered briefly why they were almost, but not quite, in alphabetical order. Surely BBG should come first, then BFD and so on? One other thing I noticed: the figures on the first two sheets, for BFD and BWD, were much the biggest. The GNet one had the next-biggest.

I stood, walked about, did more breathing. Then went to the kitchen to warm coffee, took a sup and returned to gaze. Still no inspiration.

Think, Janna. Spreadsheets were a standard tool of business, of course, and business involved moving money around. Surely these numbers were sums of money? I mean, "Cash" must simply be cash, like it said. Right?

Not really my world. I tended to leave all such calculations, on my therapy business, to Derek. He was about to receive a sheaf of my invoices and receipts for the financial year, sorted helpfully into months, for processing. At a discount, of course.

And there – another "aha" moment. I'd have to go steady, or I'd use up a lifetime's supply of those in a single weekend. Of course, I could take this to Derek. He'd surely be able to interpret it. Perhaps if I offered to forgo the discount.

He might know how to use those things in the "Tools" menu, "Auditing" and "Macro," that had their own arrow-heads pointing to sub-menus. Or "Goal Seek" and "Scenarios," which appeared next to sinister-looking sets of dots. Things I didn't like to click on, in case they scrambled up the whole lot and I couldn't get back to where I'd started. But I had a suspicion they could probably make the slew of seemingly unrelated figures make sense.

CHAPTER
THIRTY

I had to get off and push my bike on the way to Faith and Derek's. Gaggle, nay crocodile, of small children in matching yellow capes and red wellies, traipsing back down the parkside path from some outdoor activity. Parent helpers looking frazzled and virtuous in equal measure.

Inside, everything was in boxes, ready for their house move. Proudly handed over my bulging folder of the year's financial records.

"Thanks. You know, you don't have to print this stuff out anymore? You could just keep it on your computer and attach it to an email." Right. Store that one away for next year.

Derek promised to look at the spreadsheet on the data chip. Raised eyebrows, surprised mouth-shape and a quizzical "OK" at my request to switch off his Wi-Fi when he plugged it in.

"Sure I'm being paranoid, but it might be confidential. Don't want to make any trails, you know."

∽

My phone trilled later with a message to pop back round – things he could tell me. That was quick. I was about to pedal off again when I remembered Andy's advice to vary my routine. In case anyone was watching. Still felt far-fetched, but whatever.

The house the couple were selling was another end-terrace overlooking the park, several blocks down. A few hundred metres by the path – which would presumably be clear of excited kiddies this time. Mind, it would only take ten minutes or so to walk, even the long way round.

So I let myself out through the timber-framed bifold doors at the back, not the front as usual, and into the garden. Mainly laid to paving stones, for low maintenance. And there I went with the estate-agent-speak again. To the rear was a wooden gate, which led on to a narrow path running along behind the street's back walls. I held back a few straggling clematis stems and squirmed through.

A bit of mud was just something my outback boots would have to put up with. I passed down behind the gardens as far as a tarmac lane that came out further up the road, beside what used to be the backyard of a grocer's shop. Long since closed down and converted into maisonettes. It meant I could approach Faith and Derek's from the other direction than usual. There – routine duly varied. And nary an e-bike in sight.

"If you look on there, you'll see, the two figures tally up, on sheets one and three, in one way, out the other," Derek was saying, finger pointing at the document open on his computer screen. They still tended to blur in front of my eyes.

"Which means…?"

"These… entities, whatever they are, denoted by the letters at the head of each column – probably abbreviations – they're all doing business with each other."

"Right." *So what?*

"Only what's odd is how whatever's being bought and sold seems to gain in value, even though the transactions are on the same date." Faith set down two red-and-white striped mugs of black tea on the pile of cardboard boxes beside us.

"No milk now – sorry! We've emptied the fridge." He acknowledged her with a smile.

"So here, look – B-F-D pays over thirty grand to H-E-W on January 19th. Then that same value gets transferred to C-W-K the same day. That's then sold, apparently, to B-W-D, also on the same day, for nearly forty." I raised the tea, which was just cool enough to sip.

"Someone's making money off someone else, then."

"Yep. It's basically a procurement scam. These two, B-F-D and C-W-K, end up with margins, which could be profits on these deals – and seemingly hand it over to the others. Most to GNet, with smaller amounts to C-O-U and B-B-G, some to Cash. I assume that's actually just cash, as it says. No point abbreviating that."

I tucked the data chip back in my pocket, retraced my steps and came in through the back gate. Some of those abbreviations, if Derek was right and that's what they were, had more than a ring of familiarity.

Of course, HEW could be Hewsons'. The conjunction with cash raised forebodings over Adrian, whatever he'd been up to and the implications for Cara and her family. Could the goods he was moving, when I spied on him that Friday lunchtime, somehow be making money for someone else? Was that why the payments to him had to be kept off the books?

Then, COU might be Courieroo, or at least the rogue operators who'd mugged me for the lockbox. Might they be receiving cash from someone, to get up to no good? Nothing specific to point to Regal Cars, however.

∼

Time to run a quick check of the email inbox in case of any upcoming issues for the week ahead. Just the one notable message, from Emma, cancelling her session. Something had come up at work. She acknowledged the seven-day policy and was happy to pay for it.

Dinner was fish, on date and a bargain earlier from the supermarket. Pan-fried, with rice and broccoli from the microwave. Tasted OK, but the pong from its packaging was a bit pungent as I stuck it in the bin.

In fact, as I browsed and dozed through a telly movie later in the living room, I began to pick up a whiff of it in there, too. Truly, the piece of cod that passeth all understanding.

Then, I had to turn the volume up to drown out a hullabaloo from what sounded like at least two, possibly three emergency service vehicles, careering down the Botley Road.

They had to be headed somewhere nearby. Rebuilding work at the railway station had closed off the underpass, so they wouldn't go down there to get to any other part of the city. Had to hope no-one had come to any harm.

Realising I clearly wasn't meant to be enjoying peace and quiet even at that late hour, I paused the film and got up with a sigh. At least I could avoid a nasty niff in the kitchen for the morning by changing the bin liner, thus getting rid of that fish-packet. I tied it at the neck and popped out with it to the yard.

From there, I could see flashing blue lights arcing into the night sky from along the park. Either ambulance or fire brigade, probably. And yes, it must be the latter, as I could now just about smell smoke as well. Indeed, shining out amid the gloom, several blocks down, there was a faint but distinct glow of flames.

But surely... surely that couldn't be Faith and Derek's place?!

∾

"Yeah, well alight by the time we got here," the burly fire officer was saying into his radio. Two of his colleagues held a hose that snaked from the hydrant along the street and in through the front door.

A crowd of onlookers had gathered, profiles picked out by the white streetlight and flashing blue. Family from next door being ushered out onto the pavement in their nightclothes, bemused and woebegone. *Where was Derek? Where was Faith?*

The two red engines stood nose to tail in the road, between the rows of parked cars on either side, with an ambulance behind them, back doors thrown open. I could vaguely make out paramedics moving about inside, presumably getting ready for patients that needed whisking off to A and E at the John Radcliffe.

The flames were seemingly out now – I could no longer see any orange glow in the house – but there was smoke everywhere.

Presently, two of the fire crew, wearing breathing apparatus, emerged carrying a stretcher. One of the men standing on the pavement moved forward and held out a hand to that of the stricken figure, face covered with an oxygen mask, who lay thereon.

Seeing the patient was wearing a pink quilted dressing gown, I had to guess it was Faith. Yes – as they drew nearer, I could recognise her hair. And it was Derek who'd fallen into step beside her. She was evidently conscious, as she turned towards him and took his hand back while being carried along.

Well, that was a relief, at least. I approached the back of the ambulance, where Faith was being bedded in and connected up for the journey to hospital, as Derek waited and watched, his face – now I was close enough to see – a stricken mask.

"Are you OK?" He gave a slight start, but then appeared grateful to have someone to talk to.

"I'd just gone out. Couldn't sleep, went to get some milk for the morning. Supposed to be our last day in the house. Didn't want to be stuck with black coffee."

"So, what, you popped to the late shop?" He nodded.

"By the station, yeah. Let myself out the back. Must've been forty minutes, tops. I had my phone, I called for an ambulance as soon as I got back, but they were already on their way."

"I'm so sorry, Derek. If there's anything I can do?" He visibly started to brace himself for a long night and, no doubt, day ahead.

"Thanks. I've got to follow Faith to the Radcliffe."

"Of course. Is she…"

"Bit of smoke inhalation, but OK, apparently. They'll have to keep her in for a day or two." He gave a sort of rueful half-chuckle, half-sob.

"I even managed to grab our cases – they were in the back room, I went in through there, from the Ferry Hinksey Road side. Fire started at the front, apparently, while I was out." I could see the luggage on the pavement.

"Have they said how it happened, then?"

"One of the guys said it looked like arson. Accelerant squirted through the letterbox then set alight."

"My God, that's terrible!" *Arson*?! On a quiet residential street in West Oxford? The ambulance doors closed from within, the sirens started up again, and it set off, as fast as was prudent on the narrow street, to take Faith in for observation.

"It'll be a mess with the insurance. We were due to complete on the sale tomorrow." I helped him to put the cases into his car. Luckily, he'd parked a little way up the street, so he could get out unimpeded by the fire trucks.

I even offered to put him up for the night, but they'd already arranged to go to his parents' place over near Carterton, about half an hour's drive away, till they could move into Islip. If that was still on now.

"Kids went over there a couple of days ago, thank God."

He'd join them once Faith was settled, then return to the hospital later. And he agreed to let me know how she was. Somehow, I felt partly responsible. How come? Swirling currents of faint indications, half-caught clues and odd feelings of things being slightly off, at various times over the previous few weeks, were now gathering pace in my brain.

I really, really didn't want to think the arson attack had anything to do with the data chip and its enigmatic contents. But I was disturbed to find I couldn't rule it out.

I'd have to nut all this out properly, write stuff down and see if I could make any sense of it, look for links and patterns. Just like in the old news days when I worked on investigations. With Daniel.

First, though, I had to sleep. Liquorice tea, choccy and the last twenty minutes of the movie, smoke-smelly clothes in the laundry basket, facewash, night cream. Smoothed in gently this time.

CHAPTER
THIRTY-ONE

My fortnightly Monday morning spent with Dr Des in supervision, discussing various client quirks and presentations from the week, was followed by two therapy sessions that I basically chugged through on autopilot. Online processing gave me plenty of headspace for cogitation.

Floodwater in the park had been gradually receding, with a mere giant puddle now in place of the out-and-out lake from a fortnight ago. I strode out along the low-lying path towards North Hinksey village on a mission of head-clearing. Plenty of company, as others evidently had the same idea, finally able to come and go with dry feet.

So WTAF was going on?

As an experiment, I turned sharply and looked over my shoulder. Was I being followed? Not here and now, it seemed. But I'd have to start by assuming someone *was* stalking me, somehow, and for some reason linked to Daniel's murder.

OK: I'd been mugged in Temple Cowley for the lockbox, which I'd retrieved from its hiding place while out looking for the data chip. His data chip. And I was sure the muggers rode the same chunky e-bike I'd seen behind me on the way to Heptathlon.

Later, when I'd actually got it, I'd taken it to show Derek: and that same night, he and Faith had a narrow escape as their house was burned down.

If the e-bikers had been after it, or were perhaps trying to destroy it by fire, how come they'd targeted him, not me? Blithely carrying the damn thing to and fro. I shivered to reflect on how easy a target I could have been – and still could be.

But hang on. Junction Road that day had been eerily quiet and deserted: a classic opportunity for a stealth attack. I was all alone. Near-silent electric motor, no number plates, of course. All very sneaky.

When I'd got back to Bertha after finding the package in the tree hollow, the removal men had been there, on Abbey Road, chuckling as I fumbled ineffectually with the lock.

Then, as I cycled along the park to drop off my accounts – and the chip – I'd run into the kiddie-fest. The presence of others, on both occasions, might even have deterred any second attempt to snatch it.

And when I'd gone round to Derek's to see what he'd found, then brought it back with me, I was following Andy Singh's advice to "vary my routine" by walking round the back.

Perhaps I'd succeeded in giving the slip to – who? Best guess, some dodgy Courieroo impersonators, somehow linked to Regal Cars. They might have assumed it was still there and tried to destroy it – hence the fire.

As far as the spreadsheet was concerned, the letters C-O-U seemed to suggest involvement by the firm, or its rip-off merchants, in whatever kind of dodgy dealing was recorded there.

I worried about H-E-W and Cash. I'd have to tell Cara about it, at least in general terms, and press her to find out from Adrian what was actually going on in those Friday sessions after the yard ostensibly closed for the week.

If he was involved in any way, in a set of relations that ultimately led to an arson attack, I was sure it was unwitting on his part. From what I'd gleaned, he was a generally unwitting kind of guy.

But that look on his face, that I'd seen when observing from Fat Les's wooden table-and-chair set, was emblazoned on my mind's eye. He knew full well he was up to no good. Plus, his excessive rage over Kyle swallowing the lockbox key suggested some inner turmoil of conscience.

∼

In Kevin's sumptuous sitting room, we pulled the olive-green velvet chairs into position between piles of party leaflets and newsletters, delivered in boxes for the election campaign. He went straight to the nub of the issue: why didn't I simply hand all this over to the police?

"Well… last time I went in there, they seemed to think I was a bit mad. I mean, I know we're supposed to beware of conspiracy theories these days, but what if, in this case, there's an actual conspiracy?"

"Just because you think you're paranoid doesn't mean everyone's not trying to get you?"

"Something like that."

"Well, as a maxim of politics, it doesn't lead one too far astray, in my experience." He was worried at the notion that the house might be targeted, of course. I thought guiltily of the data chip, nestling in my desk drawer downstairs. Was I exposing us to danger?

"OK, leave it with me. Look, it's already shaping up to be a fraught election, insults and threats flying around." I raised my eyebrows in concern.

"Really? At local level?" He nodded grimly.

"Fraid so. Anyway, it means all Council members can opt to have security from the Community Response Team at their home address. I'll get a car with specialist officers stationed in the street outside. Let's review at the end of the week, OK?"

Shortly after returning downstairs, I looked up through the office window in time to see a small white van, with the "Oxford Council: Doing Good" livery on its side panel, manoeuvring into place beside the kerb. That was quick. I popped out to introduce myself to the two chaps sitting inside it: Abdul and Cyrille.

"We're here till six, then the night team takes over." They were to let me know if there was anything they needed. I didn't mind taking them a cup of tea or letting them in to use the loo.

Going back to my List of Unexplained And Odd Things – literally written out on A4 lined paper, on the desk in front of me – one still stood out: Emma.

Pity. I'd thought we were making good progress. "Something's come up at work," her email said. Might be true, but in my new hypersensitive investigator mode, it had the ring of a made-up excuse. One I'd encountered many times. Most frequently from Bolters, of course, whereas she was a Sobber.

Anyway, how could something work-related have "come up," days in advance? Emma was the office manager; she could simply alter the schedule. She hadn't even asked about switching to a different time. I was particularly curious about the collapse of her father's building firm – in Lincoln, I remembered – and its effects on family relations. A topic whose troubling surface we'd only just begun to scratch.

Relevant search terms soon brought up references to the bankruptcy, fifteen years or so before, of Sincil Construction and Development. With a map panel alongside, where I clicked. Might as well check I was looking in the right place.

Sure enough, a patchwork of beige and green popped up, denoting the city of Lincoln, with various district names shown within it.

Sincil, with a red blob indicating the firm's old address, was one. A sliver of blue in the middle was called Brayford Pool. Hmm – coincidence? Mind, there might be a lot of places called Brayford.

Interest sparked, I kept browsing. To the south of the centre lay two suburbs, Birchwood and Bracebridge. East of those, within the ring road, another village by the look of it, a small rectangle of settlement amid the natural space, name of Canwick.

Hang on. Again. Bloody hang right on.

Couldn't be, surely? I plugged in the chip and opened the spreadsheet back up on my computer, being careful to turn off the Wi-Fi.

I looked again at the map, then toggled through to Excel, then back. Yes, it bloody well could be. Brayford, B-F-D; Birchwood, B-W-D; Canwick, C-W-K and Bracebridge, B-B-G!

All familiar names. Not from Lincoln, or not only, but here in Oxford, too. Emma's company; the builders concreting over Cowley Marsh Rec; the disused building yard next to the Ultimate Picture Palace, and the electrical firm I'd seen installing the new internet next door at Tim and Wendy's. They were due back soon, I seemed to recall. I'd have to check with them whether they'd actually ordered it.

CHAPTER
THIRTY-TWO

I puffed my cheeks and blew a long out-breath, then bent over the screen to check again. Sure enough – they would all fit. So there could be a Lincoln connection between as many as, what, four firms in Oxford, all in the building trade.

All involved in developments which bit off chunks of green space, in fact. Plus Hewsons, Courieroo, and Cash. Denoted by abbreviations, Derek was right, at the head of each column on the grid. Brayford and Birchwood were the first two, as they were the actual builders.

Looking back over my notes from what he'd said, Brayford – B-F-D – was apparently buying material from Hewsons', then selling it straight away, at a mark-up, to Canwick. And there were dates attached to each set of transactions, seven days apart. A quick glance at the calendar confirmed they were all Fridays.

So that could be the scam, right there. I remembered Hewsons' price promise, displayed on the poster hung from the railings around their yard: to "beat any project quote."

Mind racing now.

Canwick could give Brayford a very low quote, knowing they would never actually have to supply anything themselves. Brayford would use it to buy the stuff, discounted, from

Hewsons', which was pledged to undercut the price offered by anyone else.

They could then add a margin and sell it to Canwick. Canwick, in turn, could afford to add another margin when supplying Birchwood, still at reasonable market value. That must be what I'd seen Adrian loading on the truck with his forklift.

Those goods might have gone to Birchwood, possibly even straight to the Cowley Marsh site – without ever entering Canwick's own yard. Which didn't look as if it had seen much action recently, I recalled.

The two firms – Brayford and Canwick – had to be linked. They were the ones getting the profits. Then spending them – small sums to Bracebridge, Courieroo and Cash, and much larger ones to GNet.

I went back to the map of Lincoln and scanned it in search of any district, suburb or village with a name remotely like GNet, but nixed out. The one abbreviation that didn't mean anything – not yet, anyway.

Closing the spreadsheet, I ejected the chip and put the Wi-Fi back on. Searching online for GNet brought up a Global Network on Extremism and Technology, a Greater Nottingham Education Trust, and a company called G-Net that apparently ran nursing homes. In Swindon.

I pushed the cream leather swivel chair back from the desk and took stock.

There Daniel's data chip sat, misleadingly innocuous, on the dark wooden surface in front of me. At the very least, if all those letter sets denoted building companies in some kind of collusion, working the market to their advantage, it would be evidence of corporate sharp practice.

Wouldn't that just come under a heading of business as usual, though? Bad news for Hewsons', whose margins would be getting squeezed, if not tipped into negative territory. There must be a branch manager who was expected to exercise due diligence over the project cost guarantee. Maybe he was receiving some of the cash.

But was it any more than that?

What if I'd received or gathered all this information as part of a news investigation? What would an editor say? What would Mark have said, if I'd brought it to him during his time on the *Oxford Mail* newsdesk?

There was nothing on the actual document, so far as I could see, linking it to any of the companies. The figures on the spreadsheet might be from them and might be accurate – I would assume they were. But there was no proof of its provenance.

I'd be a long way off winning scoop of the year, that was for sure. And – back in the present context – I was a long way off uncovering a plausible motive for mugging or arson, let alone murder.

Mark, though – now there was a thought. He'd mentioned an old Newsquest trainee, hadn't he, who was still in local journalism, on a paper in Lincoln? When I'd met him and Celia for the movie and dinner.

Yep – Jules Chapman, that was the name. Paths had crossed in those early days when Head Office sent a bunch of us on a weekend Hostile Environment course, run by ex-paras at a big house somewhere in Berkshire.

There'd been a scheme to start deploying us abroad to report on locals caught up in conflicts and emergencies. Never happened – financing didn't work out, I seemed to recall. Shame. Would have been good career development.

Anyway, enough on the missed opportunities of yesteryear. I dashed off a quick email to Mark, asking for the contact.

I could pump Jules for more information about the Sincil collapse and possible building trade connections between Lincoln then and Oxford now. And see if he could shed any light on who, or what GNet – in contexts other than counter-extremism, education, or social care in Swindon – might be.

Dinner? Slices of sourdough, straight from freezer compartment to toaster, with whatever was available and within use-by date. No time or inclination to pay it any more attention. Cream cheese and sliced ham, with cornichons from a jar in a long-forgotten corner of a kitchen shelf, made a decent combo on the fly if I said so myself.

The trawl netted a pack of dried dates at the back of the cupboard, kept fresh by one of those coloured plastic clippy things, which I enjoyed with a mug of warmed-up coffee. How come these had sat there neglected for so long? They were yummy.

Then my phone rang.

"Hi Janna, Chris here. Have you seen Jem?"

Classic sudden clutch of gravity in the pit of my stomach. I mean, a mother was supposed to know, right? When something was wrong? And I did. "No, he's not here."

"I'm sure he's OK, he'll just have gone out somewhere. Only he texted earlier that he'd get pizzas on his way from work. And he's not back yet."

He and Kerryn were starting to ring around friends. Message left for Denise, who was away at Hendon for a two-day training course. She would know how best to contact police and what to tell them. Ask her to ring me, I said absently, clicking the red icon to end the call.

It was, what, nearly nine o'clock now. What to do? I could hop online and book myself the Share-Wheels club car, parked in its space at the WOCC, then drive round the ring road, comb the streets of Cowley and go on to The Leys.

But shit, it was well after dark. Felt like a wild goose chase. And the idea came with a pang. How did I know I wouldn't be picked up and followed? Not by an e-bike, sure, but what about a taxi?

Another shit: the highly visible council Community Response team, parked outside the house, might be putting off any attempt to get at me as the present owner of the data chip. But what if that had made them – whoever "they" were – pick on Jem instead? To get at me through him?

Looping back: the near-abduction when he was on the brink of teenage years, still vivid, still the visceral bodily reaction. And the self-reproach for letting him go.

Then more recently, the mystery man in the toilet when he was with that Cuban dance band at Isis Farmhouse. I was a nice lady who should steer clear of Daniel, he'd said. To Jem. Someone who wanted me to steer clear of Daniel knew who Jem was. And they'd been wearing a Courieroo jacket. Shit, shit and shit again.

CHAPTER
THIRTY-THREE

Denise finally called just before one o'clock. She'd spoken to the overnight desk sergeant at St Aldates. He'd confirmed what she explained was standard procedure. As Jem was over eighteen, they'd wait at least twenty-four hours before launching a Missing Persons inquiry.

Had I ever known him to stay overnight anywhere else? Could I think of anyone he knew, like a family member or someone, he might go to?

Of course, I'd had to tell Callum earlier. Directly after hearing from the housemates, in fact. He hadn't seen or heard from Jem since the football weekend. Got me to promise to update him "soon as." So no, in answer to Denise, his dad's at Newbury was the only possible place, and he hadn't been there.

Worst thing about the night? Every time I dropped off, I'd convince myself the phone had rung. Only to discover (a) it hadn't, and (b) a mere half-hour or so had passed since the last time.

Worst thing about the morning? Feeling suddenly sleepy as the first appointment rushed up at me like a pavement towards a man falling off a tall building. Or possibly breakfast: granola going down like grit and sand, grain by grain.

On the phone, Chris again. No sign. Then Denise again, before her training course resumed for the day. Sit tight; he'll probably turn up.

Maybe at work? I got put through to a placement supervisor at BMW Mini. The security system showed he'd left the plant through Gate One at five forty-nine the previous day. He hadn't turned up that morning.

Callum called. "What have the police said?"

"They won't crank into gear till this evening, apparently. Has to have been missing for twenty-four hours." A pause, then a snort.

"Bloody ridiculous. OK, look, I'm going to call Sir Dennis." *Sir Dennis?* "My Chairman. Might sound clichéd, but he really does play golf with the Chief Constable."

Worth a try, I had to admit. But wouldn't the police just do the same things Chris and Kerryn had already tried – calling friends, eliminating places he might have gone?

Nagging away at me: shouldn't I now, at last, tell them about the data chip and its possible significance?

Then again, what did I really have that was definite and substantial? A long list of coincidences and assumptions, along with informed guesswork, and pairs of twos I was adding up to make fives. Every time I mentally rehearsed it, I pictured Andy Singh fiddling with his retractable ballpoint.

Plus, as long as the police *didn't* know about it, that might give me something to hold over whoever had Jem. I was assuming the "whoever" was connected with the whole hot mess – Temple Cowley muggers, Regal Cars, poor Faith and Derek's arsonist, maybe even the building firms with the elaborate procurement methods set out on the spreadsheet. Which I had to, I supposed.

Halfway through the eleven o'clock client, I was forced to give up, stop the session and apologise. I couldn't even feign concentration. I emailed cancellation notices to the two scheduled for that afternoon.

I was going to look for my boy. And nothing and nobody – not clients, not the police, nor any e-bike-riding thug – was going to stop me.

∽

It was early lunchtime when I trundled on to the path across the roundabout underneath the eastern ring road, opposite the Cowley works. Flower beds on either side, the effect only slightly marred by a discarded kid's bike rusting among the geraniums.

Bertha's saddle had worked a bit loose. It would need tightening up with the Allen key, which of course was sitting in the toolbox in the cupboard under the stairs at home. I'd just have to put up with it jiggling. Another annoyance in case there weren't enough already.

Across the sliproad was the entrance, marked "Welcome to Mini Assembly," behind high railings. A couple of dozen workers in dark blue overalls clustered on the steps, enjoying a quick ciggie at the start of their break. I waited for the lights, crossed again, then traced the perimeter in the bike lane of Watlington Road, keeping the plant on my left. A self-storage warehouse and a car hire depot on the other side.

A few hundred metres along, sure enough, "Gate 1." Palisade steel fencing around a turnstile with swipe-card entry and exit. Bike sheds were visible inside. This was where Jem had left the previous evening. But what happened next?

I looked around. Across and down a bit was a detached house with grey pebble-dashed facings whose entire ground floor had been converted into a pizza takeaway. It had just opened for the day. Fifteen pounds would buy you two large ones, according to a sign on the wall: special offer, available Monday to Thursday.

Wasn't this where he'd have gone for the pizzas he'd promised to bring back?

At the aroma from the ovens wafting out across the doorstep, I suddenly remembered my appetite. I could have a medium margarita and can of drink for just seven quid. In the end, I steeled myself to forbear. Detective work to do, so I'd need max concentration. Inside, I introduced myself and gave a short account of my quest.

"Shabir," the attendant volunteered in reply. From my handbag, I drew the printed-out picture of Jem I'd brought with me. Recent, though pre-dating the smart Denise-influenced haircut. Shabir squinted at it. "Yeah, he comes in regular."

"How about last night?" Shabir had not been on shift. He called his mate, who emerged from somewhere back in the kitchen, wiping his hands on a grimy blue-and-white striped apron.

"Yes, definitely." He opened a drawer on the other side of the counter and riffled through receipts held together by a bulldog clip. "Two pepperonis on the special, plus one four-seasons. All large. Twenty-five pounds, paid cash."

OK, Jem had got the three pizzas and presumably tucked them into his saddlebag. He must then have set off home. I pedalled slowly onwards, looking from side to side like a hungry hawk as I traced his likely route.

At the corner by the right-turning lights for the road towards The Leys, a shock lay in store. The Bullnose Morris, where generations of carmakers had wet their whistle at the end of a shift, had closed down. Some time ago, to judge from the vegetation poking its way through the asphalt of the pub's car park. A black-and-green estate agent's signboard announced it was for sale.

I edged down Cuddesdon Road, straining for any sign. Halfway along, the green space of Blackbird Leys Recreation Ground opened out to the left. And what was this, on the nearside edge? The council nursery, where I'd brought tiny Jem, was also closed. For sale by the same agency, it seemed. A few kiddie paintings were still stuck in the windows.

My hard-boiled private eye persona just about held up until Mirlande Richards took one look at my face and enveloped me in her arms. I sobbed unashamedly into the shoulder of her red fleece.

She sat me down for a dish of mac and cheese, which had me feeling positively faint with relief as the toothsome pasta filled my stomach.

She and Marvin had made it rather lovely, the Communi-Tea café behind the Church of the Holy Family. Multi-coloured bunting hung from the cross-beams. Grey fabric on the chairs toned with red plastic tablecloths. On the wall, a big modern oil painting showed happy folk sharing a meal and a sing-song.

A couple of customers were finishing off coffee and slices of black treacle cake, baked on the premises. "Not many in these days," Marvin said in his signature mournful voice, sad lines deepening around his face.

I began to intuit how places were closing down. And remembered why Pearl and I had been so tickled, as kids, by that comic sci-fi character, Marvin the Paranoid Android. The voice and expression could have been lifted directly.

Actually, Pearl was due in soon, Mirlande told me, off her early shift at Sanctuary Care. Denise had let her know about Jem's disappearance, and she'd passed it on to their parents.

Sure enough, she was next through the door. Still in pale blue nursing scrubs under a navy puffa jacket, she gave me a little wave, then disappeared through a door at the back to change. She'd brought clothes in a small holdall.

CHAPTER
THIRTY-FOUR

"Long time," Pearl said, with a suitably rueful smile. Now in a white blouse, beige merino cardie and tight dark blue jeans. Hair neatly gathered in cornrows. She sat opposite me at one of the tables and listened intently to a foreshortened and suitably edited tale of woe.

"And to cap it all, I think my bike saddle's about to fall off." Mirlande was refilling Pearl's cup of tea.

"Marvin will fix that for you," she said matter-of-factly, signalling to her husband with a nod. Wordlessly, he rose, went into the back room and returned carrying a big blue tradie's toolbox. My protestations were half-hearted at best, and waved away in any case. I handed over the key to Bertha's lock.

"He can do anything," Pearl said in answer to my querying look. "Loves it. Bike repairs, plumbing, decorating. Started off as a sparky at the plant, you remember, then took redundo?" I nodded. "But you've got to be an all-rounder these days. People want handymen."

I updated the story with my evidence that Jem had got as far as buying pizzas, but then the trail had gone cold.

"So you reckon he's being held somewhere here? On The Leys?" She was wide-eyed.

"No idea. But there might be some clue nearby, I thought. Just that I haven't found it."

"Right, we need some up-to-date local knowledge. I saw something earlier that we could use. Let's go outside. If you've had enough to eat?"

We walked the short distance to the green in the middle of the roundabout and sat on the bench at the bus shelter.

"See those kids?" she whispered. On the wide pavement outside the Neighbourhood Advice Centre opposite, two slightly-built young men were chatting and horsing around on those stunt bikes that have the saddles set very low. Faces covered by black hoodies and scarves. "I know one of them. And I'm pretty sure I know what he's up to. Keep watching."

Presently, Pearl jogged my elbow and pointed out two girls walking towards the shops from the technical college just around the corner. Both slim, pretty and about seventeen, I reckoned, in black puffas and leggings. One, with dark hair gathered on top of her head, wore white trainers; the other, bottle-blonde, fluffy black slippers. They sat down on the low wall outside the little budget supermarket and hunched over their phones.

One of the bikers approached them, swinging his back wheel off the ground as he cycled forwards in fits and starts in a poor imitation of stunt-riding. He stopped by the girls, bent down and talked briefly to them, then fished in the pocket of his trackie bottoms.

Fluffy-slipper-blondie passed him up a couple of banknotes. A twenty and a ten, I thought. He handed down a silver foil of capsules, which they secreted with a smile.

Well! I turned to Pearl, on my other side, cheeks puffed and ready to marvel with her at the brazenness of it, only to find her in the very act of pressing the end-record button on her iPhone camera. She leant against the back wall of the bus shelter, satisfied herself she'd captured the scene on video, and pocketed the device.

"Coming?" She got up and strode off in the dealer's direction, as the two girls headed back to college.

"Declan Donaldson!" He turned towards her with a start, nearly falling off his bike and seriously blowing his cool. Anguish etched on the thin visible sliver of his face, blue eyes below ginger brows, between hood and scarf.

"Don't call me that!" he hissed.

"It is your name."

"Not here. Ducker, right, 's my street name, innit?"

"Ducker Donaldson?!" She rolled her eyes heavenwards and shook her head. "What, and that one's Mickey Mouse, presumably?" He shrugged. The other hooded rider was already disappearing around the corner. "OK Ducker, guess what? I just caught your little transaction on video." She patted the zip-up pocket of her jacket where she'd put her phone.

"I could send it into Crimestoppers. Or I could show it to Marty Short, then he'll know his dealers are still working in front of the shops, where everyone can see. Not in the car park round the back like he's told 'em to."

A look of panic as he unwound the scarf from around his face, revealing an unhealthy, pasty complexion and uneven teeth. Not surprised – Marty Short was a name even I was vaguely aware of, as belonging to someone you don't cross. Could Pearl know him, to talk to? If not, she was a good bluffer.

"Don't do that, Missis, please. What've I gotta do, to get out from under?" Keeping her eyes fixed on Ducker, she pursed her lips, breathed deeply in and out through her nose, as if summoning patience, and nodded towards me.

"See my friend here, Janna? Her son's gone missing, on the way back from the plant last night. Jem Hodgson. You know him?"

"Jem? Yeah, he was at Spinney, with Ger."

"That's his big brother," Pearl said to me. "The one who's in Bullingdon for breaking and entering."

"Ah but he'll be out soon. Kept his nose clean in there, he has."

"Good for him. Now, back to Jem Hodgson. Snatched, maybe, then taken somewhere. You heard anything on the street?"

"Nothing, honest to God." She lifted up the side of her coat with the pocket containing the iPhone.

"Sure about that?"

"Sure as sure, I'm telling you."

"OK. Let's assume you're telling the truth. First time for everything. So – another question. If stuff like that goes down these days, is there any location you can think of, where we should be looking?" At this, he appeared relieved.

"Well yeah, there is, as it goes. That old council place, y'know, the nursery?" We nodded. "Well, it's closed down, see, so they've took away the cameras. It's on the park, so you can get clear on a bike down the paths. Plus, there's the bowling green round the back, that's been closed too, 'cos of the rain. Any big deals, that's where they go down now."

It would be an understatement to say there was a spring in Pearl's step as I followed her back to the café. Heck, there was even some renewed vigour in mine.

"That was absolutely awesome, Pearl!"

"Can't let these people get away with stuff," she replied. She pressed on a remote from her pocket and a metallic green Volkswagen Polo, parked by the kerb, chirruped and flashed its sidelights in response. "So – jump in, let's go check it out." She drove us the short distance back down Cuddesdon Road to the Rec and turned right into the car park by a sign for Blackbird Leys Bowls Club.

The council nursery name plate had been taken away, leaving only a white metal frame at the corner. We scanned along the dun-coloured, single-storey brick building with the park behind us, past verges where thistles were establishing themselves as the days grew longer. By the door, a hypericum was just starting to push out yellow buds.

Beyond the nursery was a squat structure of dark green wooden panelling, with a flat roof. Metal doors covered the entrance, a horizontal green steel bar held in place over them by twin padlocks. The Bowls Club name was reproduced above a second, black-painted set of wooden doors further down.

To the right of the clubhouse lay the bowling green itself, tufty and weed-choked as it evidently still hadn't dried out enough for mowing. To the left was a narrow-paved path leading around the back, access prevented by a locked metal gate with wire mesh.

Only, to the side of the gate, a section of mesh had been pulled loose from its post. I gingerly lifted it up and wriggled through. Pearl waited on the outside.

Behind the building was a rectangle of grass and mud. And there, on the ground in front of me, was a full-sized black men's bike, lying on its side, saddlebags attached to the rack over the back wheel. Poking out of the bag on top? Three large boxes from a pizza takeaway.

~

Chief Superintendent Yates turned up in person, creases and all, to oversee the police operation. Sir Dennis must have reached the Chief Constable and bent his niblick, or whatever golfing types do.

Pearl held on to me till I calmed down, before gently but firmly pulling away to look me in the eye for some straight talk.

"Now listen to me, babe, yeah? If Jem's been abducted or something, that's some heavy shit, right there. You're not looking at some street punk like Ducker. Even someone like Marty Short would think twice. I mean, these are serious people."

I nodded, and we shifted further away from where a police

forensic team was lifting Jem's bike, encased in clear polythene, into the back of a van.

"Sure, the cops are looking for him. They might find something on that bike. But it's like Denise always says, the law helps them as helps themselves." Andy Singh came to hover nearby, waiting for a word. Pearl lowered her voice.

"They've done it 'cos they want something. My guess? From you. I don't know what it is, but if you do, you gotta give it to 'em, yeah?" She rubbed my shoulder and we turned to speak to the Detective Sergeant. Yes, I'd go into St Aldates to make a statement. Eventually.

Pearl made him promise me a lift home, bike and all, from the Church Centre. He would arrange for a police van to pick me up "in a while."

Mirlande fussed over me and Marvin wore his gravest expression.

"Did you know there's a transmitter under the seat o' your bike?" *What?* "Reason it keeps comin' loose? Not fixed properly in the bracket. Had to take off the whole lot to refit it. That's when I saw. Underneath that fancy cover? Micro transmitter. Stuck on wi' tape."

"Christ!" *Breathe, Janna. And don't take the Lord's name in vain in front of these God-fearing people.* "Are you sure?"

"Should be. Dealt with 'em all the time. Folk get me to set 'em up on cars, phones, expensive coats an' t'ing." I looked blank. "You can track 'em online with an app, if you got the codes. Electrician these days gotta know such. Protection against thievin'. What folk worry about." He nodded sagely.

CHAPTER
THIRTY-FIVE

So bloody hell, the sod who nicked my seat cover outside the Ultimate Picture Palace was acting on instructions from whoever was spying on me. Still a sod, with knobs on. Must've forgotten to put it back on the saddle after fitting the device. Then either I missed it in the dark, or someone else picked it up. That was, what, over two weeks ago. All my two-wheeled comings and goings since then could have been tracked.

"Well, you can take it off now," Pearl said. She came outside with me as Marvin turned the bike upside down and showed us. Should I? *Think.* Where was Bertha going next? Hitching a ride in a police van to the apartment, under the watchful eyes of Abdul and Cyrille. That would deter any harm from coming my way, surely. Plus, I could always just walk if I wanted to evade detection. Vary my routine.

It had been – what was that phrase, that some American politician dude briefly made famous? – an unknown unknown. There was still a known unknown, a thing I knew I did not know: who was tracking me, and why. Though on that, of course, I was now positively bursting with informed guesswork.

No, on balance, I'd leave it in place. Then at least I'd have the satisfaction of inflicting an unknown back the other way. I knew, but they didn't know that I knew. No idea how or why, but that could come in handy sometime.

∼

I crashed straight out at home on the old leather armchair, heating cranked up as soon as I got in.

Two hours later, I was carrying a mug of peppermint tea as I pottered around, closing blinds and tidying up in the kitchen. Trying to numb the impotent rage, mounting panic and creeping despair. More pressure-point tapping in between sips.

Surely Jem would be safe and well? If he'd been taken somewhere and was now being held, to exert pressure, whoever had him wouldn't harm him, would they? That would defeat the object.

Yes, of course, I'd give up the data chip, if that was a sure way to get him back, as Pearl told me. But how, to whom, where and when? And how could I – how would I, in such a situation – be sure that would actually deliver back my boy?

Anyway, wasn't it just a matter of time before the police would find him? They'd be going door to door on the Leys. Someone would have seen something. Starting with the flats opposite the old nursery and the bowls club – though it was their back walls that faced onto Cuddesdon Road, I recalled. Front view over the paths and gardens on the other side. But surely there'd be cameras somewhere, showing where he'd been taken? Car number plates to trace? Stuff I'd seen so many times on telly.

Putting it off, but finally figured I'd better log back into emails and take care of business. Would I feel like seeing anyone the next day? Emma had cried off, but two supervisees were due online, morning and afternoon. Probably better cancel them too.

Tired eyes, so I tried switching the computer display from

black-on-white to white-on-black. Seemed more restful, somehow.

Messages duly despatched, I finished off a referral for a former client. Then sat immobile for what felt like an age, sighed, and bowed to the inevitable.

Opening the shallow drawer in the middle of the desk, sure enough, there sat Daniel's data chip. Automatically, I switched off Wi-Fi and plugged it in. As though gazing at its contents anew might reveal some hidden clue as to Jem's whereabouts.

I clicked on the Excel file, now in white-on-black mode. And wow. There, suddenly visible like a watermark running through the entire spreadsheet, was a corporate logo and letterhead.

And the name and contact details underneath, standing out clearly against the dark background, were those of the firm's office manager. I was looking straight into Emma Kesteven's data breach from Brayford Construction.

Well. That did change things. Much better story now of course, with evidence tying the figures to a highly-placed source in one of the companies whose abbreviated names headed the columns.

Presumably, there would be metadata, or distinguishing marks embedded in the coding, that would confirm the file's provenance from a company computer.

And my God, Emma. What was the deal with her? A quick glance at my notes from that first session confirmed my recollection. She never disavowed responsibility for the breach. Her problem was Lindsey's reaction: the way he kept tormenting her over it even though she'd taken the blame and apologised.

I closed the computer and walked back slowly towards the kitchen. All of a sudden, I could do with a couple more of those yummy dried dates with the last swig of peppermint tea. Purely as a thinking aid. Then I should dose myself up on lycopene, with another glug of the tomato juice, sitting in the fridge door saying "drink me."

If I was being tracked through the transmitter; if the bag theft in Temple Cowley was targeted, as it seemed; if the fire at Faith and Derek's was set on purpose, to destroy the data chip with the confidential records on it – didn't that all point to Brayford, as the owner of said records?

Then, I'd settled into a dull, aching assumption that Pearl was right, Jem had been taken to put pressure on me to give something to someone. It could only be the chip. So mustn't Brayford be responsible for that, too?

Brayford meant Lindsey, of course. He was very much in charge. What about Emma? The two of them worked closely together. If Lindsey was leaving a trail of mayhem across Oxford, including mugging, arson and kidnapping, he would have to keep it from her, surely? I strained to avoid concluding that she must know too. But found I couldn't, quite. And that could be why she'd mysteriously cancelled her session for the next day.

I returned to the office, reopened the computer and looked again at the spreadsheet. Tried switching text and background to all the different colours I could find, but nothing further was revealed.

So what was so precious, that someone would go to such lengths to prevent it from – how had Daniel put it? – "blowing wide open"?

And my God, Daniel. Could Lindsey even be responsible for his murder? Were there shock troops on e-bikes at his disposal, roaming Oxford, who would kill someone? "Serious people" as Pearl had put it? Perhaps in exchange for some of the cash recorded in that column? It hardly bore thinking about.

Callum rang. "Nothing yet, I'm afraid. I heard from Yates, the Chief Super. Search winding down, they'll start again in the morning."

"Callum, that means he's going to be missing for another night! Where *is* he?!"

His span of patience for me sobbing and wailing had seemingly expanded with age. Once, he'd have gone on Hysterical

Female Alert, told me to calm down, or given out sundry other alarm signals. Now, he just kept quiet on the other end with the occasional sympathetic murmur. Might even have been the Dolly Bird, training him.

"I know, it's awful. I'll be checking the phone all night." Well, that was something we had in common.

Of course, my two-hour stupor on the chair earlier meant I was now wide awake. A face-wash after I'd dried my eyes didn't make me any more sleepy. Completely wired, my detector parts kept bubbling up. Might have been the lycopene.

Emma, Emma, Emma. Couldn't get her out of my head. Her last session was the day before I got mugged. What did she know?

Picturing her in the chair opposite me in the office, there were one or two slight oddities in the way she'd seemed – her expressions and body language. She would occasionally gulp, lick her lips and switch her feet under the chair: left-across-right to right-across-left. I'd assumed she was fidgety because the material we were discussing was difficult, bringing up uncomfortable memories. But was there more to it?

It reminded me of that film, I'd noted at the time: the one I'd seen with Mark and Celia. *Sometimes I Think About Dying*. Was that what Emma was thinking of? Herself, or someone else? If I couldn't summon her back to my consulting room, could I take another squizz at the movie? Would that make the recollections of Emma's sessions any more vivid? The night yawned ahead, after all.

It was past its cinema release window now, having ceded screen time to a blockbuster set in the Australian desert. It might even be on my Netpix account. No – but it was available to stream. I could pay four pounds forty-five to rent it for two days on Pear TV Plus. Worth it? Well… I was having to cancel clients at the moment, so cashflow would be a bit challenged this week. Instead, I went back to the search results and found a newspaper review.

Embedded in the page was an actual trailer for the film, of about two and a half minutes, which included a couple of those odd tight cut-away shots of the character, Fran, doing as Emma had done. There – got it for free. Good job I saved the money.

The director "points our gaze towards Fran's nervous tics and tells, her bitten lip and the anxious dance of her feet under the desk," the reviewer had written. Hmm – "tells," eh? That's what they must have been. Unconscious indications from Emma that she was thinking of something else. Something she was keeping from me.

CHAPTER
THIRTY-SIX

It was fully light when I woke up for the final time, clonking my elbow on the MacBook in turning over and avoiding sweeping it off the bed by a whisker. A split second later came the jolt: what if I'd missed something?

A quick check of the phone revealed no calls. I opened the laptop to scan emails. One from Mrs Marcia Kerr. There would be a private family cremation for Daniel, then a ceremony to honour his life and work, on Friday afternoon.

The latter would be held at Hogacre Common Eco Park, in accordance with the wishes of his friends. No-one asked me. I supposed I'd become persona non grata after we last split up. At least I was being remembered now.

I'd met his mother, the first time round. We always referred to her as The Dowager. Tended to look down her nose. At me in particular, or was that just her manner? Never quite clear.

I could easily get there. It wasn't far. A patch of meadow over by the railway line at the back of Grandpont, just downriver. Hopefully it would be dry enough underfoot to avoid having to welly up. I'd have to see what else was going on. Surely to God Jem would be back by then, safe and sound?

I nearly deleted it, but there was another whose subject line said merely "Audio." OK, click.

The text was somewhat cryptic: "What you been waiting to hear. Listen with care." Attached was, sure enough, an audio file, with a .m4a filename extension. In for a penny…

"Hi Mum, it's me. Jem." I sat bolt upright on the bed. *Breathe, Janna*. The screen merely showed a horizontal audio line, peaking and troughing up and down as a slider moved from left to right.

"I'm alright, they're giving me food and water, I'm comfortable. Skylight's broken so it's a bit chilly, but there's fresh air. These people say you've got something that belongs to them. If you give it back, they'll let me go. They say you're to carry it with you, and you'll be contacted."

I steadied my now-trembling hand, used the cursor to draw the file back to the start and played it for a second time. Wasted about five minutes sobbing and wailing all over again. Then hauled myself to the bathroom, washed and dried my face and looked in the mirror. Decision time.

First thought: this should definitely go to the police. They'd be able to trace the email and catch the sender. Andy had a Detective Constable on his team who was "a whizz" at such technical things, I remembered.

I looked again at the screen and read off the sending address: impact4301@neutronmail.com. I'd never heard of neutronmail, so I opened a new browser window and looked it up.

It was, apparently, "a Swiss end-to-end encrypted email service." Located in the country specifically "to avoid any surveillance or information requests from investigating authorities."

Damn. So… maybe the police would come across him, through their normal methods. They would put out public appeals. Forensics on the bike might reveal something. But it was hard to imagine how the search would be made any more effective by receiving Jem's message. Not if they couldn't trace it.

Plus, he'd referred to "something that belongs to them." Something that was in my possession, which I should give back. As soon as Andy Singh or the Chief Super heard that, they would demand to know what it was. If I sent them the audio file, it would suddenly become very difficult to keep hold of the data chip.

It was the data chip that was valuable to the kidnappers. The moment I handed that to the police, its value would be lost, along with whatever leverage it gave me.

No – on balance, it would be safer not to involve the police. That meant playing along. I should carry the data chip with me, the message had said – and I should expect to be contacted. That way, I could get my son back.

∼

I puffed myself out on the yoga mat with six full salutes to the sun. It responded by deigning to glimmer briefly from behind the grey, then seemed to give up. C'mon, sun, show us a sign. In: play the game. Out: call the cops. Ah, you don't catch me that easily, it said. Here, take this: half-in, half-out. Gee, thanks.

A long warm shower, bringing down all those questions on my shoulders. Should I? Shouldn't I? And when? Today. Morning? Afternoon? There really would be no point in delay, if my mind was clear.

Still, as I dressed: was I really up for this? Now I knew about the transmitter under the saddle, presumably all I had to do was set off on Bertha, even just along the Botley Road and back.

Then sooner or later someone would track me down, via the app and the codes, and show up to collect. On an e-bike, most likely. I'd be contacted, as Jem's message said.

A nervous little wave to Abdul and Cyrille as I set off. Data chip slipped into the small change pocket at the waist of my jeans. Right at the top, on to the main drag. Half a mile or so along, past the WOCC on the left and St Frideswide's Church on the other side; bridging all three channels of Isis. Not a sausage.

So I turned left into the mouth of Abbey Road; circled, then headed back the way I'd come. Nerves thoroughly racked by now.

I'd planned myself a stop-off refuge in case of just this kind of impasse: good old Waitrose. I could do with a few bits and pieces anyway. Low on coffee, choccy and cheese. Right out of bananas. So I locked up at the bike racks, shouldered my bag and went straight on in through the sliding doors.

And suddenly, as I scanned the green plastic trays for fruit that would be yellow enough to eat now, not next week, out of the corner of my eye, could that be it? A tall figure in black puffa jacket and peaked smooth black bike helmet, like a cap, with a Covid-style facemask, also black, and dark shades. Shades? In a supermarket? Perhaps just someone with sensitive eyes. And concerned to avoid infection in public places, hence the mask. Unless…

I would keep a surreptitious eye out. I orbited the deli counter, snagged a small bottle of apple and elderflower juice from the fridge alongside, and peeked down the next aisle, head sticking out no further than necessary for a clear view.

The Black Rider passed across at the other end, further into the shop. I moved on in parallel, pausing to lift a double pack of Lavazza off the coffee shelf. Suddenly, away to the right, there he was.

Or was he? No. Again with the helmet, shades and mask, but shorter. Different coat, patches of khaki on grey, looked more like a Gore-Tex, and – from the bits visible above the neckline – this one was definitely black, whereas the first looked like a white dude.

A massive jolt and sudden racing pulse as I realised yes, this *must* be it. Yep, definitely, both of them, now heading my way from different directions. Either as long-lost fellow members of the Sinister-Outfits-For-Shopping club, staging a reunion, or my guys. Drawn by invisible beams from Bertha's beacon.

So I could just stand where I was, between kitchenware and the brown plastic trays of fresh bread, and we would converge. But oh, shit, how was this a good idea? These were serious people. Not nice people. And they were bearing down on me. In Waitrose, FFS. *Breathe. Get it back.*

Avoiding catching their eye, I bought some extra thinking time by dodging down the next aisle. Safety in numbers here. Motherly pensioner and solid working-dad type for company. We browsed among the cleaning products.

I had to assume they would try to get me on my own, or at least in a reasonable radius of unpopulated shopfloor, to effect a handover away from prying eyes.

You know when you embark on something, with a troubling but nameless sliver of doubt in the back of your mind? A doubt whose nature and content then suddenly reveal themselves at the most inconvenient moment? This was that moment.

Dolt, Janna! The minute you hand the chip to these two goons, why the hell should anyone give Jem back?! They'll have got what they wanted, and they won't owe you a thing! They could just... do away with him. Somehow. This isn't going to bloody work!

Again, I risked a glance from the corner of my eye. Sure enough, the pair were loitering together, watching and seemingly waiting for the aisle to clear before approaching. In unison, they looked down at a phone, then up towards me – presumably checking a picture.

Right, that was it. I was NOT doing this. Abort! Abort! Suddenly, I moved off sharply to my right. A shaft of clarity as, sure enough, sun streamed in via the big windows ahead of me. Nope – no way was I going through with it. That data chip was staying in my pocket.

Stride lengthening, I rounded the end of the aisle, set down my green shopping basket and scuttled past the startled attendants at the counter of the in-store café. Didn't dare look round but had to guess the gruesome twosome were following along behind.

Toilets to the right: no good. I could dodge into the Ladies, but all they would have to do was to wait till I came out. Even if they were squeamish about entering. In front: the emergency exit. Nothing for it but to push on through.

CHAPTER
THIRTY-SEVEN

Recrimination Road went by in a blur.
Because I was not hanging about, having dashed across from Waitrose, narrowly missing a silent electric double-decker bus, whose driver parped crossly as I flitted in front.

Then, there was quite thick foot traffic by local standards, which might have deterred any hostile approach as I dodged and wove. But also because my inner debates and laments had risen to a state of unbearable cacophony.

Within footsteps of bursting through the Waitrose side door, alarm ringing in my ears, I was convinced I'd just made a massive mistake.

I've-let-you-down, I've-let-you-down, I've-let-you-down. Jem, my best boy, Mum's let you down. How did that come to pass, the one outcome I was desperate to avoid?

Those two hoodlums would now report in. Janna's not playing ball. What then for the hostage? I'd kept looking back, but there was no sign of them. Slight relief, at least, when the Community Response van hove into view. I let myself in at home.

Sat hugging myself in the old leather armchair, rocking back and forth, keening. Literally.

One thing I could do, would do – for myself and for him. Listen to that message again. Might there be some faint glimmer of hope in it, that I'd missed? And I must hear him. I must.

Fumbling fingers pulled out my phone and unwound the headphones from around it. Opened the browser and clicked on to emails – yes, there it was.

The message was a stark one. No ambivalence or wiggle room. Quid pro quo. You give us the data chip, we'll give you him. There'd been one good chance to get him back safe. And I'd just blown it.

Listen again. Was this the last time I'd ever hear him? Would the recording be a souvenir, a keepsake? How tragic was that?

And again, tormenting myself now. Pressing the bud deep into my ear, soaking in all the sound.

Hang on.

Hang bloody right on. Could there even be something audible in the background?

I dabbed my eyes, blew my nose, sat up straight and steadied my fingertip to draw the audio back to the start. Play it again. What was it he'd said? A broken skylight. Chilly, but letting in fresh air. Was it possible that, through the skylight, sounds from outside could just be faintly heard?

Sounds? That couldn't be music, surely? I must be dreaming. Wishful thinking, losing my grip, going doolally. No, there it was. Deep in the background, but still.

And bloody hell. One of the very few pieces of classical music I could name, if you played it to me. The Spring movement from Vivaldi's *Four Seasons*. Yep, now I came to focus on it, there it was – unmistakable.

BLOODY HELL, I KNEW WHERE HE WAS!

Calm down, Janna. Lots of people must play that in lots of places. Listen again. But it could be. It bloody well could be. Surely… surely that violin with piped backing track was the one from outside the Ultimate Picture Palace, when I visited with Mark and Celia? That student, busking to the ticket queue?

And – AND – outside the disused builder's yard next door, Canwick's, which I now knew was part of this whole imbroglio. The dodgy dealings captured on the data chip itself. Too close a connection to be put down to coincidence.

I gaped and goggled like a guppy from Kevin's fish-tank, for what felt like five minutes but was probably only seconds. Then at last my brain started to catch up.

Now was the time to call Andy Singh.

A quick splash of cold water braced me for the crucial next stage. I scurried back across the road to Waitrose to retrieve Bertha. Keeping an eye out this time, for buses and lurking e-bike riders. Coast clear.

Back at the apartment, I propped the bike on her kickstand, took a deep breath to steady my hand, and gingerly reached under the saddle and its cover. I felt the lump of the transmitter, eased the tape loose and pulled. And there it was in my hand. Bronze-coloured drum shape, with wiry legs sticking out. Tiny, trouble-making thing.

I inverted an empty plastic flowerpot and used it to cover the device, still stuck to its tape, on the circular brown saucer that went with it. As far as the app was concerned, I'd be at home.

Quickest route into town was straight down Botley Road and along the pavement by the station, now in a tunnel set up for foot-sloggers to bypass the building works. There'd be some who'd squawk at a bike – you were supposed to get off and push – but let 'em.

Andy had been sceptical, naturally. But it was time to deploy the big guns.

"Well, take it straight to your Chief Super, that guy Yates who came to The Leys. I know the Chief Constable's been on to him over this. And I know Jem's there."

"OK. I'll see what I can do." I had to hope I'd reach Canwick's yard off the Cowley Road – and, more to the point, the cops would – before anything could change for the worse. Push, pedal, push.

Might they move Jem somewhere else? Or… or do something to him? Thoughts I strove to banish, while pelting along with all the force I could muster, as useless to the quest. I wove in and out among the walkers, letting their complaints bounce off.

"Sorry – emergency!"

Then across the wide pavement of Frideswide Square, skirting the café tables and cluster of red e-scooters-for-hire, opposite the brooding frontage of the arms-dealer Business School. Past the Castle Mound to my right and the hotel converted from the Victorian prison. Push, pedal, push.

Then on to Queen Street, past the Shopping Centre That Must Not Be Named. The pedestrian thoroughfare was supposed to be closed off to bikes till evening, which I'd ignore on this occasion. A Low Traffic Neighbourhood of its time.

Rival buses jostled down the High Street. Surely I could just cycle round them? Think again. Parked tradies to one side, oncoming buses to the other. Grocery van trying a three-point turn. Come *on*! OK, pavement. Sorry, walking-stick-man – needs must.

Jem – what was happening to Jem? Where was he? Languishing somewhere in the cluster of rundown buildings behind that palisade fence around Canwick's yard? Or had I got this completely wrong?

At The Plain, the four-way roundabout that forms the gateway to east Oxford, I took the middle exit for Cowley, with its dedicated bike lane, and flicked up another gear. Push, pedal, push.

Yes, I was close now: there was Shiraz, the Persian restaurant where we'd eaten that night. And, as I followed the road's slight leftward arc… yes again, thank God. Police, outside the cinema and builder's yard, establishing a perimeter and ushering back the public.

I stood panting by the bike racks, took my helmet off, pulled my sleeve across my damp brow and locked Bertha to the rail. Presently, a pair of coppers in peaked caps and fluorescent green jackets approached the front gates. One cut through the padlock with bolt cutters and opened them up.

If only x-ray specs had been invented for real. Was he in there? Inside one of those squat blue brick sheds with tin roofs? The one further away had a high barred window on the facing side. Could the broken skylight be on the far side?

Just then, a plain white van came nosing the wrong way up Jeune Street, in front of Canwick's, and pulled to a halt. A murmur among the gathering crowd of onlookers as, from the back, black-swathed figures began to clamber out. Blimey, armed support. Take that back about the taxes.

Glad they were on our side. They looked dead scary this close, with robocop helmet-and-goggle sets, body armour and those big pointy shooters.

The gun squad swarmed into the yard and took up positions around the buildings. Around me on the pavement, phones got whipped out as the good folk of Cowley Road sensed an opportunity to impress followers on their socials.

Crouching down behind a triangular wooden council flowerbox, on the corner opposite the cinema, I suddenly spotted Andy Singh. One of the green-coats from the gates squatted beside him and handed over a radio. They exchanged nods, and he spoke into it. Barking a command, I had to assume. This was it!

"Armed police!" came the cry familiar from television dramas. But shit, this was for real: distant but distinct from, what, about forty metres or so in front of where I stood.

My insides felt like a sponge being squeezed. I was in urgent need of a pee, but that would have to wait. Eyes on stalks, straining for any clues.

They seemed to have got inside all three of the buildings I could see. One had a steel roller door at the front for deliveries, but they'd gone round the side of it.

Seconds ticked by, each feeling like an hour. No sign.

CHAPTER
THIRTY-EIGHT

Then, suddenly, at last, a stirring of movement. One of the weapons team emerged from the narrow opening to a passage through the buildings, lifting goggles onto the top of his helmet and dislodging his nose-and-mouth mask.

And behind him – YES! My Jem! Walking unsupported across the yard, upright and apparently unharmed. Other armed support officers around him, now in relaxed mode.

I dashed forward, only to be restrained at the line of blue-and-white tape by a burly uniformed PC. "I'm his mum! Jem!" That smile. That wave. That face. That hair (thanks, Denise).

Copious cuddling. Relief at last. Relief doubled when I could finally drag myself from his side and pop into the cinema to use their loo. A glug from the cold-water tap didn't come amiss either, after my earlier exertions on Bertha.

Andy Singh caught my eye and signalled me to one side for a chat. A medical team was checking Jem over, taking blood pressure and suchlike, before he could be pronounced fit to go. He sat on the floor of the ambulance, feet on the street, as they ministered to him.

"OK, I'll come clean," the Detective Sergeant said. "Soon as you called, we put up a drone with thermal imaging, showed there were two people in there. So your story checked out."

"Mmm." I was concentrating on beaming at all and sundry. He wasn't going to get any sense out of me there and then.

"And you were right on the money with taking it to Yates. The Brass were all over this one. Course, we know about the WPC and your boy there. All very sweet. Talk of the station."

"Bless." Behind him, I saw a metallic green VW Polo edging down the Cowley Road, traffic returning to normal. Denise emerged from the passenger seat as, presumably, Pearl went off to find a parking space. She was in jeans and a puffa jacket, so evidently not back on duty yet.

"We even got the guy holding him. Tried to make a break for it out the back on an e-bike. Found his knife inside. There'll be dabs all over it."

"Great," I mouthed absently. He could have been telling me the moon was made of green cheese.

"So the Chief Super'll be pleased. But it's a big chunk out of his budget. Tac support doesn't come cheap. At some point, he's gonna want to know what this hot lead was, and where it came from." Over his shoulder, I could see Jem getting a huge, enveloping hug from Denise.

"Right." OK, now I'd have to go back on guard. It felt like putting on an extra pair of clothes, like waterproof trousers over my jeans. My new investigator kit. He narrowed his eyes and looked at me askance.

"It's good to share, Janna, you taught me that."

"Sure."

"Look, it's a right result, and everyone's happy. But I did go out on a limb, just remember that, yeah? Come and talk to me." And with that, he turned on his heel and went back to share congratulations with his troops.

∽

Pearl parked in a side road opposite Cowley nick while Jem went in with Denise for a debrief. I phoned Callum's office and left a message with his PA, passing on the good news. Though he'd no doubt heard it from Sir Dennis by then.

"Won't take long – promise," Andy had said. Sure enough, Jem soon emerged, the dregs of a chocolate shake, pressed on him by an awestruck well-wisher back outside the cinema, in hand.

"Sorted me out, that has." He finished it off, popped the container into a nearby litter bin and let himself into the back alongside the off-duty WPC. He had a couple of days' stubble and was still in his work clothes, a white business shirt now rather grimy around the collar. All things considered, though, he looked pretty damn good. Good to me, anyway.

"So he's been putting a brave face on it," Denise began, as Pearl indicated left onto the Cowley Road.

"Feels OK, really. I didn't mind telling them about it." *That's my boy.*

"But apparently there were – what? – about six of them? And one of 'em had a gun?"

"On those e-bikes, yeah, just seemed to come out of nowhere, suddenly they were all around me. By the nursery on the park, you know." Sympathetic murmurs all round.

"I'd have been bloody terrified," Pearl said.

"I thought they wanted to nick our pizzas at first. I mean, sure, I was bricking it. But there was no other way to react. I couldn't get away on a pushbike. I thought, I'll just have to do what they say. It'll sort itself out."

"And then they put you in a car?" She sounded incredulous on all our behalves.

"With a cloth bag over my head, yeah. Smelt of strawberries." There was a chuckle from the assembled throng. He was so cool! My therapist parts were momentarily worried. Would there be a delayed reaction to the trauma? But that could wait.

"But then later, when they... had you. In there," Pearl persisted.

"Oh, they made me comfortable. Brought in food and water. Mind, I've had enough supermarket sandwiches for a while."

"And what, they just sat and watched you?" She'd crossed the ring road and was passing the giant grey metallic wall of the plant on our left.

"Well, there was always one of them in the next room. It was kind of a suite – two rooms and a toilet, all behind a locked door. Cops just burst through it."

"And you had no idea where you were?"

"Not really. I mean, the car journey wasn't that long. And I could just about hear traffic, through the broken skylight. So I guessed it must be somewhere in Oxford."

"And they told you not to shout out, you said?" Denise referred back to his interview with Andy Singh, where she'd sat in.

"Yeah, that was the big no-no. That and trying to get away, of course." We each emitted noises somewhere on the spectrum between rueful chuckle and sympathetic murmur.

"That's how I worked out where he was, from the recording they sent me, the sound of the busker coming in through that skylight."

"I know, amazing," Pearl said, turning right by the Bullnose Morris.

∼

We gazed at the spreadsheet on the screen of Jem's MacBook. The Richards sisters shared the big old red upholstered armchair – Pearl on the seat, Denise perched on one of its wide padded arms – below a poster for an Oxford gig from some band, Cavetown I thought the letters said. It showed a blue-and-orange cartoon moth sitting at a table, holding knife and fork. Reminded me I hadn't eaten.

The housemates were just calming down from their excitement at Jem's return. Chris sat next to me at the dining table while Kerryn leant in the doorway to the kitchen beyond.

I'd performed the trick of reversing to white-on-black to reveal the Brayford logo and Emma's letterhead, to suitable gasps and exclamations. "So this is what it's all about? These… dodgy dealings?" Pearl shook her head. I'd explained how money circulated to generate surpluses in the Brayford and Canwick columns.

"If I was Hewsons' I'd be a bit cross," Kerryn said.

"Me too. What I don't know is, what's GNet? I mean, all the others are connected – names of Oxford businesses, and bits of Lincoln, bizarrely." From his recumbent position on the threadbare blue sofa, Jem's head snapped round.

"GNet? They're the enemy!" He sat up, put on his specs, leaned across us and clicked back to the first page of the spreadsheet. "Yeah, that's how they're always denoted – GNet. Must be the same one." We looked blank. "Gallium Network," he pronounced triumphantly.

"You'll have to give us a bit more to go on, babe," Denise said. Jem breathed deeply in and out. He'd showered and changed on arrival back at Falcon Crescent, but then crashed out for half an hour as the ordeal caught up with him. Now, though, he was wide awake.

"Only one of the biggest troll and bot farm operators on the entire worldwide web." Suddenly, connections fused with absolute clarity. This was what Daniel had prophesied would "blow wide open."

"Fu-uck!" Chris, voicing what we were all thinking.

"So right," Pearl began, "Brayford and Birchwood are doing these developments that gobble up green space and promote car traffic…"

"… And they're like, scamming money out of Hewsons' and giving it to this Gallium, to do – what? – trolling and botting?

How come? I mean, what even are those?" The puzzled faces around me reflected Kerryn's question.

"Because that's how they can influence political decisions to get *their* schemes approved over others. Riling people up on social media to oppose Low Traffic Neighbourhoods," I said triumphantly, enjoying the clarity at last. "Without that, the tenders would go to other firms, who put in bids that are more environmentally friendly."

"It works by astroturfing," Jem said. "Imitating grassroots campaigns, only fake. Look, let me show you. Here's a report Beate sent me to read as homework, before I started working for her." He opened a pdf on his desktop, a report by the Oxford Internet Institute: *Social media manipulation by political actors an industrial scale problem.* Typed in "Gallium" as a search term and the file flicked onto page 416. We craned over to read.

In one case, the mysterious GNet had apparently created an entire Facebook account, built up eighty thousand followers over a period of years, then started using it to influence an election somewhere in the north of England. The same methods were suspected in other countries – all Gallium's handiwork.

Kerryn handed round mugs of tea. Mine had a faded picture of characters from a children's TV series that I'd watched with Jem when he was small: goggle-eyed yellow dog, boy in blue with strange white hat, and pink-haired princess. What was it called? *Adventure Time,* that was it. Fiction, meet your match in fact.

The report gave another instance, of competition between rival online gaming franchises, where social media messaging had insinuated one of them was a secret surveillance trap set by government agencies. A trail of false and misleading claims about it was traced to Gallium's door although, the report noted, the agency itself denied responsibility.

"We had a product launch a few months ago, a conversion kit for classic Minis, to switch them to electric motors," Jem said.

"Suddenly, we're getting all this crap online about them blowing up."

"What, like – exploding?" Chris asked. He took a deep swig of his tea, as if to douse the flames.

"Yep. Well, catching fire, while people were just driving along in them. You know, like spontaneous combustion. But all false."

"So how come people believe it?" Denise voiced the question on all our minds.

"Well – they put out these messages, on Facebook, X, Insta, whatever. Then someone like Gallium will have bots programmed to repost them, thousands of times. Plus, they're using AI to add text comments now, so they look more authentic."

"Right – and that's how they suddenly seem to be everywhere," she said.

CHAPTER
THIRTY-NINE

In the contacts app on my phone, I still had the login and password for my old Twitter X account. We opened it up on Jem's screen and entered search terms linking Oxford and traffic. Bile and bluster billowed out.

The others used their phones to experiment on their Instagram and TikTok accounts. Searching pictures and videos brought up similar patterns. It was just like the trawl I'd done a couple of weeks before, only more current, more active and still more angry. Cryptic handles and usernames, thousands of likes and reposts as if from nowhere.

"Hallmarks of GNet," Jem said. The strong impression was that Low Traffic Neighbourhoods were part of an elite conspiracy to undermine people's freedom of movement; to confine mobility to a privileged few and discriminate on grounds of race, class and religion.

Prominent among the posts were links to the campaigns being waged by independent candidates opposed to the LTNs in the forthcoming council elections. "I feel a bit lost," Chris said, looking up from his screen. "I mean, what's this got to do with Jem being kidnapped?" I decided to try out my big theory on them.

"OK, here's how it all fits together. Brayford and Birchwood are two building companies…"

"Might even be the same one, just with two names," Denise chipped in.

"Indeed, maybe. Anyway, they pay Gallium to ratchet up the anger on social media over the LTNs. That puts pressure on councillors, worried about their seats, to approve developments that appease opponents, like taxi firms. These companies know that and they know to expect it. So they put in bids that include buildings and roads that bite off chunks of green space."

"Cancel that," Kerryn said. She went and sat down on the sofa next to Jem. I bit off a chunk from one of the Hobnobs she'd brought. Slightly stale but, dipped in the tea, manna from heaven. (I mean, how do biscuits hang around uneaten for long enough to *go* stale? Must have iron self-control, these young'uns.)

"Right. And if it came out, the tables would turn," I went on, brushing away crumbs. "If these building companies – or company – were *seen* to be manipulating local opinion, and the council, it would toxify them. They'd lose contracts worth millions. In fact, tens of millions." I took another swig of tea. Pearl shifted in the armchair. Jem leaned across to the laptop and toggled back to the Institute report.

"So that's motive, right there, on that chip," Denise said.

"Better believe it. And it's led to them sending men to mug me for it in Temple Cowley, burning down my accountant's house to try and destroy it, then kidnapping Jem to make me give it to them." To add emphasis, I counted off the incidents with the index finger of one hand on the middle three of the other.

"So what are *we* gonna do?" Pearl jumped into the lull that followed the five minutes' worth or so of my answers to their follow-up questions. "You've been through some shit, Janna. So's Jem. What now?"

"You could give that data chip to the police and like, get them on to this Brayford. Make *them* squirm for a change."

I totally got where Chris was coming from, but still felt conflicted, as in Waitrose. "I've spent so much time thinking about that. Denise, what would happen if I did hand it in?" She re-crossed her legs on the arm of the big chair.

"It'd go to Corporate Crime." She registered our blank looks. "Specialist unit. I'm putting in for attachment there next year, once I've finished my beat requirement. Well, I did Economics at uni, so…"

"What would they do then?"

"Well, they'd look into all the connections and decide whether a crime had been committed. Then they'd like, decide whether to investigate. And whether it's linked to any others, ongoing."

"How long would that take?" I thought of the looming Council deadline, the confirmation meeting to approve the Brayford scheme for the Osney Mead bridge. Next Monday, I seemed to remember – the only substantive decision still to be taken before the election.

"Hard to say. I mean, they're a top team, I'd love to go there. But I know they've got a long backlog; all the specialist units have."

"And d'you need the data chip to get the people who took Jem?" Pearl asked. "I mean, didn't they pick up that guy at the yard, who was holding him?"

"Yeah, there'll be enough to charge him. But the others?" Denise pursed her lips, deep in thought, then gave a slight shake of her head. "It's often difficult to get information from a single suspect. The more the better, then you can play 'em off against each other. That's the course I've just been doing."

"The stuff on the chip, plus that recording of Jem from your emails: that's what could link it with Brayford and those builders," Chris said. He was – what was the phrase Andy Singh had used? – right on the money. But now my boy was out of immediate danger, I felt a surprisingly strong residual loyalty to Daniel, and the cause he'd asked me to take on if anything happened to him.

Excellent as the Corporate Crime unit might be, there was no way it would blow this open in time to stop the development. Heck, by the time they made up their minds the bridge might have traffic on it, to judge from what Denise had said.

It fell to Jem to break the silence that followed. "Course, we could always just go ahead and post the whole thing online."

There was a stunned pause, then everyone else spoke at once.

"So how would it work?" Pearl, when people's initial reactions subsided, practical as ever.

"Well, there's lots of things we can do," Jem began. "This is what I've been doing at work, in my placement. I've got loads of contacts with online groups we can use on all the apps, lists of followers and stuff. Activate them to spread the word."

"Right. But these people here just literally abducted you at gunpoint. You don't wanna mess with them," Kerryn said, homing in on a flaw in the scheme. "I mean, Janna reckons her accountant's house got burned down. Don't want that to happen here." She zipped up her dark red top to full extent, and dipped her chin inside it at the neck.

"What about the flat?" Pearl nodded in answer to Denise's question.

"There's a flat in the Church Centre, gets used for locum priests and suchlike. Mum and Dad look after it. It's decent."

"Right, so I could go in there and use my mum's X account to put a bit of that stuff from the chip online every day. If there *is* someone watching the house, they'll soon realise I'm not here."

"But wouldn't that make Janna the target?" Pearl, looking after me, bless her. Must admit I hadn't *quite* wanted to spell that out to myself, but now she'd done so, I concentrated on suppressing a shiver so the others wouldn't see.

"I'll be OK, I've got the Council Community Response van

outside mine, over in West Oxford." *Well done, Janna.* Otherwise, this was shaping up as a decent plan.

"What, and that would spread, the stuff you put out?" Chris asked.

"We can do thunderclaps." Mystified looks all round. Jem in explainer mode. He was getting good at it. "OK, so we coordinate, get as many users as we can to post at the same time, then all like and repost each other's straight away. Like a thunderclap. Same on the other apps."

Denise led us in thinking through the logistics. We'd have to assume we were under surveillance. The Falcon Crescent house had been added to the police patrol driving route for The Leys, but they would only pass every half-hour or so. Jem would have to be smuggled to the Centre.

"We need a decoy," Chris said. "Your bike's back now, Jem, they dropped it round earlier. I could put some of your clothes on, and your helmet, then cycle out somewhere on it. If anyone's targeting you, they'd think I was you, and follow me. Pearl could drive you round the corner, when they're not looking."

"Well hang on, wouldn't that put *you* in danger? Where would you go, anyway?" Kerryn's brow furrowed in concern.

"I could go and fetch pizzas for dinner, from down by the plant. Same route as Jem was on."

"And I could get the patrol to follow. At a distance, but close enough to come to the rescue," Denise added.

"So Jem hides out in the Church Centre flat, away from prying eyes," Pearl said, piecing it together out loud. "And from there, he uses Janna's X account to run a social media campaign – what? Putting out info from that spreadsheet?"

"Yeah, we could tease it, use a small amount in each post and say on Monday all will be revealed. Be in time for that council meeting, wouldn't it? I mean, we could tag all the councillors, make sure they see it in their feeds." Jem looked flushed with excitement.

I couldn't suppress misgivings. But Marvin and Mirlande

would look after him. And the thought of using his newfound skills to strike back at our tormentors was appealing.

"Right. The hunter becomes the hunted."

"Sure. So now it's my turn to be the hunter," he replied with a grin.

CHAPTER
FORTY

Big hugs all round. I let him go before he pulled away, and he went last to Denise. He pocketed the data chip. We agreed to keep in touch. He'd collected his wash things and enough clothes for a few days away. Brought a tear to my eye, seeing him leave the old family place again without even being able to spend the night. I'd hoped we were bringing him safely back home after his abduction – but that moment would have to wait.

The bike helmet covered up Chris's dark blond hair, several shades lighter than Jem's. And sure, they were of similar height and build. It should work. He pedalled away and Pearl peeked out through the nets at the front.

"Coast's clear, as far as I can tell. Time to go." One more quick hug, a few last "take cares" and "good lucks" and they were off.

She came back in time for pizza. Only when presented with the open box did I realise how hungry I was. Stale biscuits hadn't quite cut it. I shoved in the soft, yielding slices, topped with melted cheese and piquant pepperoni, like they were going out of fashion.

Chris hadn't been aware of anyone following him. Neither had the police patrol, according to Denise, who had a quick word with them on her mobile. We had to guess the heat was off for the moment, at least.

I got hold of Kevin while we waited for dinner. Shocked amazement at Jem's abduction, relief that we'd found him, of course. I promised to give him the full story as soon as there was time.

He offered to get the Community Response team to fetch me back from the Leys, in a van big enough to pick up Bertha, from where I'd left her locked up outside Canwick's, en route. She'd get too used to being ferried around at this rate. Wouldn't want her to seize up on me.

Pizza, relief, security at home, and central heating: a combination that set me up for a decent night's rest. At last.

~

Downward dogs and legs up the wall were a struggle the next morning. Ideally, I'd have gone running, but trips out of the apartment would have to be carefully rationed.

A supervision session came and went. Online, so I surreptitiously refreshed my X account now and then on the other screen while the supervisee was talking.

As the hour was nearly up, suddenly there it was – the first post of Jem's campaign. I stifled a squeal of excitement, closed the session, and read closely. "How come @oxfordcouncil is destroying ancient woodland to build a new road bridge? Who's pulling the strings? #oxfordbridgescam #localgovernmentcorruption."

There was a line of figures from the spreadsheet, also showing company names: Brayford, Birchwood and Canwick. It promised "more secrets to come." X-handles were appended for several councillors from the committee that was due to meet on Monday to give the scheme final approval – or not.

As I gazed at the MacBook screen, the "like" and "re-post" figures climbed steadily. Jem's thunderclap. That'd start shaking things up.

∼

Miri was adding oil and cottage cheese to a bowl of whisked eggs. I'd squeezed Bertha out through the back gate and along the lane, leaving the transmitter under the upturned flowerpot. Parked and locked up, then snuck round the back of the WOCC to wave at her through the glass of the kitchen door. It felt safe to venture out, being a busy time of day, and fun to vary my routine, especially after seeing Jem's first post of the campaign. Also fun, I had to admit, making her jump.

Her eyes widened at news of his abduction and how I'd figured out where he was being held. "So, guy who did it, they get?" They did. One of them, at least. She was more animated when told about the Temple Cowley mugging, which I added as an afterthought. Well, it seemed relatively small beer. And old news.

"Janna Rose, I leave town for week, this happen?!" Shaking her head, she set down her mixing bowl with a clatter. "These guys, police get them too?" I had to admit not.

When I got to describing the neck tattoo I'd briefly glimpsed on the one who'd scooped up my bag, she turned visibly pale, took several deep breaths, and seemed to lean on her wooden spoon on the worktop.

"Never do I think to see such thing here," she said from the back of her throat, looking back gravely at me. "Is Serbian gang mark, this cross. Bad, bad people, Janna."

"Oh, I'm so sorry, Miri, I had no idea." I leant over to stroke her upper arm. Through the fine black merino, I could feel her trembling. She looked down into the mixture, got herself to breathe deeply, then turned to me again.

"These gangs, force us from home. Burning, bombing, on

doorstep, bang-bang-bang!" She pronounced the second "b" in bombing. Made it sound even more sinister.

We stepped out and went for a quick walk around the children's playground, Miri leaning on my arm at first, then steadying.

Back in the kitchen, she crumbled feta cheese into her mixture and laid sheets of filo pastry into a baking tin, brushing the layers with more egg-and-oil as she went. We shared a hug, she gave me a cookie that had emerged too misshapen from the oven to put on sale, and sent me off with a coffee. I'd come back afterwards to see how she was doing. I might even score some of that pie.

I had to warn Cara what Adrian might have got himself into, with his cash-in-hand overtime on Friday afternoons. But she waved away my concerns.

"Oh, he's not doing that no more. Tomorrow, he'll say no if they ask him, and tell his boss if it's not put a stop to, he'll report it to Head Office."

"Great, good for him."

"Well, everything's gotta be above board, innit? Then you know where you are."

"Indeed."

"Then, tomorrow night, he's going to get us all our dinners delivered from Courieroo, to celebrate!" She beamed. Even the troubled young scion of the family had calmed down, seemingly, since he'd spent a week of the school holidays with his gran. "We've had our disagreements, me and Mum, but I'll say this, she's always been good with Kyle."

Ah, but how did they make her feel, those disagreements? What negative cognitions were activated, and how could they be turned positive, as she balanced the emotional demands of motherhood and daughterhood? Such were our themes for the rest of the session.

Miri had set the egg and cheese filo pie to cool. *Gibanica*, she called it. Might have been Serbo-Croat for "smells delicious." An aroma reminiscent of Banja Luka, it seemed.

"Always many, many people around at home. Cousins, friends of cousins, cousins of friends. All play out in fields, back in mother's kitchen, all Summer long."

"Happy times?" She nodded.

"Then, one day, war come, all change. Bang-bang-bang!" She should really see someone for the PTSD, but it wouldn't be me. Doesn't do to mix therapy with friendship. I could picture Dr Des knitting his brows.

The Godalming trip had taken her down memory lane, apparently, but there was a twist. "We light bonfire in yard, for sit and drink and talk. Like old days. But rain. Always in England, rain." After another hug, I got away with a promise to stay safe and keep away from men with tattoos, and a slice of the pie in a plastic box for later.

∼

There was a new post on X from Jem, a variation on the previous theme with a different set of figures from the spreadsheet. My account followers had leapt up fourfold, I reckoned. His networks were obviously going full tilt, liking and re-posting. The figures ticked up satisfyingly as I watched.

Email from Jules Chapman, in Lincoln. Aha. He'd attached several stories from the *Echo*. Sure enough, the meltdown of Sincil Construction and Development had been big news as the Credit Crunch was deepening into the Global Financial Crisis.

At one point, the firm's boss, Bob Kesteven – Emma's father – had turned up at a building site in the city to see for himself whether it was true, as contractors had complained, that a perimeter fence had been erected overnight, complete with locks and security guards to keep them out.

It seemed the bank had pulled the plug on a big project

without telling him, putting several dozen people effectively out of work with no notice. The snapper had done well to capture the mixture of anger and defeated confusion on his face, I thought.

But wait. I looked again, this time over Bob's left shoulder. There, in the background, a face that might even be familiar. Sans beard, and obviously much younger – but that couldn't be Lindsey, could it? Probably just someone who looked like him. Still…

I only had my recollection from the Osney Mead launch event to go on. I clicked on to the *Oxford Mail* report. The main picture was the smoke demo, but sure enough, there was one of him too. I toggled between them. Mm. Could be. But how come?

I warmed up half a mug of coffee in the microwave and rang the mobile number Jules had appended to his email. Got through straight away and exchanged pleasantries.

"Ha – remember that Hostile Environment course?"

"Wow, that's going back a long way. You ever had to use any of that stuff?"

"Well… I've never been shot at, anyway. Bit of a sticky spot during Covid with some anti-vaxxers in Sleaford, but luckily the cops turned up. You?"

"Not really. Mind, if I ever have a therapy client cut up rough, I'll remember the self-defence class."

"Kick 'em in the goolies and shout like crazy!" We completed, in unison, what had been the catchphrase of the course leader. I know, what larks.

"So – you wanted to know about the Sincil debacle. Trip down Memory Lane. Big story here, in its day."

I took a swig of coffee. "Yeah, thanks for that. Y'see the piece with the picture of Bob Kesteven, at that shopping centre site?"

"Poor chap. Course, they call him Bob the Builder. Well, used to. Ah yes, OK, I've got it. Never did get built, that centre. Houses there now."

"Right. Who's that standing there behind him, d'you know? The young guy?"

"I think that might be the son. He was helping to run the business by then, I seem to recall. Baptism of fire."

"Quite. Only, he looks like someone I met recently here in Oxford. The boss of my client. Lindsey Miles, he's called."

"Never heard that name. Actually, now I remember, he was called Giles. Giles Kesteven, that's right."

"OK, thanks. Not Lindsey then."

"Bloody hell, I've just realised."

"What?"

"Well… Kesteven is an old name for part of Lincolnshire. Quite a few people round here with that surname. Here's the thing: Lindsey is another. They meet in the city, the historic boundary is just down from the office."

"What, so Lindsey and Kesteven are both *places*? In Lincoln?" I put down the mug with a clatter and a bit spilled out. Damn. Reached for a tissue and mopped up.

"In the county, yeah. Lindsey to the north and east, Kesteven south and west. They're still used for the names of district councils."

I looked again at the pictures of Giles in Lincoln and Lindsey in Oxford. OMG. Sudden visitation from that intense feeling you get when Something Is Up. *Should I say it out loud? Deep breath.*

"I think Lindsey Miles *is* Giles Kesteven." *And OMG again, didn't that finally make sense of what Emma had told me, in that first session, when she'd handed in a resignation letter at work?!*

"Right. I haven't seen Lindsey's pic, but those names would be an outrageous coincidence. Then of course there's the Miles/Giles thing, soundalike. And your client, Bob's daughter, works with this Lindsey?"

"Works *for* him, I think would be more accurate." Jules gave a low whistle, audible down the phone. *"It can't be a resignation letter, because you still love me."* That was it. Manipulative sod.

"I s'pose if Giles was staying in the trade, he would've

wanted to avoid any connection with Sincil. So, he might've changed his name. I mean, the whole thing caused a massive stink."

"Thanks," I mouthed absently. "If you find anything else on Giles Kesteven, would you mind sending it my way?"

"Will do. And remember: always aim for the goolies." And with that, he rang off.

CHAPTER
FORTY-ONE

So, bloody hell, Emma and Lindsey, eh? Or, more to the point, Emma and Giles. She was working for her big brother, the one who could "do no wrong" in the eyes of their parents when they were growing up.

Going back through my notes from Emma's sessions, Lindsey came over as a domineering figure. She was the Office Manager, quite a senior role. But he'd routinely humiliate her by making her do menial tasks. "Taking out rubbish" was one I'd noted down. Speaking disrespectfully to her and calling her "woman."

So all the episodes she'd recounted had really been the acting-out of deeply dysfunctional family relations. The toxic legacy of parental favouritism and withholding, then the shared anguish of material comforts suddenly snatched away. Blame and recrimination poisoning the atmosphere.

That must at least partly account for the intensity of drive and ambition that I'd felt steaming off Giles at the launch. To restore the status and prosperity he'd been brought up to regard as a birthright.

And to think, Emma herself never let on. Strange girl! Plenty of brains. Surely she must have realised I could have been much more help to her if she'd been straight with me?

Then, where did that leave the overall situation? The investigation, as I supposed I must now call it? Brayford sat at the centre of a web of companies, clearly connected through their Lincoln names. They were scamming Hewsons to get money for under-the-counter payments to Gallium. As well as cash to the likes of Adrian and, presumably, the posse of self-employed e-bike riders roaming the city streets, causing mayhem.

Gallium was manipulating social media, in the tense atmosphere of an election, to keep up pressure for developments that ran counter to Oxford folk's general preference for environmentally friendly policies. Developments that could make millions for Brayford and its twin, Birchwood.

If there was such a web, then Lindsey, or rather Giles, was the spider. So what was Emma – a fly, caught in the sticky strands of familial duty? Or another spider? How much did she know about the mugging, arson, and abduction? Or even Daniel's murder?

As the low afternoon sun projected the slatted Venetian blind of the office on to the far wall, I noticed the frame around my certificate had come loose again. Damn. Knew that Blu-tak was too old and dry.

With a sigh, I got up to take a closer look. There was a glint coming off the bookshelves at the back of the room, I momentarily registered. Er… hang on, from books? Nothing shiny there, just dull tomes about therapy. (Well, OK, *interesting*, but you wouldn't take them on a week's holiday to Marbella.)

The frame was a write-off, basically. Well, it had done decent service. I turned to the shelves. And what was this? With a start, I stared in bafflement at a slim, white plastic cuboid object that now nestled between *Break Free From OCD* and *No Bad Parts*.

What the hell?! Near its top was a circular pattern of successive minutely inset layers, at the centre of which sat a tiny but clearly discernible transparent bubble. That was what had briefly caught a shaft of reflected sunlight just now.

It *looked* like… well, much as I tried to avoid it, I couldn't help concluding that there was one thing, above all, that it did look like. A micro-camera. Which pointed only one way: to Brayford. That was how they'd pulled that stunt at the launch, with the screen showing live shots from around the room. Micro-cameras for invisible security systems.

And there was only one person from Brayford who'd been in this room. Emma bloody Kesteven, that was who. But how could she have put it there, and when? I'd led us in here each time when she arrived and seen her off at the end of every session.

Then I remembered. Shit. The time I'd got up to answer the doorbell to that misguided Courieroo delivery man. That was in one of her sessions. And shit again – what if that was actually a stunt, to get me to turn my back and leave her alone in here?

Come to think of it, that might explain why Colin at number thirty-two was flummoxed by it. They never ordered food deliveries. Could that e-bike rider have been sent purely as a decoy?

Blimey! All that time Emma was in my therapy room – in this office – she was pretending. While actually spying on me. The vixen! But why? What went on in here, that anyone would be remotely interested in watching? Or interested in watching remotely?

I'd have to alert clients over a possible breach of confidentiality. Bloody nightmare. Dr Des would advise. But none of them was well-known or involved in anything compromising – just private.

Then it hit me. Of course – the spreadsheet. When I'd opened it on the MacBook, it would have been in full view of that sodding camera. That's how they knew I knew. To them, it went from a known unknown to a known known. And to me, an unknown unknown to a known known with, at that stage, a few known unknowns and one more important unknown unknown. Or something.

The point was, only after I'd opened it up in here did Derek and Faith's house get burned down, and Jem get snatched at gunpoint on his way back to The Leys.

Another thought. That was in Emma's second session, the fake delivery. She'd actually had the brass neck to turn up, in person, for two more. Sitting there for an hour at a time, apparently taking a full part in her therapy. Just without telling me Lindsey was her brother. And she couldn't have done anything else because we'd both been in here together for the whole time. What was her game?

Gazing out of the front window with the last gulp of the coffee, I noticed a car tucked in behind the Community Response team's van that hadn't been there for a while. Next-door neighbours, Tim and Wendy, were back.

What was next up from a sneaking suspicion? A galloping one? No, didn't work: no alliteration. Maybe a steaming suspicion. You can go steaming in somewhere, can't you? At speed.

Of course, I'd now remembered the grinning electrician, who'd been there when I got back from the trip to Isis Farmhouse to see Jem. From Bracebridge, one of the Lincoln-named contractors, fitting that box to the side of Tim and Wendy's. And I had a steaming suspicion that was nothing to do with their internet.

Wendy came to the door, looking a bit flustered. Well, they'd just got back after a month away. But I'd adopted a kind of rueful-and-slightly-grim facial expression calculated to show we needed to talk. Or maybe I just looked a bit deranged. Anyway, she felt it prudent to hear me out.

We soon confirmed they had ordered no new internet connection. She padded round with me in sheepskin slippers to look at the contraption, squatting at the base of the side wall and connected to the mains, apparently, via a side-feed from their doorbell. Twin grey stalks, that might be aerials or antennae, made a V-shape, poking up out of it from the back end.

"Well, it's nothing to do with us." Her kindly old face creased in consternation. "I'll get Tim to unscrew it when he comes back. He's just popped out."

"I'd leave it there, actually." The antennae, if such they were, meant it could be linked somehow to the camera Emma had planted in my office. And that could be linked to all sorts of things. "Police might want to have a look at it."

"Police?" Now she looked even more worried, poor old soul.

"Look, don't do anything for the moment. I've got a friend who's a detective at St Aldates, I'll ask him. But some strange things have been going on while you've been away." I caught her eye. "Nothing that need concern you – just... strange." Best I could do on the spur of the moment. I left her to stew. But sure, it would be good to get clarity as quickly as possible – for all our sakes.

The rest of the afternoon passed in a brown study. I picked away at jobs, writing up client notes and responding to emails. Then turned to searching online for any more information about the Sincil collapse. Not much, as it had taken place over fifteen years earlier. The *Lincolnshire Echo* material was comprehensive. The number of jobs lost, all told, ran into hundreds.

I clicked on to the sites for Brayford and its apparent sister companies here in Oxford. Sure enough, they shared a similar look and feel. Nothing explicit to say they were linked, besides the names, but then nothing to indicate they weren't.

Brayford itself was evidently the largest concern. Its activities spanned numerous construction-related areas. As well as building and building design, there were pages for their security systems, and their "long track record" of installing kit for clean energy generation.

Clients could engage Brayford and "monitor project progress in real time" via drone-mounted surveillance cameras, another page said. Yet another highlighted the company's expertise in the controlled use of explosives. "Renovate or detonate: your choice," this one proclaimed. "Is it better to refurbish an existing structure? Or knock it down and start again? Our expertise in controlled explosive technologies can shorten lead-times, making demolition the cost-effective option."

There was a page on the Osney Mead development, complete with the artist's impressions they'd printed out for display at the launch. And plenty of Lindsey himself, posing in hard hat on various sites in scenes of bonhomie calculated to convey shared ambition with "stakeholders."

CHAPTER
FORTY-TWO

The Botley Road was full of traffic. More bikes and pedestrians than cars now, since the road past the station got blocked off. Buses would jostle in from the west, stop just short of the obstacle and decant morning commuters, who would then have to walk the rest of the way to work or catch another ride on the far side.

It felt like a safe time to hustle across to Waitrose and stock up on food. Plenty of potential witnesses to any attempts at interference by shadowy riders. Jem reckoned six of them had cornered him at the nursery on the way to The Leys. Just three more and there'd be Nine, like in *Lord of the Rings*. They tended to dress head-to-toe in black, too, for that matter.

Surely they couldn't sprout wings as well? I'd be safe as long as I didn't hang about in any dark corners. Or take up arms to defend any ramparts. Come to think of it, the data chip was probably the equivalent of the One Ring. Wouldn't it be handy if it made the bearer invisible?

The social media maestro had been posting vigorously. Any followers – now well into the tens of thousands on my X account – would be in no doubt that a major revelation about corruption and development in Oxford was in the offing.

I'd spoken to him the previous evening on WhatsApp. Apartment warm, bed comfortable, Mirlande's catering lavish, accounts growing steadily.

∽

If I wondered whether and how all that online activity was affecting events in the "real world," Kevin was happy to enlighten me.

He'd got an invite to Daniel's funeral ceremony at Hogacre Common, due to take place that afternoon at two. It seemed his credentials as an old radical trumped his reluctance to commit himself on the Osney Mead scheme.

"So I heard from Lindsey Miles yesterday." We sat side by side on the capacious back seat of an electric Mini Countryman, operated by the council's Community Response team. And made at the Cowley plant, of course.

Normally, I'd have enjoyed cycling to the Eco Park, especially as we'd had quite a few dry days. Just down the river and south a bit. But it felt safer to accept Kevin's offer of a lift. Ahmed and Cyrille offered a reassuring burly presence up front. "What did he want?"

"He wanted to know what you're doing with your X account." He folded his navy cashmere Crombie coat, which he'd taken off as we entered, and placed it on the seat between us.

I heaved a deep sigh.

"That bad, eh?"

"What's in those posts is all stuff from one of Lindsey's own documents. It shows he's been up to no good." *Sounding too defensive, Janna.*

"What kind of no good?" *Where to start? Why not the stuff from Jules?*

"Brayford is named after a part of Lincoln. That's where

Lindsey is from. His real name is Giles Kesteven. He worked at his family's building firm there till it went belly-up in the GFC."

"Mm. Good for us who got out in time, not so good for the rest. I'm sure quite a few adopted new identities. I s'pose there's nothing illegal in it, necessarily. But sure, you've got my attention. Go on."

"OK, well there are at least three other firms in Oxford that also have names from Lincoln: Birchwood…"

"The developer from Cowley Marsh Rec?!" Now he did raise his eyebrows.

"Yep, that's one of them."

"Right. They're supposed to be in competition with Brayford. Now you're telling me they're in cahoots?"

"Looks that way. Also Bracebridge, which is an electrical contractor, and Canwick's, a builder's merchant. Jem was being held in their disused yard off the Cowley Road when the police rescued him."

"When you heard the music in the background and tipped them off?"

"Indeed. Anyway, these firms are working together to operate some kind of scam on Hewsons'."

"What, the builder's yard on the trading estate, by us?"

"The same. Taking advantage of their 'price promise' to undercut any other project quote. Point is, they're using the money to pay a"… *what did Jem call it?* "troll and bot farm operator, Gallium Network."

He breathed out with an audible "pff". "And what do they do? Or do I not want to know?"

"They're the ones riling people up online against the LTNs, putting pressure on for developments that bite off green space. For new roads, like the one at Osney Mead."

"And the firms that put in the bids with those elements…"

"Are Brayford and Birchwood, right." The big car trundled through North Hinksey village, skirting the honey-coloured walls of St Lawrence's Church, and filtering left on to the ring road.

"And you've been tagging my council colleagues in these posts, apparently. They're getting quite upset. Lots of their constituents follow those accounts."

"Yeah, well, those are the ones in that sub-committee meeting on Monday, who'll have the final say on the development." *Jem's idea. Good to know he'd struck a nerve.*

Hedgerows zipped by, sprouting abundantly from the combination of damp spring and lengthening daylight and shrouded now in white-blossomed mounds of hawthorn and blackthorn.

"Thing is, I reckon Lindsey is behind all this other stuff that's been happening."

"Stuff?"

"Jem being abducted. At gunpoint. The guys who mugged me in Temple Cowley. Arson at Derek's. My accountant's."

"What, that house down the park?!" I nodded. Not sure if Kevin's eyebrows could be raised any higher. And I hadn't even mentioned Daniel's murder. There were definitely a few missing links there. Didn't want to over-egg it.

"And this is all based on – what, exactly?"

"The document I found, from clues Daniel left. Well, it's a spreadsheet, an original. On a data chip. That's what they've been trying to get back." I caught sight of his sceptical expression. "It's definitely from Brayford, with their logo and everything. And it shows all these dodgy dealings."

"So that's the evidence." He nodded. "What have the police said?"

"They arrested the guy who was holding Jem captive. They'll have charged him by now. But I've no idea whether he'll point the finger at Lindsey. Or Giles."

"Who are in fact the same person." I nodded. By now, we'd turned in down Abingdon Road, past the end of Donnington Bridge and the college playing fields on the right, then left into

Grandpont. Nearly there. "Well, thanks for filling me in. I take it *you're* not in any danger? I mean, just coming and going?"

"Long as these good chaps are with us," I replied, nodding towards the front seats as Ahmed parked the car. I could have mentioned the hidden camera in my office, the transmitter under my bike saddle and the antennae on Tim and Wendy's box next door. But that would have risked sounding a bit unhinged.

Kevin signalled me to wait before getting out, propped his two index fingers on his lips, breathed deeply in and out while looking through the window, then back at me. "OK, to state the obvious... Beyond chatting in the back of a car, you can't be going round accusing people of stuff without proof. I mean, from what you've said, Lindsey could be some kind of criminal mastermind. And there's just this one spreadsheet? Does it even show anything illegal? I'm not saying you're wrong, but you'll need more than that."

"What about the connection with Gallium? Shows they're manipulating democracy. That'd put people off."

"Sure, that doesn't smell good. *If* it can be shown to come from him. And that sub-committee'll be tight on Monday. It's not a foregone conclusion. That's why Lindsey's feeling agitated. Just promise me one thing – don't take any risks, huh?"

CHAPTER
FORTY-THREE

We walked along a verdant corridor, past the South Oxford Adventure Park on our left, with its grassy mound, slides and swings, and the now rapidly drying football pitch of Hinksey Park FC to the right.

Following the heavy tread of Ahmed and Cyrille, Kevin and I climbed the steps to the bridge over the railway. Dark green metal surfaces presented a study in the urban graffiti trends of several decades.

By now, we were among quite a crowd heading the same way. Down the steps on the other side, then on to a path through woods, to a white rectangular sign, divided between two halves. To one side: Pembroke College sports ground. To the other: Hogacre Common Eco Park. Further paths, then a second sign reminding the visitor the site had been leased to the community since 2011 for a jar of honey a year.

A red-brick pavilion with a tall pointy roof, pillars and portico around the front door, stood to our left. And inside it, at last, the refreshments table. Staff behind, in white shirts, black v-necks and neat, burgundy-coloured waist aprons, pouring for the masses. A plug-in stove at the back radiated some minimal warmth.

Over to one side, an artist's easel set up with a big print of Daniel's photograph, laughing on some family occasion. Yes, it did capture his sense of fun. And, just about discernible (at least to me), the glint in his eye. His undertow of mischief; even – when occasion demanded – menace? No, too strong. Iconoclasm, certainly. Sprite-ish heedlessness, perhaps.

Pausing briefly for polite greetings with Marcia, I signed the Book of Condolences, snaffled a plastic wineglass of *sauvignon blanc* and a handful of herby mini crostini slices. I needed something toothsome to help digest Kevin's advice. Had it been a telling-off? More of a talking-to, probably.

In fact, on reflection, there were two pieces of advice: get more evidence, and don't take risks. But what if those could not, in fact, be acted on at the same time?

The Extinction Rebellion activists stood around by the hedge on the far side, cradling drinks from Marcia's table. Did Mick sleep in that light blue woollen beanie? He was already reminiscing with Kevin about Stopping the War, or some such.

I reckoned I'd judged it about right, in long dark blue heavy cotton dress, leggings and my outback boots, with smart red lambswool cardie, navy Gore-Tex and new necklace. Hair would do for another day or two. Nothing a bit of back-combing couldn't sort out – and for once it didn't have to be revived from coming out of a bike helmet.

As it was outdoors and semi-formal, no-one had gone smart. Well, not *smart* smart. Sure, Kevin was in grey suit and open-necked blue city shirt under his posh coat, but that was his trademark image. Marcia set the tone for waxed jackets and patterned silk squares among the county set.

But we were all in the shade when Tara turned up.

"In the real world, 'Martin'," Amelia confided. "Not trans or anything – just reckons Tara sounds more interesting, I guess."

"Rumour is, he's adopting a new surname to go with it," Squirrel said. "Ra-boom-di-yay."

Tara was to be the Celebrant in the humanist ceremony for

Daniel. A childhood chum from darkest Surrey who'd renewed their friendship over various environmental causes, it seemed. I'd never heard of him, as either Martin or Tara.

So, from the ground up: orange Doc Martens, black laces. Orange, black and white tartan drainpipe trousers; knee-length calico frock coat in a kind of Persian design, predominantly red and turquoise. Long string of wooden beads around the neck; straps of two cloth shoulder-bags, also in different patterns, crossing over his chest.

Well, good luck to him for the outfit. Showed originality anyway. But was he a colourful character? Or just a colourful dresser? We might be about to find out. Tara climbed to the concrete platform at the top of the steps in front of the pavilion doorway. He'd better be good, he was now blocking the way to the drinks. He paused to consult a smartphone, his wrists revealing various bands and bangles.

"Friends!" We were gathered to honour our colleague, comrade and – for many – guiding light. Encouraging to see such a big turnout (fifty or so, I reckoned.) "Daniel, in his environmental activism, showed a questing intellectual curiosity. How could he do the greatest good for the greatest number?"

Tat shifted his weight from one foot to the other and swigged deeply of his beer.

"He rose above the emotional blackmail of special pleading. Instead, he considered the future of humanity at large, and our planet. In transition away from petty local disputes, to focus on the bigger picture."

"That's that Effective Altruism crap," Mick growled. I'd heard the phrase but knew no more about it. Perhaps I'd ask Tara when he'd finished. Or Mick. Or both – then I'd doubtless emerge further enlightened. Or confused.

There was more in like vein, then Tara moved to wrap up. "So we pay tribute to his leadership and extend our horizons. Wherever we believe Daniel is now; whatever form his spirit has taken… The struggle continues in his memory."

We applauded, as Marcia dabbed discreetly at her eyes with a tissue. The speaker had the good sense and good manners to clear the way to the bar, and we lined up for another bevvy.

"I like what you've been doing on your socials," Wiz said, behind me in the queue.

"Yeah so, what's it all about then?" That was Squirrel. "Some big reveal about Brayford and the bridge of doom?"

We reached the table and recharged our glasses, then I ushered us towards a corner of the small meadow, mad from the farting crowd, and brought them up to speed.

"Right, so *Brayford* is paying for all that tosh about LTNs and fifteen-minute cities?!" Amelia hadn't minded mixing lager and cider herself, when staff at the drinks table reacted uncomprehendingly to her request for a snakebite. (Good job she didn't ask for a screwdriver.) No, it was the lack of blackcurrant to go with it that had aroused her ire. The right mood to be hearing about social media skulduggery.

"Well, it's got people fired up," Mick said. "We reckoned that road was bound to go through. Might be looking dicey now."

"Yeah, there's an activists' meeting Sunday night at Isis Farmhouse, if you can make it?" Squirrel looked at me expectantly, as if eyeing a hazelnut. "We'll be planning for the demo at that council hearing the next day."

Up at the front, a three-piece folk band had struck up. Comely young fiddler in long purply frock, accompanied by burly bearded chap on squeezebox, and a callow youth with one of those little hand-held ratchet things by way of percussion.

I noticed Wiz giving her the evil eye. Might Daniel have transferred his affections? Not massively clear what they were doing here otherwise. The music wasn't his taste, so maybe she was.

So – an activists' meeting. Not usually my kind of scene. Of course I'd be wary of going out there on the bike, with or without the transmitter. And I could hardly ask the Community Response team to escort me. Still, it felt like I'd qualified for admission to some kind of inner sanctum. I'd think about it. Time for another tack. "What's all this about Effective Altruism?"

Mick rolled his eyes heavenwards and shook his head. "Don't get me started."

"Tara reckoned he was recruiting Daniel," Wiz said, above the music. "He did some stuff with them, up at Wytham. Seminars and shit."

"They bought the Wytham estate a couple of years ago, did you know?" Tat chipped in. A fine old country house, in a hamlet just across the ring road. Used to have a nice pub, but Covid put paid to that. And no, I did not know they'd bought it.

"What they don't understand is, *all* politics are local. I mean, to the likes of Tara, *we* are a petty dispute." Mick was obviously well-versed in the arguments. "But how do disputes begin? I mean, how does any of this stuff get opposed in the first place? People taking action in their communities, that's how."

The band reached a crescendo of hey-diddle-diddle. The fiddler smilingly acknowledged the applause, shaking her chestnut mane of curls back over her shoulders as she outstretched arms with instrument in one hand, bow in the other. Very comely.

"Plus, this is Oxford," Wiz pointed out. "Famous place. What happens here – lots of people get to hear about it."

Tat and I stepped aside and hunkered down for a moment or two over iPhones. He shared the Facebook event invitation page for the activists' meeting. I sent it on to Jem via WhatsApp, with message: "New material for posts. Keep up the good work." And a smiley face. And a star.

CHAPTER
FORTY-FOUR

Whenever I got home from one of these shindigs, it seemed, I had only to sit on a comfy seat for a few minutes to get my breath back, and my eyes would close of their own accord.

I woke up with a start in the venerable brown leather armchair, fixed myself a cup of builder's tea, and took stock. All in all, it must go down as a good day. I'd reflected on Daniel, of course, on the way back in the car. Fell so quiet that Kevin at one point said, sardonically, "Chatty, aren't we?!"

Where *did* I think Daniel was now, and what form *had* his spirit taken? Perhaps it could be glimpsed in the sense of comic mischief, combined with strong convictions, that seemed to animate both the rebels and, latterly, Jem and friends from The Leys.

So that was positive. The social media campaign was getting through. Lindsey was nervous, the committee said to be in flux, and the activists making plans. And meeting at Isis Farmhouse on Sunday night.

Then, I remembered, this was the day when Adrian had planned to tell his supervisor at Hewsons' a few home truths.

Put a stop to the dodgy trading, or he'd report it to Head Office. Good for him. And big of him, foregoing extra cash.

He was going to treat the family by ordering a dinner delivery from Courieroo, I remembered. Found myself hoping Kyle hadn't ruined his appetite by swallowing any more household items. Nice to recall he had a gran who was good with him.

Actually, thinking of dinner, I suddenly realised I was hungry. It was that time, after all – approaching half past six. Marcia's hospitality, generous in the liquid department, had been light on comestibles.

My slice of Miri's egg and cheese pie was still sitting in its box in the fridge. I put on the oven at a low temperature to warm it through. Every bit as yummy as I'd imagined. But poor Miri! Just me describing that tattoo had been enough to give her paraclysms. Revisiting traumas of war, still fresh three decades on – because, presumably, they were unprocessed.

Nostalgia in Godalming around a campfire in the rain was never going to cut it. She really, really should see someone. I was sure I could find her a pro bono therapist through The Listening Project. Ye gods, it must have been a terrible experience for her. People being burned out of their homes. Like poor Derek and Faith, in fact. I should check up, see how they were doing.

Or – worse, apparently, in Banja Luka – bombs being planted on doorsteps. "Bang-bang-bang," Miri had said. Twice, I recalled. Yep – definitely unprocessed trauma.

It was at that point that my veins turned to ice. Oh, no. Oh, no, no, no, no, no.

Here I was, blathering on in some stream-of-consciousness-thingy, about grans, and shirts, and pies – when… could it be? No, surely, wildly implausible. What was chilling was that I found I couldn't altogether rule it out.

Might Cara and her family be in danger?

I propelled Bertha as fast as I could down the back lane, turned on to Botley Road towards Osney Court, and flicked up through the gears. Push, pedal, push.

Left my dinner, delicious or not, half-eaten on the kitchen worktop. Because the thought, once summoned to mind, could not be un-thought. In fact, as I went steaming along, I was steaming up inside with ever greater forebodings.

What the hell had I been playing at, encouraging Adrian to threaten his bosses at Hewsons'? With dobbing them in at Head Office, for a scheme that was integral to Bayford's social media campaign? The one run by Gallium Network? On the brink of a crucial council committee now said to be "dicey"?!

Push, pedal, push.

Hadn't Emma, accursed spying Emma, warned me explicitly of the dangers of "crossing" Lindsey? Lindsey who'd sent a delivery rider, at least seeming to come from Courieroo, with takeaway food to my house.

Courieroo, whose name and merch were in use by countless pirate operators. Operators of e-bikes, shadows of the road, which could go anywhere at any time.

Lindsey who'd thought nothing, it seemed, of ordering a mugging, an arson attack and even a gunpoint abduction, as he chased millions in revenue. Push, pedal, push.

Millions that would no doubt represent some kind of cathartic payback from a cruel world that had sent his father's business, the rock of his childhood existence, spinning into oblivion. More unprocessed trauma.

I got as far as the Carpet Warehouse car park on the near side, looked back over my shoulder down the westbound lane, and, seeing it was clear, pedalled to the midpoint. Then paused to puff and pant, allowed a bus to go by from my left, crossed the city-bound lane, and made landfall on the far pavement.

Dismounting, I pushed the bike in through the driveway and down the ramp to the apartments' private car park. Now, if I could remember which door was Cara's…

Sheds to one side with big green wheelie bins, stacked with bulging black plastic rubbish sacks. To the other, grey metal containers with broad openings near the top, presumably for recyclables.

Up on the wall to my left, the ubiquitous notice, alerting passers-by that the area was under video surveillance. I stood, getting my bearings and dredging memory banks.

Then, suddenly, it happened.

A flash, from around the corner, in the wing of the complex set further back from the road. And BOOM.

For a few instants, I felt as though my ears had blown out completely. Eyes blinking but seeing only white.

Found myself kneeling on the ground, Bertha crashed down to one side. Deep breaths. Slowly, it seemed, sound and vision began to return. First shapes, then colours.

Then the insistent ringing of an alarm. Or more than one. I staggered to my feet and emerged onto the concourse facing the block housing Cara and Adrian's ground-floor flat…

And what was this? Floating in the air, black shreds, or fragments. I held out my hand and let some fall on it. Sight now clearing, I looked more closely down at my palm. Could they be? Yes, they were. Definitely. Bits of feathers. Black feathers. From a bird.

In what still seemed like the middle distance, I was dimly aware of the door being opened to the apartment on the bottom left corner of the building. Cara's plump, artless face, mouth in a shocked "O". And beside her now, with luxuriant hair and ginger-tinged beard, Adrian. Big old, good old Adrian. Between them, around waist-height? Well, if it wasn't Kyle. The young tyke.

I plodded across towards them. Yes, all there. All safe. But OMG, what a mess on their doorstep. Bits of – what? Chicken chow mein? Or did any food look like that, after being blown up?

Blown up. Their food delivery from Courieroo, intended as a family treat, had been blown up. On their doorstep. Where was this, Oxford – or poor Banja Luka of thirty years ago? But they were safe. They were OK.

Cara reached out to me and I instinctively enveloped both of them in my arms, little Kyle burrowing in for his share of the cuddles.

"What just happened?" Adrian, unwitting as ever.

"I think a crow just tried to nick your dinner. And I *think* that might just have saved you from being blown up." *Blown up.* Still couldn't believe I was saying it. They hugged tighter, before we all pulled back.

Cara looked down at the doorstep and the battered remnants of their front door.

"Good job we was in the back." She turned to me with a sheepish expression. "Rowing again, we was."

"Couldn't agree whose turn it was to get the door, could we love?"

"Sounds a bit silly now." *Silly?* It was mind-boggling. But my mind was already starting to move on from being boggled. And when it did, it went straight back to its previous train of thought: Lindsey.

Lindsey whose building firm boasted on its website about its mastery of *explosive technologies.* Explosive. Bloody. Technologies.

CHAPTER
FORTY-FIVE

Andy Singh looked at me askance. "Quick word?" He led us off to a nook between two small hatchbacks in the Osney Court car park. Behind, a confusion of blue lights, police tape stretching around a perimeter, firefighters attending to the stricken apartment and forensic team waiting to be allowed on site.

Neighbours, who'd come out to drop jaws in worry and wonderment, now reassured and filtering back indoors for the night.

"Gotta say, I'm surprised to see you here. Care to enlighten me?" *Long story, short version.*

"Cara's one of my clients. I see her at the Community Centre, through The Listening Project."

"Right, got it. And didn't I see your name in the file on that suspected arson last week, the house down the park?"

"That was my accountant, Derek."

"Bit of a coincidence. Put it another way, you're a common denominator. And that might make us start to look at things in a different light."

I ended up promising to bring him fully into the picture. He was on weekends, and clearly in for a late night on this one, so I'd meet him at St Aldates at noon when he planned to report in.

∽

I munched the rest of Miri's pie. Or should that be humble pie? I'd allowed (even encouraged) that family to endanger themselves, when caution was clearly a better policy. Fine for Adrian to opt out of Friday "fishing." But, knowing what I knew, I should have advised against confrontation.

I video-called Jem on WhatsApp. Signed off sick for the week from BMW Mini. Who'd been most understanding. Looking after himself – regimen of press-ups, sit-ups and so forth, within the confines of the Church Centre apartment. And being looked after by Mirlande, with a steady supply of tasty meals.

"I've got a full-on operation going here, Mum. It's bussin' – loads of groups jumping on board, on all the apps. I mean, it's Oxford, it's famous, whatever happens here, people wanna know."

"Yeah, but look, this started as me picking up Daniel's great exposé. Now it's other people being exposed. Derek and Faith's house burned down, you being abducted. Now there's Adrian and Cara. And their kid."

"Well... let's give it the weekend, then there's that meeting on Monday, right? See what happens then." Next visit to the bathroom, I took a long, hard look in the mirror. The Temple Cowley mugging aside, I'd kept behind the frontline of this war with Lindsey. Was it time to go back there myself?

∽

The squad car pulled up smoothly outside St Aldates nick and I hopped out. Gave my name at the desk, Andy appeared and showed me through to an interview room. Denise was off weekend shifts for now, so another WPC sat in. Wasn't it supposed to be a sign of ageing, that police looked younger all the time? This one might have been fresh out of training school.

"So – talk to me."

I'd rehearsed my spiel – literally with Kevin the day before, and in my head during wakeful hours overnight. This time, I left nothing out.

Andy exchanged glances with the WPC, sat back, breathed deeply and gave me a searching look. "So the abduction, the arson attack and that mess last night are all to stop this coming out, this – what? Campaign, I s'pose, to put pressure on the council to approve the scheme for Osney Mead?"

"That's how it seems."

"And this is all based on a spreadsheet, that you reckon is from the company, Brayford? That you found in a tree by the river?"

I could see how it sounded. But each incident was serious in itself. Presented with them as a sequence, his copper's instinct was clearly telling him Something Was Up. Beyond the fevered imaginings of a lone female.

"OK. We're gonna need to get people to look at the transmitter, the camera, the receiver with the aerials next door, and that data chip." He read them off his notes. An improvement on last time. At least he'd used the retractable ballpoint for writing, not just to click a mounting sense of incredulity.

A forensic team would fit better with the Chief Super's budget if it could wait till Monday – no overtime. So I agreed to preserve the evidence for the weekend. I'd have to tell Tim and Wendy not to do anything to that box. Meanwhile, I had some questions of my own.

"What about the guy you picked up at Canwick's?"

"With your boy? Yeah, he was bang to rights. Looking at a decent stretch for that – abduction and false imprisonment. Course, we've got Jem's statement."

"Right. And the others? I mean, he didn't do it all by himself."

"Yeah, no, he's not pointed the finger. Not yet anyway. I can apply to re-interview, but I'd need fresh evidence."

Denise was right, then, seemingly: more information would flow if police had the opportunity to play off each suspect against several others.

CHAPTER
FORTY-SIX

I lifted the flowerpot from its brown plastic saucer. Nestling beneath it, the transmitter, a little bronze drum with prongs, still on the patch of thick silver tape. I stuck it under Bertha's saddle, then put the cover back on.

The Extinction Rebels had created a Facebook Event page for their activists' meeting. It now said: "With special guest speaker, Janna Rose. The campaign to expose Brayford Developments, whose proposed Bridge of Doom would destroy ancient woodland and bring more cars to Oxford. Just what we DON'T need."

Over on X, Jem's posts on my account were now getting thousands of likes and re-posts. Users were seemingly intrigued by the mysterious sets of figures from the spreadsheet. Copious conspiracy theories and bile swishing around on there too, with the LTNs made out as a plot to undermine the English way of life, an elite design to do down plain old ordinary folk, with racist overtones against car drivers in general and taxi firms in particular.

I'd pulled on jeans and trusty outback boots. White t-shirt under loose, thick old cotton shirt in a mainly green pattern. Navy Gore-Tex, no necklace. Definitely not a necklace occasion.

Lunch? Sliced cheddar on toast with microwaved baked

beans poured over the top. The hot tomato sauce softened the edges of the cheese, making a pleasing contrast with the crunch of browned bread. Tea to wash it down. Builder's.

Mid-afternoon, I'd taken the MacBook into my office and set it down on the desk. Dealt with one or two emails from clients and supervisees, then clicked on to Facebook and marked myself as "going" to the evening meeting at Isis Farmhouse.

Then back to my stalwart leather armchair with the iPhone for a couple of calls on WhatsApp followed by a sleepy spell browsing over stuff in the Sunday papers. As we used to call them. Reviews 'n' recipes, not doom 'n' gloom. OK, OK, biscuits were involved as well. And strong black coffee.

So now I was ready to go. I unlocked Bertha and wheeled her out on to the pavement. Ahmed raised a hand in greeting.

Only another few days and the election would bring an end to their tour of duty outside councillors' home addresses. Surely the Oxford public could be trusted to be civil to their representatives once they had actually voted them in. Or at least not physically attack them.

Set off down the park, counting off the trees, past the diagonal sloping paths that led up from either direction to the cross-streets with their red-brick Victorian terraces.

After the excitement of my ride in the police car back from St Aldates, the rest of the weekend had dragged by. By the end of Saturday telly, I'd written off this little jaunt as a bad idea. A Netpix costume drama set in a kind of stylised Jane Austen world reassured me I was a person of good taste, humour and discernment. Then the dear old BBC pulled me up short with death and suffering in a casualty ward. Kevin's words rang in my ears: don't go taking any risks.

By the end of Sunday morning yoga, including a vigorous set of Downward Dogs, I was back on. Kevin's words rang in my ears: get more evidence. *Ah, but he didn't actually say that, did he Janna? Just that you'd* need *more. Can't go blaming him, if it all ends in tears.*

Scaffolding now covered Faith and Derek's place. Maybe the new owners were getting in their renovation straight away. Wasn't the Chinese word for crisis the same as opportunity?

I veered off rightwards through the narrow-triangle-shaped council car park, past the meter that doubled as a leaning-post, well it did now – and stopped at the pavement's edge. Stacks and pylons from the electrical switching station frowned down from behind their coils of razor wire on the opposite side.

Once across and pedalling along the cycle lane, I clocked the car rental offices on the left. Probably the last bits with anyone actually at work at this time on a Sunday evening. Or maybe they'd stopped bothering now.

Did some box breathing. In for four through the nose, hold for four, out for four through the mouth. *Don't want to go too fast. Then again, let's not literally fall over for lack of forward momentum.*

Reached the mini roundabout with Willow Walk, the path to North Hinksey village, away to my right. Straight ahead: King's Meadow, a stub of industrial estate with anonymous offices and/or workshops. I turned left and headed off down the main drag.

Heating gas storage yard to one side, aforementioned cryogenic cylinders on the other. Cash-and-carry, fast-food truck, fish market, trade butcher. All deserted.

What was it Gran Tucker used to say to me? "Go and ask the butcher if you can play with the bacon slicer." I had to use my own judgement to stay safe, she meant – not just rely on others. The grown-ups. The Queen's Centre hove into view on the left, with the coffee roasters café opposite. I looked around and back over my shoulder. Nothing coming.

Then a mysterious big, grey, windowless metal shed. "Waterside House," a sign said. Might it conceal a rocket assembly line? Or a pistol-shooting range? Or wait, hadn't I spoken to someone once who worked in there designing computer games?

To the other side, an oblique-facing office block squatted inelegantly behind its own triangular patch of scruffy asphalt. A road headed off at right angles down towards a bunch more buildings, and ultimately, I'd reminded myself while looking at maps online earlier, a shallow Thames drainage channel, the Bulstake Stream.

From the tallest in a row of scrubby trees opposite, a bird, possibly a robin, proclaimed territorial rights. "Cheerily-cheer-up-cheer-up!" All very well for you to say, Mister.

Still, birds and the bees, eh? That time of year, I supposed. I'd have to watch myself or I'd start to get those daydreams again, featuring *me* as a gran, with Jem and Denise and their nestlings.

Bit early for bees still, mind. Give it a month or two. Although, wasn't that a buzzing sound I could hear as well? Who'd have thought a ride down the industrial estate could turn out to be such a nature trek?

Hang on. Buzzing?! Oh shit.

Suddenly there were two of them in front of me. Not bees. Must have appeared from the shadows of some building on the other side as I looked round and saw the two coming from behind.

CHAPTER
FORTY-SEVEN

I slammed on the brakes and went to pedal off towards the condemned buildings down the side road. Think again. Looming from that direction: a dark red hatchback, a Toyota Corolla hybrid. The kind Regal Cars used, but no logo.

I turned again to face the pursuing pack. Or flock. Crows eyeing an unattended takeaway on a doorstep. All in black, helmets and tinted goggles, like sunglasses, with nose and mouth coverings ranging from a scarf wound round the lower half of the face to Covid-style masks.

The pillion passenger on one of the heavier double e-bikes dismounted and took a black cloth whatsit from the pocket of his Courieroo-branded puffa jacket. He'd pulled down the zip, revealing, above the line of his black t-shirt, a distinctive neck tattoo: cross-shaped with transverse stalks on the ends.

Tattoo man strolled towards me with apparent calm. As he drew near, I could see the object he was carrying was a hood.

One of the riders who'd materialised from in front of me swung a long leg over his single bike and straightened up. Could he be the tall Black Rider from Waitrose? Almost instantaneously, a pistol appeared in his hand, as if I'd blinked and missed the supple, well-practised motion by which he removed it from his waistband.

I felt hands grab my upper arms from behind and pull me back off my saddle. Bertha fell with a crash to one side. Outnumbered and outgunned: no possibility of fighting back, goolies or no goolies. Nor, now, of outrunning them by pedal power. *Never gonna happen anyway, Janna, these things all have electric motors.* Only one thing for it: shout like crazy.

"Help! Help!" As soon as I cried out, I realised it was hopeless. All those office blocks, trade outlets and industrial units, awaiting the return of human eyes and ears, hands and brains, the next morning; but, for the moment, unseeing and unhearing.

Tattoo man pulled the hood down over my head and I felt myself being half-hustled, half-carried along towards the car. Sound of doors opening, then I was shoved on to what must be the middle of the passenger seat, with a rider on either side, still holding me with iron grip. Doors closed.

A screech of tyres as the car accelerated away. No-one spoke. I tried again to regulate my breathing. In for four through the nose, hold for four, out for four through the mouth – making it to two or three if I was lucky. As I inhaled, I noticed a faint but definite odour inside the bag. Strawberries.

Then suddenly, in the car, mayhem.

"Fuck!" and "Shit!" from the front. Another screech of tyres. Two big bangs, as the car suddenly slowed and I was thrown forwards into the back of the front seats ahead of me. Yelling and cussing all around.

Doors opened, and the hands on my arms vanished. I reached up and pulled off the hood. Blue flashing lights, back and front. We were right outside the *Oxford Mail* office.

"Armed police! Drop the weapon!"

∼

Of course, Andy Singh had wanted to intervene much earlier. I had to remonstrate with him to let the black riders actually do something. To me. Otherwise they might just have been out for a spin, enjoying the view.

I mean, there'd have been no point in their physically harming me, as long as I had that data chip. Whatever they did would be to get it back. Desperate calculation: but it was a desperate time. The attack on Adrian and Cara was a clear signal that we'd reached the stage for risk-taking. Something had to be done to bring all this to an end.

"That'd be way too dangerous, Janna. And massively unpredictable. I mean, I have to think about public safety."

"Well, at that time on a Sunday, there'll be no public there, will there? Whole place'll be deserted."

"You're the public, in case you didn't realise."

He'd gone off to consult his DI while I agreed to wait on the line. Or the patch of digital ether, I supposed, since, yes, this was one of my afternoon WhatsApp calls on the iPhone.

"OK, we'll deploy units on to the estate, then we can get the drone team to keep across any movements. So we'll know in real time what's happening, and be ready to respond. If it's nothing, well and good. You'll go on your way and we'll just stand down."

"What if they try to get to me further downstream?"

"Uniform have got bike patrols out on the riverbank, so I'll have them briefed." At that point, there was a clutching downward feeling in the pit of my stomach. Getting police deployed on my account had made it serious. And irreversible. No squinnying out then.

But he'd gone out on a limb for me once before, and I'd been proved right. Better yet, it got him credit with the Chief Super. So now we'd be sharing a limb. Although, at his end, a different image had sprung to mind.

"I'm still not happy. Effectively, we're using you as bait."

"I s'pose. But you said yourself, the man you got for Jem's

abduction won't talk. And there's no evidence against anyone else. Unless they get caught red-handed." Yup – quite the range of metaphors.

Bertha was in danger of becoming spoilt. As the cops wrapped things up, she and I got another lift in one of their vans.

Somewhat revived by copious administration of choccy and black coffee, I talked to Andy again later as promised. They'd flung a "pro-spike stinger" across the road, apparently. That's what burst the car tyres.

When the blues-and-twos hove into view, emerging from their hidey-hole on King's Meadow, the gang realised the jig was up. The armed response team zooming up behind them must have been persuasive, as well. So, had they pointed the finger?

"Matter of fact, a couple of 'em *have* mentioned Lindsey." *Yes. Got the bugger. At last.* "Seems he's been running that Cowley Marsh site like a cash dispenser. Sending the riders out like you thought. They reckon he's behind the arson and the bombing as well."

How did I feel, hearing it from someone else? A thrill of justification, certainly. An avalanche of relief. And oddly tearful. I'd expended so much nervous energy in getting myself to believe it, first of all, then convincing others. The Leys crew; the Extinction Rebels; Kevin.

Of course, Andy had been sceptical that first time. Me babbling about conspiracies, 20-year-old lockboxes and taxi drivers. But the evidence had kept building. There had to be some back story, some common denominator as he'd put it. And if it wasn't going to be me, it must be something or someone else. So, was Lindsey going to be arrested? And when? Taken to St Aldates, presumably?

"That's tomorrow's job, I'd have thought. Desk Sergeant won't want to put him up for the night. So yeah, probably first thing. Should bring him in by about nine. In confidence though, eh?"

"Sure. Good day's work then?" *Get you, Janna Rose, sounding all tough 'n' nonchalant. Not foolin' anyone, you know that don't you?*

"Decent. Five arrests. Car driver and four others. We're charging 'em tonight. One pair did manage to get away, I'm afraid. Seems they abandoned their bike, waded across the stream and scarpered. We went looking but had to call it off. Too dark."

∿

Socials were bangin'. (Or was it bussin'? Something like that.) The Extinction Rebels were agog at my comments on their event page. A new post brought followers the sensational news that Janna Rose, who'd been leading the online campaign against the Bridge of Doom, had been attacked on the way to the Isis Farmhouse meeting. By armed thugs.

Jem kept up the pressure via my X account, teasing our Big Reveal in time for the council committee meeting the next day. Biggest job, it was already clear, would be reassuring people I was OK. I spoke briefly to both Pearl and Kevin on the phone. Promised to stay safe.

Emails and Facebook messages were rolling in from concerned old friends. Lovely to hear from them, yes I was fine. I could fill my diary with good resolutions to meet up. Yes, we really mustn't leave it so long. I replied to everything then hurriedly closed the computer before any more could arrive.

CHAPTER
FORTY-EIGHT

Dr Des was not overjoyed at having our session curtailed. Actually, the police forensic team's arrival was timely, from my point of view. There hadn't been much thrupping in the week since our last session, and I was still wondering how to explain. I made some excuse and we hurriedly resolved to pick up next time.

Wearing those blue powdery-looking plastic gloves, two earnest young chaps (Vinay and Maybe Will) removed and bagged up the micro camera from the office shelf and dusted for prints. No, I hadn't touched it, I assured them, but they took mine "for elimination purposes." They'd be on the transmitter from under the bike saddle anyway.

I knocked up next door for them and explained to Wendy that they'd come for her mystery box. Briefly considered adding, "Don't worry, not a euphemism," but she was frazzled enough already.

I was scooping up the last crumbs of granola between forefinger and thumb, in between sips of freshly swooshed coffee from the moka, when the call came through.

"So – did you get him?"

"Certainly did. Good long steady shot. The car had to pull in quite a way down from the station door, so it was a perp walk, you know, like in America."

"And you managed to get through to Anthea this morning?"

"Yes, that worked thanks. She was quite forthcoming, off the record. So don't worry, it didn't come from you!"

"Excellent. Well, you should have no problem getting a slot, then?"

"Definitely. We've got the lunchtime bully on BBC One after the national news, we'll use some of it then. And we'll be with you in about an hour for the interview, OK?"

Yes, Lauren Kemp: my second WhatsApp call the previous afternoon (besides Andy Singh) and text message last night. So I'd be on telly – again. In my office this time, bookshelves in the background.

Good job I'd finally made time to wash and blow-dry that morning. I flipped the iPhone camera to selfie mode and refreshed my lippy.

With Lindsey under lock and key at St Aldates cop shop, and BBC viewers set to be entertained by video of him being led inside, it was time to fire the big gun. I texted Jem via WhatsApp to post the whole spreadsheet on my X account. From there, Lauren could easily get screen grabs for her evening report.

~

The mood among demonstrators outside council HQ that afternoon was celebratory, almost playful. As a special concession, Mick had come in a cheeky beige bucket hat with the legend, "Just Stop Oil" on the side instead of his blue woollen job.

A small grey dog wandered around, wearing a fluorescent green bib with the words, "No to the bridge" felt-tipped on the side. People held up their devices, reached and pivoted in search of a stronger signal, in the notoriously sparse digital coverage of central Oxford, as they marvelled at online revelations of Bayford's financial chicanery.

Members filed in for their committee meeting under the watchful gaze of Lauren's camera. Banners and placards condemning the Osney Mead scheme – including the wheezing anthropomorphised Planet Earth – formed a vivid backdrop.

Kevin happened to be passing. He and I stood side by side on the pavement, looking down on to the little pedestrian precinct outside the building entrance where the protesters waited. "Didn't I tell you not to go running any risks, Janna Rose?!" But with his trademark twinkle.

"Mm. But you also told me I had to get more evidence."

"Did I? I'll be due some of the credit here, then. Saved the council from serious egg-on-face."

A ripple of excitement in the crowd and yes, sure enough, the news was out. The committee had taken less than twenty minutes to complete its business, with the development proposal – warmly supported by a majority of members just a few short weeks ago – now unanimously... rejected.

Lauren's report on the decision led the regional news at half past six. Yet another fetching jacket, daffodil yellow this time to match the turning of seasons.

"The Chief Executive of Brayford Construction, Lindsey Miles, arriving at a central Oxford police station this morning," she began. In the picture, you could see the moment he realised he was on camera, brow knitting and pale blue eyes glazing over with a layer of frost.

He was "one of six men arrested in connection with a series of recent incidents across the city. Police sources wouldn't be drawn on alleged links with the controversial bridge project."

File pictures showed Lindsey speaking and the artist's impressions from the Osney Mead launch event. Then the report cut to the moment of jubilation among activists at the council committee's climbdown. Amelia gave a brief in-vision comment, paying tribute to the power of grassroots action.

There were shots of Faith and Derek's house, scaffolded and still visibly singed, along with wobble-vision, presumably from viewers' phones and harvested from social media, of police and firefighters outside Adrian and Cara's flat.

Exterior views of Canwick's yard, over a brief account of Jem's abduction and the man charged, led on to the industrial estate, with the Toyota Corolla cordoned off by blue-and-white police tape. Then it was me, sitting at my computer for an establishing sequence and speaking in head-shot.

"Internet activist Janna Rose says she was targeted by an armed gang because of her online opposition to the bridge proposal."

"The worst moment was when one of them pointed an actual gun at me," I said. "Then when they drove off with me in the back of the car. But I knew the police were on to them by then."

We saw the spreadsheet, taken from my X account: white-on-black, revealing the company letterhead. An Accountancy Professor from the Business School appeared, briefly giving a similar interpretation to the one Derek had offered when I'd shown it to him.

Lauren stood outside Bayford's office, signboard clearly visible over her shoulder, for a closing piece-to-camera. "The building firms at the centre of this dispute, Brayford and its sister company, Birchwood, hold as many as two dozen ongoing contracts, worth tens of millions of pounds, with councils across our region. Councils that will be anxiously following the progress of this case and any criminal proceedings."

There was just enough daylight left for a run to Folly Bridge and back. Something I'd been grievously missing over the past week. I'd even watched the piece ready for the off, perched on the edge of the sofa in yoga pants, trainers, t-shirt and fleece.

Should I chew? Nah. Bad habit. And I wouldn't want anything to detract from the sweet taste of vindication.

CHAPTER
FORTY-NINE

So, Daniel, we did it. Our last joint news investigation. Lauren took the glory, but you and I did the work. We exposed wrongdoing, in the public interest. We'll always have that.

I padded along the path across the park. Mind, Lindsey had been a formidable opponent. Must have been completely in the shadow of his father when he was in Lincoln. There was nothing else of significance on him from there, according to Jules Chapman.

His email had arrived among another tranche of anxious enquiries from friends and contacts as to my continued health and wellbeing. "Just a bit of parish pump stuff, attached FWIW," it said. The young Giles Kesteven was listed in *Echo* reports as a winner of age-group judo championships, several years running.

Even Emma was mentioned, with a couple of third-place finishes in the girls' section. Hence her interest in unarmed combat on the telly, presumably.

Then, there was a picture of Giles aged about sixteen, in the khaki of Lincolnshire Army Cadets. A bunch of them were helping to build a dry-stone wall. Old principle of local news, one of the first dinned into us in training: every excuse you can find to name someone in the paper, do it – that's one more sale. Or more than one, since family members buy copies as well.

I stopped for a minute on the industrial estate, watching as police oversaw the Corolla being taken away on a low loader. Good job Lauren got those shots when she did. Good timing on her piece outside Bayford's office, too. The sky was dulling over now, whereas earlier she'd got a helpful bit of sunshine to go with her jacket.

Sandwiched on the back seat, about this time yesterday, how confident had I been that Andy Singh and his team really would turn up and prevent me being taken away, as Jem was, to put pressure on for the return of the data chip?

Logically, very. Nine out of ten. Well, eight point five, certainly. But did I have parts that had squawked in anguish, telling me I was rushing headlong in that car towards a sticky end? Of course.

I got a second wind by the time I reached the Bodleian Admin building, where 24 hours earlier the unmarked cop cars had parked up, tucked in behind an outbuilding, while Andy monitored the drone feed from above.

Lengthened my stride a bit as I passed the graffiti under the railway lines and the trees with their plastic-covered notices about the campaign against the development. Some kind of goosey kerfuffle caused an outbreak of honking and splashing on the opposite bank. Perhaps they'd heard they could stay after all and were celebrating.

Slowing down on the way back towards Osney lock, I passed the footpath, on my left, that skirted the Queen's Centre. Shiny new padlock on the gates around the wheelie bins, I noticed – since naughty Extinction Rebels had sliced through the previous one with bolt cutters.

Then hung a right on to the footbridge across the weir. Raging torrent below. Rain had eased recently, but at this point, the river was still draining floodwater from way upstream. It would take a few more weeks of dry weather across the catchment for normal levels to return.

Puffed out, I slalomed around the anti-cycling railings and walked past the lock-keeper's cubicle. I'd just get home in the last glimmer of daylight. Maybe with a bit more running once I reached The Boater.

There was a little waist-high nook at the far end of the lock-keeper's garden, where a fresh-water tap was installed. Passing mariners could use it to fill their on-board bottles for washing and drinking, as they waited for the lock. I didn't look in as I passed it. Well, you wouldn't.

Suddenly, from behind, my left wrist was grabbed and twisted up hard between my shoulder blades. All the remaining air left my lungs. I tried to turn round, to get my wrist back in front of me, and breathe back in. But the first was made impossible, the second much harder than comfortable, as my throat was gripped in the crook of a strong right arm.

"Y'know, when confidential material gets mislaid, then turns up somewhere, the polite thing is to return it to its rightful owner." The low voice came out of a mouth so close to my ear that I could feel the bristles of beard. Shit. Lindsey.

He steered me along the path, then turned and, with his haunch, pushed open the metal gate in the compound surrounding the hydro power plant. *Oh no, not the hydro.* I could hear the enormous turbine rotating inside, propelled by the raging current: whump-whump-whump-whump.

"Visiting hours are over by this time. Good job I've got the keys. We installed it, you see. So now, you and I can have a special private tour." I was being pushed towards the glass-and-wood cubicle that housed the throbbing machinery. I felt the grip on my neck slacken momentarily.

"But the police…" It immediately tightened again, making any further speech impossible.

"What, you thought I'd still be in St Aldates?" He trapped me with his bodyweight against the rail on the far side of the compound. Metres to our right, the door to the hydro stood ajar.

"Right, let's review the evidence, shall we? Poor Emma, having her letterhead exposed all over Twitter. She'll have some explaining to do. To me, that is – her boss." He moved us along, the metal bar pressing into my left hip.

"No, that wasn't me, putting those figures in the spreadsheet. Let's see, what else? Ah yes, those riders the police have in custody. 'Lindsey paid us cash, Lindsey told us to do it.' A man in my position, wealthy and successful? Bound to attract false allegations, I'm afraid. Sign of the times. Envy, I suppose. Course I was sorry to hear about the fire. And that terrible bomb. But I was elsewhere at both times. And I could prove it."

Once again, we edged along closer to that open door, the hydro now almost drowning out his voice: whump-whump-whump-whump. "So they let me out on bail. Had to. What, didn't your BBC friend include that in her report? Yes, we're just clearing up a few misunderstandings, the police and me. Won't take long, I'm sure."

Fuck, fuck, fuck. But how come he was *here*? Hiding, in that crevice on the lock-side, lying in wait? How the *fuck* did he know where to find me?!

"'Spect you're wondering how I knew where you were." What was he, a friggin' mind reader now, too?! "Lots of things we can do with technology these days. Construction's transformed since my father's time. Clients love our drone surveillance service, did you know? Spy in the sky. Lets 'em monitor their projects in real time. All through an app you can operate from a smartphone."

Finally, he manoeuvred me to the open doorway of the hydro. I looked down on the giant white steel blades, transforming the cascading floodwater from across the Thames catchment into electricity for the households of West Oxford.

"Now, what's admirable here is the construction. Proud of this one. Massive extra torque on this mechanism, you see, from all the rain this year. But it's rock-steady. The tech itself, in this case, is pretty basic. Same principle as a kitchen blender."

He used his body weight to force me to look down on the massive propeller. Whump-whump-whump-whump. "Imagine the purée you could make with that." *Grapes and banana.* I gathered my rapidly ebbing strength to wriggle against the iron grip. But it merely tightened still further.

"No point struggling. It's a chokehold. All I've got to do is press a little harder, and out you'll go." Sure enough, there was now even more pressure on my trachea and the carotid artery behind it. I gasped for breath.

"But you want me to do that, don't you? Render you unconscious. Then at the point of... impact, you won't feel a thing. You'll just float off downriver, through the night. Well, bits of you. Obviously."

Desperate calculations convulsed my mind in rhythm with the great plunging steel fins, slicing through the water. *Shout like crazy – no, impossible. Noise too loud anyway, no-one to hear.* Whump-whump-whump-whump. *OK, different tack. Struggling means tightening. Could stopping mean loosening? But as soon as I stop struggling, I'll be thrown into that hydro. Like a blender. Yogurt, grapes and banana.* "Impact."

What should I do? Roll the dice... last best chance. Yes. Do it. With a final shred of conscious volition, I made myself go slack in Lindsey's arms. Pretended to pass out. Felt him stagger slightly as my weight tipped downwards, my knees suddenly turning to jelly.

Right, this was it. With every sinew in the quadriceps of my right leg, toned through all those years of Downward Dogs, I tensed, straightened back up and in one movement brought up the heel of my trainer sharply into contact with his goolies.

He gasped, relaxing the grip of both hands just enough for me to pull free. Chest heaving now I could finally breathe properly, I sprinted back across the stone-tiled platform around the hydro cubicle and the adjoining pebble-dashed precinct, then out through the still-open gate. Turned sharp left and started running towards the lights of The Boater, glowing up ahead on the corner of South Street. If I could make it there, I'd be safe.

But I'd reckoned without the gate at the other end of the compound. By the time we reached the door above the turbine, we'd been closer to it than the first. And of course, Lindsey had unlocked that one, too.

Still several metres ahead, he shot out onto the path in front, steadied himself on the wooden railing above the swollen river below, fixed his pale blue eyes on me, and began a long stride in my direction.

Shit. I turned abruptly and set off back the way I'd come, downstream. Surely there'd be someone in a narrowboat or something, who'd shelter me and raise the alarm? I had a head start. Surely I could reach one before he caught up? I danced around the railings, up onto the footbridge across the weir and glanced down the riverbank to my left.

And shit again. Barrelling toward me, vaguely outlined in the twilight but unmistakable from its already-audible buzz: an e-bike, with black-clad riders back and front. Of course – the pair that got away from the industrial estate the night before. Must've got hold of another machine.

Only one way to turn – right, onto the path alongside the Queen's Centre and back to Osney Mead. I'd have to hope someone was late finishing work at one of the offices or workshops or cycling back from town. Someone I could turn to for help.

I passed the yard around the wheelie bins, with its new padlock. In the gathering dusk, a streetlight was suddenly illuminated on the road ahead, glowing pink then white. I didn't dare turn to check on the pursuing Lindsey and the e-bike riders. *Run, Janna. Just run.*

CHAPTER
FIFTY

About ten metres short of the road, I began to believe I'd make it. Then, from the right, a pearl-white streamlined hatchback appeared as if from thin air, drove up onto the pavement and stopped with a screech of tyres. The end of the path was blocked.

Instantly I recognised it as a Tesla. Of course: Emma. Shit yet again. Still at Lindsey's beck and call, still doing his bidding. Cutting me off as freedom beckoned.

The front window opened and sure enough, there she was. She leant across from the driver's seat and called out: "Get in, Janna! I'll get you to safety!" *What*?! I pulled up short, blinking. How did this make sense?

"Come on, I'm your only chance here. Let me help you!" Decision time again. Was there something in her expression, the urgency in her eyes, that swayed me? Or remembering the sad life story she'd begun to reveal in our therapy sessions?

Right, quick decision, all or nothing. I leapt forward, tugged open the door and jumped in, Emma accelerating into a high-speed U-turn even before I'd slammed it shut behind me.

"Lucky I found you. I knew he was over here somewhere. I paired our phones a while back, so I can follow the drone on his app at the same time." She stole a glance across at me. "He doesn't know that, by the way."

I looked back at her, breath coming in short gasps, mingled with sobs of… what? Relief coupled with shock, starting to deal with echoes in my head of words like "impact."

"He doesn't realise it's over." At the roundabout, she went right onto Ferry Hinksey Road, slowing down now but still flicking her gaze between the rearview mirror and the lane ahead. "He's totally lost it, this past week or two. You confronting him like that, he couldn't handle it."

Once again, I glanced across, this time catching that same subdued, almost resigned cast of countenance, visible in eyes and mouth, that I'd noticed in low moments during our sessions.

The lights were green at the top and she hung a left onto the main road. My breath was returning to normal. So, Emma had turned, eh? In more ways than one. I began to imagine the indignities she must have endured as Lindsey "lost it."

Another minute or two and she indicated left again into our road and cruised slowly along, coming to a halt just short of the apartment and the parked Community Response van. She stopped and looked properly at me, full in the face. "Can people change, Janna? I mean, really change?"

"Of course. I've seen it, many times. And I'm pretty sure I'm seeing it right now." She nodded, took a deep breath and looked at me again, eyes and mouth set in determined mode.

"He has to be stopped. That's what I see."

"What will you do? Talk to the police?" Another nod.

"When the time comes, yeah." I breathed deeply in and out. That tension from when I thought she was there to cut off my escape, then hardly daring to believe she'd come to my rescue, finally dissipating.

"Right. Well, look, thanks, Emma." I put a hand on her wrist. "I guess I can only begin to realise what that's cost you. But you just saved my life back there, I'm sure of it." She looked away, raised the other hand to her mouth to cover a sob, and nodded again.

I glanced back as I let myself in. She gave a small wave then looked over her shoulder and reversed up to the alleyway, turned and drove off.

I slumped onto the sofa, legs suddenly wobbly. Sobs rose uncontrollably. Sat there for minutes on end, shoulders heaving, feeling sorry for myself. Bloody hell, less than half an hour ago I was looking down onto that propeller. Those blades.

At last, I got up to blow my nose and splash my face. Halfway through drying, a sudden hideous thought. *Jem*. I bounded back through to the living room and seized my phone. Straight to voicemail. Shit. OK, try Denise on WhatsApp.

"Janna!" Oh, thank God. She and Jem were fine. He was just charging his phone. She got me to calm down. Horrified to hear about Lindsey. She'd call colleagues at The Leys cop shop, just round the corner, and get them to put on extra patrols outside the house.

Relief warming me from within, I shrugged on my old zippy fleece against the evening chill. Suddenly felt ravenous. No biscuits left, unfortunately. But I could toast a piece of sourdough, lather it with butter and squidge honey all over it. Washed it down with last night's leftover peppermint tea, microwaved for half a minute.

Right, now for Andy Singh. Head of steam building up, not just from the tea. I mean, sure, here I was safe and well, but no thanks to bloody Thames Valley Police. They'd let the bugger go! And not even bothered to tell me.

No, it was Emma I had to thank. Mind, she'd handled her car impressively. Accelerated into that U-turn like she was taking a hairpin bend at Silverstone.

As I picked the phone back up, I paused. Something bothering me, what was it? Something *missing* from that episode. No seatbelt on, was that it? Slammed the door then clung onto the lip of the glove compartment as we careened round.

No. No, there was something else. Ah – no vroom. Not like the cross red hatchback on the Cowley Road a couple of weeks ago, in that row with the taxi man. Of course, there wouldn't be – electric car. That was it. *Now* I would call Andy Singh.

"I know how Daniel was killed, and I know who did it." Precious, deadly, horrifying moments of clarity as I'd dialled and held. Yes, I knew. After wondering and puzzling all this time, through all those wakeful hours. I profoundly wished I didn't. Wished it was otherwise. The facts were getting in the way of a good story. But wasn't that both the journalist's vocation and curse? To report without fear or favour?

"Really?! Go on."

"Have you had any more witnesses come forward, from those posters you put up in The Boater?"

"Er, no, as it happens, I don't think…"

"You wouldn't. No-one saw anything because the streetlight was out. It was still dark then, at that time – clocks hadn't gone forward."

"Right…"

"And no-one heard anything because the car that ran him over – the car that crushed him to death – was powered by an electric motor. A Tesla. Driven by Emma Kesteven."

It had been dry for most of the time since the launch, just a few drizzly days. So there was apparently a good chance that forensics would find traces on the chassis and wheel-arches. They would also remove and test the wheelie bins from outside the Queen's Centre.

That part of the puzzle had fallen into place at the same time. Of course, Daniel was unconscious by the time he was being run over. "Everyone was calming down that taxi man. Lindsey would have grabbed him, then hustled him back through the door into the corridor, where the protesters had lain in wait, and got him in a chokehold till he passed out."

"Right. Well, that would fit, certainly."

"He was a youth-level judo champion, did you know? In

Lincolnshire, under his real name, Giles Kesteven." No, Andy had to admit, he didn't. And I told him exactly how I knew about Lindsey's way with chokeholds.

"Bloody hell, are you OK?" Sure, keep listening.

"So Emma was sent to fetch a wheelie bin. They put Daniel in it, then she had to wheel it across the weir, past the hydro and onto the corner of South Street by the pub. Where she'd parked."

He kept getting her to "put rubbish out," Emma had told me, in one of her sessions. Even though it wasn't part of her job description, as office manager. Lindsey himself would only have been gone for a couple of minutes. Then he could reappear in front of Lauren's camera.

"I'm sure he told her Daniel was already dead by then. Far as she was concerned, she was just making it look like an accident."

"We'll see," Andy said grimly.

CHAPTER
FIFTY-ONE

"Emma Kesteven was asked when she realised Daniel Kerr had been merely unconscious as she drove over him, not already dead as her brother had claimed. It was when she watched coverage from the police news conference by BBC South Today, she said, on her computer, days after it went to air."

Lauren momentarily looked down, making a show of consulting the notes she'd taken during the hearing, then up again at the camera. "She was horrified, she told the court. And devastated." Bloody weird experience, seeing the artist's impression of me giving evidence. Quite flattering, though, actually. Especially the eyes. "Psychotherapist Janna Rose treated Kesteven before she turned out to be the killer. The office manager had been subjected to 'a regime of coercive control,' she said."

∽

When Emma's legal team approached me, I was glad to help. Making a clean breast of things: yes, she had indeed planted the micro camera in my office, at Lindsey's behest. He'd figured out that Daniel would turn to me, his old collaborator on news investigations, to pick up if anything happened to him.

Why had she kept the other two appointments? "Those sessions with you were the first chance I'd ever had to talk about the real me—what was really going on in my life, how I felt about things?"

We were sitting in a sun-filled legal office in a modern block near Heptathlon, off the Botley Road. Emma was out on police bail pending trial at that stage. "I couldn't tell you, but I so desperately wanted to keep coming back. When it turned out he wasn't already dead, like Giles said, I just couldn't face it. Couldn't keep it together anymore."

The solicitor, I noticed, had topped up her office supply of tissues for the occasion.

~

Under cross-examination, Lindsey tried to dismiss our encounter at the hydro. First by denying he was there, then, presented with evidence from his phone and the drone app, affecting to "suddenly remember" it. "Just a bit of horseplay," he called it.

The e-bike pillion passenger with the neck tattoo turned out to be an army veteran, an old mate from Lincolnshire Army Cadets. The chap had been on duty with K-For in Kosovo, got drunk and was taken by a Serb paramilitary gang to a tattooist in Mitrovice. They made sure it was in a conspicuous place, so, sure enough, his superiors saw it, and he was promptly dismissed for conduct prejudicial to good order and discipline.

When schools went back, police retrieved recordings from the security camera outside the Temple Cowley primary, which fortuitously the caretaker had forgotten to switch off for the holidays. It clearly showed him searching through my bag, pulling out and pocketing the lockbox, dumping it in the road and zooming off.

It seemed he'd convened a group of former military men who

then acted as Lindsey's private army. The gun brandished at both Jem and me was a service weapon, kept by a tall ex-soldier (the one from Waitrose) as a souvenir. Though he denied it was ever loaded.

Another pleaded for leniency, claiming he'd tried to warn me off through an approach to my son in the loos at Isis Farmhouse. It seemed to cut little ice with the judge.

The sheer weight of testimony against him gradually washed away Lindsey's denials like floodwater. Back to Lauren in vision, outside Oxford Crown Court, to summarise the sentencing.

"Mr Justice Harmon told him: 'I am satisfied that Mr Kerr's death *was* the intended outcome of your actions.' He was jailed for life on the murder, with a recommendation that he serve at least fifteen years, and a further seven for conspiracy and fraud, to run concurrently."

She'd gone back to her smart dark plum-coloured jacket, to match the serious nature of the story. And I finally got to ask where she got her hair cut.

Given the mitigation, Emma would go down for seven, after admitting the lesser charge of manslaughter. With good behaviour, she could be out in four. In the witness box, after she'd testified against her brother, she was asked if there was anything she'd like to add.

"I know I've got to go to prison, and I should; I did a terrible thing," she replied, voice slightly quavering, then steadying herself. "But in another way, I'm free now, for the first time in my life. And I'd like to thank my therapist, Janna Rose, for showing me how."

I'm told she looked towards me in the public gallery, but I didn't see because, right about then, I got something in my eye.

Emma had a new ambition: to change careers and become a therapist herself, specialising in EMDR. Would I continue seeing her for therapy while she was inside, then ultimately be her supervisor? Of course. Wasn't there something in those conference recordings about EMDR in prisons? Have to take another look.

∼

Denise was all smiles. Jem was wearing that smart shirt she'd chosen for him, from the Tap Social gig: floral pattern, dark red on navy. We'd gathered at the Communi-Tea café to celebrate their anniversary of getting together.

Yes, I would have another couple of wings from the jerk chicken platter, thanks very much. They were delicious. And I'd made peace with the bathroom scales. Or at least called a truce.

I snatched a moment for a quick chat with my old friend before we split. "Thanks so much for stepping up, Pearl, when Jem was missing."

"This is the Leys, Jan. We look after our own. Even when they go swanning off and seem to forget we ever existed."

"OK, I deserved that."

"Just make sure that boy of yours doesn't go hurting my baby sister. Else he'll have me to reckon with."

∼

Andy Singh reached out, arranging to meet for coffee at the Community Centre café.

"Nice to get the vibe of this place. All useful background," he said.

"Nice lemon cake, too."

"Indeed." He took a sip of macchiato and looked me in the eye.

"What I wanted to talk about—I reckon we're good together, you and me." Gosh. Must admit, I'd had a sneaking feeling that something like this might be coming. And he did look the part, in a natty blue linen jacket over a dark polo shirt. Tidy haircut, too. I gave an encouraging smile.

"We have a budget for specialist civilian input into investigations. Could I put you on the list?" Oh. *That's* what he wanted. "That way, when we're puzzling over motivation, or how suspects might be acting out trauma or suchlike, we can call you in. Decent rates, so I'm told."

"Right." Well, yes, there were aspects of detective work that I quite liked, now I came to think about it. Could do without my son being abducted, or my neighbours being bombed or burned out of their homes. To say nothing of being held over the rotating blades of the Osney Community Hydro. But Lindsey was a one-off, surely? The reality would be much more prosaic. Plus, I could use some decent rates. Might splash out on a new pair of yoga pants. "OK, sure."

"Great! I'll tell the Chief Super, and we'll see what business we can put your way." I waved him off and returned to my faithful Bertha. *Looks like it's just thee and me, old girl, for the foreseeable.* Could be worse. Yeah—could be a lot worse.

The End

ABOUT THE AUTHORS

Jake Lynch and Annabel McGoldrick met at Yorkshire Television when both joined as reporters in 1992. Jake went on to be a Political Correspondent and Foreign Correspondent, ending up as a newsreader on BBC World. He switched to an academic career at the University of Sydney, where he teaches in the Master of Social Justice degree. Annabel is now a psychotherapist and supervisor in private practice, specialising in Eye Movement Desensitisation and Reprocessing, with Internal Family System. She runs international training courses for other therapists. The couple were jointly honoured with the 2017 Luxembourg Peace Prize, given by the Schengen Peace Foundation, for their contributions to Peace Journalism.

To learn more about Jake Lynch & Annabel McGoldrick and discover more Next Chapter authors, visit our website at www.nextchapter.pub.

Printed in Great Britain
by Amazon